WHEN HEARTS COLLIDE
by Marilyn Jaye Lewis

"Lewis deftly erases the line between 'erotica'
and 'literature.'"—Ian Grey

"An unmistakable feminine perspective to matters
of the flesh." —The Guardian, London

D1022885

WHEN HEARTS
collide

Marilyn Jaye Lewis

an erotic romance

When Hearts Collide
Copyright @ 2003 by Magic Carpet Books
All Rights Reserved

No part of this book may be reproduced, stored in a retrieval
system, or transmitted in any form, by any means, including
mechanical, electronic, photocopying, recording or otherwise, without
prior written permission from the publisher and author.

First Magic Carpet Inc. edition March 2003

Published in 2003

Manufactured in th United States of America
Published by Magic Carpet Books

Magic Carpet Books
PO Box 473
New Milford, CT 06776

Library of Congress Cataloging in Publication Date

When Hearts Collide by Marilyn Jaye Lewis
ISBN 0-9726339-1-X

cover design: stella by design contact: stellabydesign@aol.com

For Iris and J.Q.

CHAPTER ONE

In the bedroom of her Manhattan apartment, Dorianne Constance smoothed each of the shimmering black stockings up her long legs and hooked them securely into the clips of her garter.

This is crazy, she thought, pulling a black silk slip carefully down around the curlers in her hair. We're just meeting for lunch—why I am doing this? I'm only setting myself up to be disappointed by him again.

And yet she continued.

The straps of the slip fell into place over her delicate white shoulders and the length of it tumbled lightly down the curves of her body. It came to rest at the middle of her thigh, where the hem of her cashmere skirt would hit.

A pair of shiny black pumps went on next. The ones with the spiked heels. Shoes that looked conservative on first glance. But a closer inspection of just how spiked the heels were, revealed a different story about the secret hopes of the young woman wearing the shoes; the place inside Dorianne that dreamed of being less conservative one day, perhaps of letting go, of accepting his terms this time.

Dorianne inspected herself in the mirror. Her padded bra pushed her breasts up into two full, inviting mounds and the black lace edging of the slip highlighted those fleshy mounds enticingly. She looked sexy. She knew it.

I wonder if this is going too far, she sighed.

All this suddenly pronounced cleavage would be plainly visible at the top of her black suit jacket. She wasn't planning on wearing a blouse underneath it, just the slip. And Dorianne wasn't the type of woman who felt comfortable exposing any part of her flesh in public. She was a beautiful woman; she could admit that. But she wasn't like any of the famous women she interviewed for a living; women who made an art out of seeming blithely unaware of being half-undressed in the finest places, while the men in the vicinity drooled all over themselves in vain.

This bra is like wearing a sign that says I'm desperate, she thought. But who do I think I'm kidding? I feel desperate.

As Dorianne unrolled the curlers from her hair, she wondered what Kent would look like after all these years. She tried to prepare herself for the inevitable—that he might be old and gray now. He might look tired or sexually unappealing. Kent was twenty years older than Dorianne was, which would have made him fifty on his most recent birthday. Maybe he would seem ordinary to her today, like any other newly divorced middle-aged man of the world who was obviously too old for her.

Oh, but back when she and Kent had been lovers....

It was nearly a decade ago, when Dorianne had been just getting out of college. Then, the twenty-year age difference between them had seemed sexy to her. A little scary, a little intimidating, but always secretly thrilling. And Kent had been just hitting his stride in his career in publishing. That, too, had made him extra exciting to Dorianne. He'd been one of the founders of *Babylon* movie magazine, which became an immediate sensation. And he had many lucrative book deals. He was earning over six figures a year and moving in some fancy circles. It had seemed to Dorianne back then that doors opened so easily for Kent, as if he held a god-given key.

The lifestyle he led—the endless cocktail parties with famous people as he became more and more famous himself; his travels all over Europe, Asia, Australia; talk shows and book tours. It was all very glamorous to a young, inexperienced college girl who was hoping to be a successful journalist. But to make their affair even more unnerving, Kent was old enough to be Dorianne's father and from day one, he would never let her forget that, especially in bed.

Kent Cryer had been the only man who had ever controlled Dorianne and without knowing she was doing it, she had permitted it to happen.

Kent was a man who needed to be in charge and Dorianne had been swept away by his larger-than-life persona. When it came to the bedroom, she was inexperienced and he was a man who knew what he wanted. He would tell her what he expected her to do and what he wanted her to wear. Kent wasn't kinky, necessarily. But he was quirky, she remembered, and demanding. He'd exposed Dorianne to elements of her own sexual needs that she'd found unsettling when she'd been only twenty. He'd expected an obedience from her that had been unheard of in her liberal, politically correct upbringing.

What had really thrown her, though, was how erotic it had felt to give in to Kent's overpowering will in bed. She would never admit it to anybody, not to Kent and sometimes not even to herself, but with him, Dorianne had discovered a world inside her that secretly liked having an older man tell her what to do. To put her through her paces in every imaginable position until she was exhausted.

Dorianne fluffed her chestnut hair now, the soft curls falling gently around her shoulders. She checked her make-up in the mirror—just a hint of mascara on her black lashes and a touch of plum on her lips. She enhanced the conservative look with a simple strand of pearls around her exquisite neck. And as she slipped on her pearl earrings, she was surprised to notice her hands shaking ever so slightly.

His needs had frightened her because they'd aroused a lust in her body that had been overwhelming and unmanageable.

"But I'm not twenty years old anymore," she reminded herself in the mirror. "And this is *just lunch.*"

She straightened her black suit jacket and smoothed her black cashmere skirt.

"Kent Cryer was ten years ago," she added. "I'm not that girl anymore."

Dorianne Constance was a woman now and an impressive success. She was earning a six-figure salary in an unlikely field, and she was well aware that other people, especially men, found her success intimidating. Most journalists never made it to the top—least of all, by interviewing movie stars and presenting them to the fickle readers of movie magazines in the most flattering light possible. That was what had made Dorianne a success. She helped forge blockbuster careers by turning 'working actors' into 'enigmatic movie stars' in the minds of the public. One interview with Dorianne Constance could set a shrewd actor on that meteoric rise to fame. Dorianne didn't flaunt her success, but she had a healthy appreciation for how she was perceived in public. And that need for respect spilled into her private life, as well. It wasn't that she had to have the upper hand over men, she just wanted to be on equal footing now. At thirty, she was more in the habit of doing as she pleased instead of doing as she was told.

Dorianne grabbed her patent leather clutch, pulled her apartment door closed behind her and felt it securely lock.

She waited for the elevator to take her down to the lobby when, without warning, she suddenly felt all her attempts at detached, cool-headed assuredness beginning to crumble and the pressure of her memories of Kent, the thing she had been trying most to avoid, threatened to burst her bubble of calm and break her heart wide open.

When the elevator opened on her floor, Dorianne was relieved to find that it was empty. She rushed in as if she could escape herself— the silly girl who had been standing there, waiting. Always waiting. As the elevator door closed, Dorianne tried hard to keep her sudden tears at bay, to keep the past from overtaking her. But the memories flooded her like a tidal wave. The two tortuous, naïve years she'd spent as Kent's lover, as his secret, illicit mistress. The shameful truth of their affair had been that Kent had been a married man back then with no intentions of getting a divorce from his wife. And Dorianne had been his perfect little fool, believing all his lies. After two long years of humiliation, after too many nights of feeling unneeded, used, cast aside and left out, Dorianne had finally reached the breaking point. She hadn't been able to endure the heartache anymore, no matter how much she'd enjoyed making love with Kent. She had forced herself to break it off with him the night she'd turned twenty-one and the decision had nearly smothered her with grief.

Now she remembered the heartbreak and humiliation perfectly. The expensive birthday gifts he'd bought for her lay unopened on the unmade bed in their hotel room. "I can't see you anymore, Kent," she'd blurted in a sudden tantrum of tears, as her resolve to leave him yet again began to crumble. "If and when you decide to leave your wife for good," she'd bluffed, "you can call me."

But with no coaxing whatsoever that night, Kent had agreed to Dorianne's ultimatum: If and when he ever left his wife, he'd assured her, Dorianne would be the first to know. He'd walked out on Dorianne then, leaving her alone with her unopened birthday presents, crying in the hotel room he'd paid for. Just like that, it had ended for good.

But they were both working at *Babylon* by then. Kent himself had seen to it that she'd been hired. It became torture for Dorianne to have to confront the reality of Kent Cryer every single day—the married man that she still loved; the married man who no longer gave her the time of day, who'd used and humiliated her and written her off. Dorianne had thanked god when Kent finally sold his interest in *Babylon* and moved with his wife to Paris.

Now here she was all these years later, making it on her own in a world Kent had discarded, and Kent had finally called. He'd been true to his word. He'd left his wife. He was free now, divorced, living again in New York, and he wanted to see Dorianne. And she was still single, looking for love.

She wanted to see him; she knew she did. But she didn't want Kent to get the best of her again. Dorianne swiped a tear from her cheek and pulled her resolve together as the elevator doors opened. She stepped out into the lobby, on to solid ground. She would handle this. It was just lunch.

*   *   *

Early autumn in New York was Dorianne's favorite time of year. The air was crisp, but not cold enough yet to have to be encumbered by a heavy coat. Her doorman hailed her a cab quickly and through some miracle, traffic was light and Dorianne was at her destination in no time.

Ernesto's was a very upscale Italian restaurant, one of Dorianne's favorites. The lunch crowd consisted primarily of business executives, male and female, who worked in midtown Manhattan. But the décor was elegant and subdued. There was a feeling of privacy about Ernesto's. It was possible, at least at a secluded table in the corner, to feel a hint of romance, even during the busy lunch hour.

Dorianne had arrived too early. Rather than wait impatiently for Kent in the doorway and risk feeling like a nervous fool, she asked to be seated at her table. This way, she figured, she would have the added benefit of seeing Kent first, of taking him in, before he'd have a chance to see her.

Ernesto's dining room was already buzzing with customers who had that hard-edged urban air of sophistication and financial achievement. They noticed Dorianne as she was led to her table in the corner by the *maitre d'*. Her soft chestnut curls, her flattering black suit and her long slender legs in those impossibly high heels—heads turned and conversations faltered, as if an unseen sea were parting while Dorianne moved across the crowded room.

She knew she had a presence about her, a cultivated look of success that caught people's attention. Yet she felt her confidence beginning to crumble again. The anticipation of seeing Kent after all these empty years, as the seconds ticked away and his arrival became imminent, was making Dorianne's pulse race and her palms sweat. She was finally forced to admit to herself that a lot was riding on this lunch. Regardless of how he'd treated her, this was a man that Dorianne had prayed would come back to her.

And finally, the moment came. Dorianne recognized Kent the minute he walked into Ernesto's. She watched the *maitre d'* escort him toward the table. She saw that he still had a full head of hair, but it was entirely gray now. And he'd put on weight— maybe as much as twenty pounds. He was dressed impeccably in a suit and tie, but Dorianne noticed something less dynamic about him, the way he carried himself now, as if he had surrendered to a subtle defeat. She wanted to see that masculine magnetic attraction she remembered finding in him once, but it was no longer there.

In the few seconds it had taken Kent to cross the room and stand before her, to smile warmly down at her and say hello, Dorianne knew without a doubt that, for her, the spark was gone.

"Hello, Kent," she said graciously, masking her disappointment like a pro. "It's been a long time."

Kent sat down in the chair next to hers, closing in the space between them. "Well, Miss Constance, you certainly have grown. Look at you. You look sensational."

Dorianne studied his face up close now. The Kent she used to know was still in there around the edges of his eyes.

"Thank you, Kent. You don't look so bad yourself."

"I wish I could believe that," he laughed good-naturedly. "But I'm afraid too much good living finally caught up with me. I can't *budge* this weight off. It's part of getting older, I suppose. It got to the point where I had to choose; do I spend the extra hours in the gym, or spend them just enjoying life? I guess it's obvious which choice I made. But you, my dear, look fabulous. How old are you now, about twenty-two?"

Dorianne smiled self-consciously, caught off guard by his charm. No one had been able to make her blush in a long time. "No," she answered. "I turned thirty about a month ago."

Kent let out a mock sigh of disbelief. "Well, then I must be getting *really* old. If I remember correctly, I had a few years on you."

"A few," she nodded.

Kent reached for Dorianne's hand and held it affectionately. "No kidding, Dory. You look sensational," he said quietly. "Are you happy?"

"I'm happy enough," she answered honestly. "I'm having a good life. My career is going great."

"I know all about that. I've seen your byline everywhere and I read your last book a couple months ago. I liked it. But do you have time to do anything besides work?"

"Not really. I do work an awful lot." Dorianne glanced down at her hand being held in Kent's and something about the intimacy felt reassuring. "But I'm okay with working. These are the years where I need to be giving it all I've got, so that later on, I can really enjoy the rewards. Don't you think?"

Kent, the once larger-than-life go-getter, looked at her almost wistfully. "I don't know, Dory. There are things about life that should be lived in the moment. If you don't make time for them in the present, they have an odd way of always being just a little ahead of you in a future that doesn't come." Then he stopped himself from going further. "Well, I didn't come here to tell you how to live. You seem to be doing a good job of it on your own."

"What *did* you come here for, Kent?" Dorianne was taken aback by the sudden accusatory tone in her voice, by her gracelessness. She tried to control herself. "I mean, it was certainly a surprise to hear from you after all this time. And to learn of your divorce."

Kent didn't flinch. He looked her in the eye. "I can't believe the divorce was a surprise to you, Dory," he said. "As I'm sure you've always known, it was a long time in the making. Listen, why don't we order first? I'm famished. There'll be plenty of time to talk about why I came here after we eat."

Dorianne agreed. She set aside the creeping feelings of anxious insecurity and tried to treat Kent simply as an old friend. They ordered lunch and Kent convinced her to join him in an expensive bottle of red wine. When the glasses were placed in front of them and the wine was being poured, Dorianne realized it was going to be a long lunch. Normally, she didn't drink in the middle of the day, even one glass of wine tended to make her too tired to work and then the day would be shot. But Kent could still be pretty persuasive so together they ordered the bottle of wine.

What was she afraid of anyway, she wondered. Would her career go down the tubes because she gave up one afternoon to have a harmless lunch with an old flame?

Or maybe she was afraid of something more serious; that the wine would coax her into letting down her guard with Kent, that he might get the best of her. The sexual magnetism she'd been hoping to find in him seemed to have fizzled out, but maybe she was afraid that the wine would confuse her hungry libido, that she would find herself indulging in a little sex anyway strictly to please him.

Or—and her heart beat a little faster as Kent lifted his wine glass and his eyes met hers—maybe she was afraid that underneath the added years, Kent hadn't changed a bit. That the sex between them would be the same as it ever was, with Kent's will overpowering hers in bed as he urged her to please him in those ways, those positions, that she'd always found so secretly thrilling. He would tell her to bend over for him. He would go at her from behind until her legs wanted to give out, and then what? Would her lust overwhelm her? She was sex-starved. She knew it.

Once it was unleashed again, she would be consumed by it. It was going to be death by lust for Dorianne and all because of a bottle of red wine.

Kent lightly touched glasses with hers and said, "To old times, honey."

His choice of words made Dorianne feel unwittingly exposed. And as the enticing taste of the wine filled her mouth, she felt herself get warm between her legs. She knew lunch would likely be very long indeed now and perhaps push dinner clear into the following day.

The waiter let Kent and Dorianne take their time with their meal and he didn't rush them. He only appeared to refill their wine glasses. As if he sensed what was underway, he gave them privacy and space.

But they didn't talk about what was now uppermost in Dorianne's mind; they didn't talk about sex. Mostly, they talked about work. About writing, about deadlines and the pressure of success—how difficult it could be to say 'no' to more and more work. The conversation was mechanical, perhaps even superficial, but it progressed with ease and helped Dorianne feel as if she were somehow still in control, keeping her growing passion undetectable.

"You really took the ball and ran with it, didn't you, Dory?" Kent said. "You've become quite a success."

"I couldn't have done it without your help, though. You know that," she said.

"That's not true. I gave you an opportunity, a break. You were the one who turned that opportunity into a gold mine."

Dorianne had been just a few weeks shy of graduating from college with her heart set on a journalism career, when Kent had told the editor-in-chief at *Babylon* to throw Dorianne a bone. She was offered an assignment: interview the up and upcoming hot Hollywood property, Evan Crane. If the interview went well, it might turn into other assignments for Dorianne.

"Remember how nervous I was, Kent? My god, *Babylon* movie magazine—your baby. I thought that the pressure would kill me. And it turned out to be a piece of cake."

"You had it in your blood, Dory. For a lot of kids, it would have been a tough job. Even I was surprised at how good you were. Your very first interview, landing on the cover. Who was it you interviewed?"

"Evan Crane. Practically a nobody back then."

"Evan Crane. That's right. And then his movie went mega-millions and he became a bona fide blockbuster star. If that wasn't an auspicious beginning for you, what was?"

"I guess I have Evan Crane to thank for my career, too, then. If he hadn't had the decency to become such a spectacular success, I might never have landed that cover story."

Kent scoffed and took a sip of wine. "The word 'decency' in the same sentence with the name 'Evan Crane' is a little bit of a joke, don't you think?"

"Why? Is there something indecent about Evan Crane?"

"He can't act, for one thing. God knows he practically slept his way to the top."

"And that's indecent?" she asked, his caustic remarks rubbing her the wrong way. "It's not as if he were married while he was sleeping his way to the top—if that's what he was doing. I only know he never had sex with me. You, however, slept with me for two years while you were supposedly committed to someone else. In some circles, that could be considered indecent."

It stopped Kent cold. "*Touché*, my dear. I get the feeling you've been waiting a long time to say that."

"Maybe," she conceded quietly, feeling stupid for losing her cool.

"I'm sorry for sounding so bitter. But you know it's not my style to sum up anyone's life with such mean-spirited clichés."

Kent smiled at her but it wasn't a kind smile, it was patronizing. "Come on, Dorianne. You of all people must know what it takes to succeed in Hollywood. You've interviewed every major star from the past decade. Regardless of all that Pollyanna stuff you write about them, no one in Hollywood gets to the top by being a nice guy—or gal, for that matter."

"There's no blue print for success for any of us," she said. "All of those people in Hollywood—every story is just as valid as yours or mine. I don't really care who's nice or not, who anyone has sex with, or what their motivations might be while they're having sex. My only interests are in my own career and in my own sex life."

"And how is that sex life going?" Kent cut in.

Dorianne glared at him. He was trying to trivialize her point of view. "Frankly, it's non-existent right now," she said. "How is yours going? Is it exciting to be single again? It must be comforting to be able to have the same sex life you've always had, only now you don't have the added worry of getting caught by your wife."

Kent backed down and pondered his wine glass. He couldn't look her in the eye. "Okay, Dory. I deserved that. But it's not how you think it's been. It's not like there was a long string of girls I was screwing while I was married to my wife."

"You can't fool me anymore, Kent. I'm not twenty years old. Do you think I've lived the last ten years in a vacuum? That I haven't heard the stories? I may not be the type to respect or repeat gossip, but that doesn't mean I don't hear it."

"But just because you hear it doesn't mean it's true, Dory."

"No, it doesn't. But knowing you as well as I did once has

enabled me to make some educated guesses."

"Well, as much as I didn't come here to tell *you* how to live, I certainly didn't come here to have you tell me how to live my life, either."

Before Dorianne's very eyes, the lunch was falling to pieces.

"What *did* you come here for, Kent? Maybe we should have that conversation right now. Was it just to torment me?"

As if Dorianne's words had pierced Kent through the heart, his confidence faltered. "No," he answered. "I didn't come here to torment you. I came here to apologize to you."

Now it was Dorianne's turn to be stopped cold.

He went on, slowly regaining his composure while he spoke. "I came here to say that I've spent a lot of sleepless nights looking at the person I'd been for most of my adult life and I didn't like what I saw. I haven't been very kind to people, or fair, or understanding. I cared only about my work," Kent confessed. "About my success, my income. I see that now, and I wanted to try to make amends with the people I cared about while I still could, before any more precious years were wasted."

Dorianne stared at him.

"It was my decision to divorce Katherine, not hers," he continued. "It was time to admit our marriage was one of habit and convenience, that there wasn't any love between us at all. In fact, I'd come to the realization that there was no love left in my life anywhere. Everywhere my mind turned, I saw only empty relationships and I didn't want that to be how I spent any more of my life. That's why I came here, Dory. Not to torment you, but to apologize to you because life's too short and too precious and I behaved pretty reprehensibly toward you. So, I apologize."

Dorianne didn't know what to say. It was something she'd been hoping to hear from Kent for a lifetime it seemed, and now that she was hearing it, she found herself peculiarly unprepared for it. She wanted to say something, anything, but words wouldn't come.

"You were so young and trusting back then, Dory," Kent went on. "I don't think I fully appreciated it until recently, what you were doing to yourself by sleeping with me. Betraying your own values because you loved me and assumed I would have your best interests at heart. I think I only had my own interests at heart—well, let's say 95% of the time. I don't think I was an all-out monster. Or maybe I was."

"No, you weren't a monster, Kent. You were far from that."

"Well, I wasn't fair to you. You're right, what you said just now; it was indecent. I never should have so much as kissed you while I was married to someone else. I guess I just assumed I could have everything, do anything, because I was in my prime and earning more money than most of my peers. I think I could only gage my sense of self-worth by how much money I had in the bank.

"I know this is going to sound trite, Dorianne, but I want you to believe it. While you and I were having that affair, you were the only one I was interested in. You were the only one in my world. I think I only had sex with my wife about once or twice a *year* during those days with you. In fact, I was a little obsessed with you. I thought about you constantly. You were such an open lover and your body was so exciting. Making love with you was one of my greatest pleasures, Dorianne. Being away from you was torture, but whenever we were apart, craving you was a torment I couldn't get enough of. Then being with you again was heaven. I haven't had any other affairs that have come close to making me feel what I felt when I was with you. When you ended it, it almost tore my world apart. But I had my pride, and my work, of course.

I could get lost in that. And I pretended that somehow Katherine would be enough for me—that I didn't need you. But it wasn't the case. It's true, the stories you've heard about me, and they're probably all true. I screwed a lot of women after you ended it. I didn't care anymore."

Dorianne tried to overcome her shock. "Kent," she said, "I don't know, I suddenly feel so inarticulate. There's so much I've wanted to say to you all these years, and now I can't seem to put my words together."

"That's all right," he said quietly. "There's no rush. Take your time. I want to hear what you have to say whenever you feel like saying it. I honestly do."

He reached out tentatively, then and lightly touched the black lace that peeked out from Dorianne's suit jacket, tracing a warm finger along the edge of the lace—just at the top, where the cleavage of her soft breasts was exposed. An unmasked desire flooded his face when he looked into her eyes.

Dorianne could hardly take the intensity of his gaze, the passion of it burned into her. And his touch was intimidating. She felt exposed on every level—emotionally, psychologically, and sexually. Yes, she wanted him again but he was coming on too strong now. He was going to gain the upper hand and she had her reputation to think of.

"You really do look sensational," he whispered up close to her face, "do you know that?" His fingertips discreetly brushed across her breast as his hand moved down and disappeared under the table, under the tablecloth, coming to rest lightly on Dorianne's knee.

"You're as appealing as ever—in fact, even more so. I wish I could show you right now what it is I still feel for you, Dory."

His hand brushed lightly against her smooth, stocking-covered thigh. Dorianne discreetly crossed her legs, pulling away from his touch. Not wanting to encourage his hand to move any higher.

"I do feel it, you know," he persisted. "I want to excite you again, I want to remember what that sounds like. You always made the most erotic little sounds when we made love, remember, Dory? That's something I want to hear again. I want it to fill the room."

Dorianne wanted to flee the restaurant. Not to run away from Kent, so much, as to run away from her own heart. She felt very confused. It was finally happening; Kent was coming on to her again and she felt herself giving in to him. But was this what she wanted? Was this good enough? To be seduced in broad daylight, in a restaurant of all places? Was his bold, heroic confession just a way of knocking her off balance so that he could move in for the kill?

Kent saw plainly that she was conflicted and he eased up on her.

"I'm sorry, Dory," he said, his hands retreating to his lap. "I shouldn't have said that just now, it was inappropriate. It takes for granted that you were still interested in making love with me. I know it's been a lot of years."

"It's all right, Kent," she assured him, although she knew she wasn't being very truthful. It wasn't really all right. But before she knew it, more words were coming out of her mouth. Was the wine making her say it? Was it the force of pure lust pushing through her resolve? " Listen," she said, "do you want to come back to my apartment and talk? I don't live too far from here. We could be alone there. This restaurant is suddenly suffocating me."

"I don't want to impose on you."

"It's not an imposition, Kent. There's so much I want to say. But not here, not like this. I feel like we're on display."

Kent agreed. He paid the tab and together they left the restaurant, openly holding hands. He wasn't a married man anymore; he could touch her out in the open like this.

Dorianne felt light-headed. She knew this was what she'd wanted, to be alone with Kent in her apartment. She knew that he was going to seduce her and that she was going to give in to him. Still she couldn't convince herself that it was the best idea.

CHAPTER TWO

"Mr. Crane, it certainly is nice to meet you."

The petite blonde woman, who extended her hand to Evan Crane in the entryway of Café Madre on Sunset Boulevard, spoke with a clipped and formal-sounding British accent. But she hardly looked formal. She wore a pair of five inch high open-toed platform sandals, a pair of blue jeans slung low on her narrow hips, and a flowing white baby doll blouse that exposed both her modest cleavage and her small belly—complete with pierced naval.

Her wavy blonde hair was cut quite short and looked dramatically unkempt—a look Evan knew must have taken the woman at least an hour every morning to achieve.

If not two hours, he thought, with a bit of contempt.

He felt that wall of privacy going up inside him. He was already pushing her away and they hadn't even sat down to lunch yet.

"I'm Christine Miles from *Rex* magazine," she continued excitedly. "You know, I have to say, I've been a big fan of yours since I saw you in *The Devil Gets His Way*, when I was about thirteen," she gushed. "I know that doesn't make me sound very professional, does it? Saying I'm a big fan of yours when I'm supposed to be here to interview you."

Evan smiled charmingly, thinking to himself that it was going to be a very long day. "That's okay," he said. "I never get tired of meeting my fans, whoever they turn out to be."

"They're holding a table for us toward the back," Christine said, well aware that the energy in the restaurant had heightened considerably the minute Evan walked through the door. "I thought a little privacy might be nice, unless of course, you prefer that table by the front window?"

"A table in back is fine," he assured her. "Contrary to what they might say about me, I don't need to be on display twenty-four hours a day."

"Great!"

Again, Christine gushed so enthusiastically, Evan wondered how old she could possibly be.

All eyes were upon the famous movie star as the hostess showed them to their table in back.

"So you saw *The Devil Gets His Way* when you were only thirteen?" Evan ventured. "That must make you pretty young."

"I'm almost twenty-three," Christine chirped, as she sat down across from Evan in the spacious booth. "After all, that movie *was* ten years ago."

She spoke as if the mere idea of 'ten years' were a lifetime to her.

"I hope you enjoy your lunch, Mr. Crane," the hostess said, ignoring Christine's presence altogether, as if Evan were dining alone. "If there's anything you need, don't hesitate to ask."

"Thanks," he replied. "I'm sure everything will be fine."

"I aim to please," the hostess continued. She had a dazzling smile, with perfectly bleached teeth. "My name's Claire, by the way, just in case you need me."

"Well, thank you, Claire. I'm sure we'll be fine."

As if it pained her greatly to tear herself away from Evan, Claire walked back toward her podium at the front of the restaurant.

"Where were we?" Evan asked, as he watched Christine take a small tape recorder from her handbag and prop the microphone up on the table.

"You were asking me how old I was and I told you that I'm almost twenty-three. I hope this doesn't make you too uncomfortable," she added, indicating the tape recorder.

"No," he assured her. "I'm used to it," he said, feeling himself losing patience with Christine and with the whole idea of the interview.

"Well, of course you're used to it. Silly me. You're an old pro at this."

"Yes, I'm hopelessly old," he joked. "And how long have you been a journalist, Christine?"

"Oh, just ages," she replied in her stiff British accent. "Since I was nineteen. But I've only been with *Rex* magazine for about a year. My boyfriend, Eddie, plays bass for the Space Lillies—you know them? They're a band from Manchester originally. They did that CD, *Put The Girl Out.*"

"I think I may have heard of them," Evan said, fidgeting with his menu.

"Well, since me and Eddie are 'an item,' as they say, I got the gig at *Rex.* I'm not ashamed to admit it. He's enhanced my profile. Since Eddie and I moved in together there've been a lot of perks, my life has *so* gotten better."

"I'm sure it has. Love does that to a person."

Evan's sarcasm soared clear over Christine's head.

"Yes," she replied uncertainly. "Being in love is great, too."

Evan tapped his menu lightly against the tabletop. "Should we order a drink? Or is it too early in the day for you?"

"Oh, a drink would be *fabulous*. I'm still on London time, you know. I only got in yesterday morning. I was supposed to see a band open at The Truent last evening but by then, it *felt* like four in the morning and I had to crash. My whole body feels topsy turvy."

They ordered their drinks and Evan resigned himself to giving up an entire day to this hopelessly naive social climber who called herself a journalist. Surrendering to defeat was the only way he would survive it.

Throughout lunch, Christine asked the same tedious, unenlightened questions all the journalists asked: "Is it true you were only four when your father left your mother? How did it feel to work with a legend like Robert Trask in *Catastrophe in the Valley*? Was it intimidating? Is it true that he eats lobster for breakfast? Why did your engagement to Lisa Wilson *really* end? Was it her idea to break up? Did you know she's engaged to Paul Rydell now, from the band, F-Stop 4? Do you ever regret dropping out of high school? How did it feel to be abandoned by your father at such a young age? Did it make you closer to your mother? Was it sad when your mother died? Is it true she was married five times? Who are you dating now? Why are you afraid to get married? Is it true that you slept with Norma Pearl last year when you were on location with her in New Zealand for *Trust Not the Innocents*? Are you in love with her?"

Evan desperately wanted a cigarette—anything to escape the tirade of useless questions for even a few minutes. When the lunch dishes were cleared, he asked Christine to excuse him while he went out front for a smoke.

"Oh, I'd just *love* a cig. I'll come with you," she chimed. "Better yet, why don't you come back with me to my hotel? We can sit in the lounge there and smoke to our hearts' content. I wouldn't mind another cocktail, how about you? What do you say?"

Her hotel. Evan wondered if they would wind up in bed together before the day was over. It might be a nice diversion from this inanity, he figured. "Sure, your hotel would be fine," he said. "Where are you staying?"

"At the Hotel Beverly."

"Do you need a lift?"

"No, I have a rental car," Christine said.

"All right, then," Evan agreed. "I'll meet you in the lounge of the Hotel Beverly in about twenty minutes."

What a relief it was for Evan to be alone in his car for the twenty precious minutes it took him to drive to Christine's hotel. He wondered when the whole interview process had become so tedious. In the early days of his career, it had been incredibly exciting to be interviewed by *anyone* from the press. Now it was a necessary evil, an integral part of maintaining his career.

As he idled at a traffic light in his black Mercedes, he thought back ten years to when he'd starred in *The Devil Gets His Way*. It had been Evan's breakthrough film. His life had never been the same since then. Had it really been ten years? In some ways it felt like fifty—in others, a mere heartbeat ago. His mother was still alive back then and she'd been so proud of his success.

Evan remembered the interview he'd done for *Babylon* magazine to promote the film. It was a high point in his early career, when he was still living in New York. Back then, he was giving up a huge portion of his income to afford the best public relations firm on the east coast and they were the ones who had landed him the *Babylon* interview. Evan had been on cloud nine about that.

"Dorianne Constance," he said aloud now, and it made him smile. He'd nearly forgotten how much fun she'd been. "She was so *young* back then," he remembered. It didn't seem possible that it could have been ten years. It had been her first serious assignment so they had both been very nervous for different reasons. It wasn't like it was now, with Dorianne Constance being a well-known writer and Evan secure in his career.

"I only got this job because Kent Cryer is my boyfriend," a twenty-year-old Dorianne had confided to Evan halfway through their interview.

The twenty-five year old Evan had been impressed. "Really? Kent Cryer is your boyfriend? I saw him on television just last night."

"Yes, he's my boyfriend and he owns *Babylon*, so he got me this job. But don't say anything because he's, you know, he's married."

"I won't say anything," he'd assured her—and he never had.

Evan remembered how exhilarating it had felt when Dorianne's interview with him had wound up on the cover of *Babylon* just as *The Devil Gets His Way* hit theaters across the nation, and how Dorianne had made him sound interesting, intelligent, and as if he had a future in films.

Evan pulled his Mercedes up the palm tree-lined drive of the Hotel Beverly and turned his car over to the parking valet just as Christine pulled up behind him in her rental car. He realized that Christine was actually older than Dorianne had been back then, but no one would ever guess it. Christine seemed like a child and Dorianne had been so self-possessed, even under pressure.

"They don't make them like that anymore," Evan sighed. Then he put on his charming movie star smile for Christine and escorted her into the lobby of her hotel.

*   *   *

"Can I get you a little more wine?" Dorianne asked Kent uneasily as they sat together on her living room sofa. The autumn sun barely lingered in the late afternoon sky, casting a warm glow over the elegant room. "I know I have a good bottle of red tucked away somewhere."

"No," Kent replied. "I've had enough wine."

"You know," she confessed, feeling like a nervous schoolgirl trying to make conversation, "besides being hopelessly in love with you way back when, I also idolized you. I owe you a lot. You were my role model. I watched you achieve so much and I just assumed that that was what was expected of anyone who wanted to be a successful journalist. Of course I know now that you were different. That most people never achieve the kind of success you achieved. You really have something special, a gift. You're not like other people. I didn't really know that at the time."

"No, there aren't many who are crazy enough to be as driven as I was."

"I'm crazy enough. I think I'm still trying to be like you in a lot of ways, when you get right down to it."

"I know you mean that as a compliment, Dory. But there's an awful lot of regrettable things about my alleged 'success' that I hope you don't try to duplicate." He put an affectionate hand on her knee. "But look who I'm talking to; Miss Integrity herself. You wouldn't betray a fly, would you? Tell me, Dorianne, were you born good? Or did your parents have to knock it into you the old-fashioned way, like everyone else's?"

Dorianne was caught off-guard. The warmth of Kent's hand on her knee again felt as arousing as it had ever felt and she couldn't ignore it. "I was—you know," her voice faltered as she tried to answer him. "I was like any other kid. My worst fault was being so stubborn."

Dorianne tried to uphold her end of the conversation, but her mind flooded with memories of a much younger Kent and a long ago sofa in an expensive hotel suite—the night he'd first seduced her.

His hand had been on her knee then just like it was now.

Back then it had thrilled her young ego that someone as successful as he was would pay her so much attention. She'd been painfully naive. She'd had no idea she was being seduced by Kent, that he'd deftly steered the conversation to sex by disguising it as a confession. That he was luring Dorianne into his web with his made-up stories about his wife being too uptight to give him the wilder things he craved. And, convincing Dorianne that she was his trusted confidant, he'd gone into explicit details about the sexual acts his wife supposedly disdained and why she disdained them.

"It's makes her feel dirty to show herself to me like that," he'd said. "Dirty and exposed. But the human body is a natural thing. Why should it make her feel dirty? I'm sure it wouldn't make you feel that way. You're too smart to waste time feeling ashamed about something your body likes, right?"

"Right," she'd said.

Yet she had felt a little ashamed—for being sexually aroused by the secrets he was entrusting to her. And ashamed for quietly hoping that his hand would move further up her thigh when she knew he was a married man.

When it finally did, when his hand had moved up under her dress, it had felt like fire and she'd spread her legs willingly for him, eager to show him that her desire to expose herself to him didn't make her feel anything but delight. Soon, she had let him strip her completely naked, fondle and caress her in ways she'd only dreamed about or seen in dirty magazines. She gave him everything he'd asked for, in every immodest position that she believed his wife had denied him.

"My goodness, Dorianne, are you blushing?"

Kent broke in on her reverie. She smiled self-consciously and said nothing. Then, at almost the same moment, they both noticed how Dorianne's cashmere skirt had ridden up her knee, enough to reveal where her black stocking was clipped into her garter. Her exposed thigh seemed impossibly white. She blushed even more at the sight of it and tugged at her skirt.

"What are you thinking about, Dory? You have quite a look on your face."

"I was thinking about old times," she finally confessed.

"There's nothing wrong with that. I've been thinking a lot about that, too."

Kent leaned over and kissed Dorianne on the mouth, taking control as he always did. He held her face gently and looked into her eyes. "I'm different now," he said quietly. "I don't know how else to say it. I want you just as much as I ever did, even more. I hope you can trust me."

Dorianne felt overwhelmed. Still, she let him unbutton her suit jacket, and with trembling fingers, she removed it.

As he had done in the restaurant, Kent traced a finger lightly over the black lace framing her soft breasts. "Was this beautiful lingerie for my benefit," he wanted to know, "or do you always look this pretty under your clothes?"

"It was for you," she admitted softly. "Even though I was undecided about whether or not you should see it."

"Thanks," he said, leaning over to kiss her again. "It looks stunning on you. I'm glad you decided to let me see it."

Dorianne pulled him close letting his hands roam over her concealed breasts while they kissed. She broke away from his kisses to lower the straps of her slip down her arms, until the slip was down around her slender waist. Then she reached behind herself and unclasped the padded bra. Her full breasts spilled out, her nipples were excited and erect.

Kent took in the site of Dorianne's naked tits, heavy on her slim frame, and he couldn't disguise his lust.

She leaned back against the sofa to let Kent explore her.

He took her breasts in his hands and gently squeezed them, tugging the nipples lightly until Dorianne began to writhe with obvious desire. He guided one of her nipples to his lips.

The sensation was exquisite. Dorianne moaned softly as Kent sucked her nipple determinedly in his mouth. The pressure tugged at her breast and she squirmed impatiently on the sofa. She knew that before long she would be completely naked for him, opening herself for his insistent passion as she always had.

She felt Kent reach around for the zipper on the back of her skirt and she tried to help him unfasten it, but he, too, was impatient. He pushed her skirt up instead, clear up her thighs, exposing that impossibly white flesh between the tops of her stockings and her black silk panties. He slipped his hand up the back of her panties and squeezed a sizable portion of her firm, round, womanly behind.

The feel of his hands grabbing her ass made Dorianne want to kiss him passionately. Her bare breasts, the nipples stiff and tender now, pressed full against the crisp cotton of his shirt. She felt his fingers slip to the front of her panties, dip inside the silky crotch of them, to where she had already soaked herself in anticipation of being touched there.

She spread her legs apart for him and he moaned in appreciation.

His fingers slid into her easily, she was so wet, and they filled her, probing her vagina deeply while he kissed her; circling inside the swollen tender passage of her hole, massaging her into a keen heat.

When they finally broke free of the kisses, they were both breathing heavy.

He slid his fingers out of her.

"Lie back," Kent urged her quietly, as he shoved aside the sopping crotch of her panties.

She did as he asked, hardly believing her own excitement, loving the feeling of having her pussy exposed to him. She spread her long legs wide as Kent leaned down and planted his hot mouth right on her erect clitoris. He sucked it in between his lips, stroking it ceaselessly with his tongue and driving her deeper into ecstasy.

She was panting now, groaning with pleasure when he suddenly stopped.

"Why didn't it ever occur to me to just divorce Katherine and marry you, Dory? What was I so afraid of?"

"I don't know," Dorianne replied breathlessly, still held in the erotic throes of lust, her thighs spread wide for Kent, her slick female arousal dripping plainly in front of his face.

"I think I was afraid that if I were with you, Dory, I wouldn't have been able to play the field. I could never have cheated on a woman like you. I wouldn't have been able to screw all those women who were always throwing themselves at me. I would have loved you too much. What a fool I was to pass up love. What a waste," he lamented, pushing a finger deep into Dorianne's engorged hole, making her moan again. "Playing the field is just empty sex," he lamented, letting the finger slide in and out, "and there's nothing lonelier than empty sex, is there?"

Dorianne felt Kent's mouth return greedily to her aching clitoris and she answered as best she could.

"No," she whimpered softly as his tongue licked the tender flesh over and over, a second finger pushing into her hole as he licked her. Then he sucked her clit hard, and worked his fingers up inside her hole vigorously.

"Yes," she gasped, answering him finally, clutching her knees to her tits, keeping herself spread for him, coming now. "Yes, yes, yes."

And to herself, she said, "Empty sex must be the loneliest sex there is."

*   *   *

Christine's room in the Hotel Beverly was as ordinary as it could be—a king-sized bed, a desk, a chair, a television set, and a chest of drawers. A closet, a bathroom; nothing at all like the multi-room suites in the five-star hotels Evan was accustomed to staying in all over the world. But it didn't matter. He was only here for what would amount to a mere moment in the scope of his career. He wouldn't even be spending the night.

Christine wobbled slightly on her five-inch platform sandals. She'd managed to put away quite a few cosmopolitans in the lounge and then Evan had bought her dinner. The first thing she did when she and Evan were alone in her hotel room, was kick off the clunky shoes. When she was in her bare feet, Evan couldn't believe how tiny she seemed. She was about five feet tall to his six-foot-one frame. For a fleeting instant, he had the impression he was alone in a hotel room with a child. It made him want to ask her for some ID.

That would be crazy, he realized. Someone had rented

her a car at the airport. They've been serving her cosmopolitans all day in the bar. She writes for a famous foreign magazine. If she were underage, surely someone would have discovered it by now.

Still, it seemed as though everything had a way of making it into the tabloids and hounding him. The last thing he wanted to experience was a scandal involving an under-aged girl. His career would be over.

"Are you really twenty-three?" he asked her, trying to sound as if he were only half-serious.

"Well, I will be on my next birthday, which is right before Christmas," Christine replied, shooting him a curious smile. "Why? Do you think you're too old for me? I've been with plenty of men older than you." As she said this, she opened the top drawer of the dresser and casually tossed a condom packet onto the bed.

Evan felt very sorry for poor Eddie Bailey, the bass player for the Space Lillies. He certainly had himself a devoted woman in Christine Miles—traveling with condoms, no less. But then maybe Eddie was just as faithless to Christine when he was on the road with his band. Evan figured that, in the long run, it wasn't any of his business. Christine had been the one to suggest coming up to her room, not Evan.

"It's one of my fantasies," she'd confided to Evan during dinner—although Evan had assumed it was the cosmopolitans causing her to be so candid. "I've always dreamed about having sex with you, you know. Think of it: me and Evan Crane"—she said this as if she were talking about a third person who wasn't even present—"one of the sexiest men alive."

Now here she was in front of Evan, taking off all her clothes, preparing to do something that suddenly seemed very mechanical to him.

These were the moments when Evan felt most like a trained animal act in a circus. 'Handsome Evan Crane,' he was always called in the tabloids. The editors at *Babylon* had been the ones who'd dubbed him 'The sexiest man alive,' back when *Catastrophe in the Valley* had been released. It was catch phrases like those that made Evan feel removed from his own name, and it had gradually turned him into a commodity even in bed.

"Aren't you joining me?" Christine asked. She was totally naked now and sitting in the middle of the king-sized bed. The pink nipples on her small breasts were soft and unexcited. Her pierced navel winked at Evan. A tattoo sliced across her ankle and another one climbed garishly up her pale thigh. And between her legs, Evan could plainly see that only a hint of blonde pubic hair had managed to escape a professional waxing.

Evan gave it some thought. He couldn't get past the fact that she looked like a child and he had no desire for a young girl's body at all. He was thirty-five years old already; he wanted grown women, with meat on their bones.

And Evan knew he would merely be some sort of trophy for Christine, a prize; just one of the many mementoes from the never-ending cavalcade of her sex life. But if he backed out now and humiliated her, he could only imagine the hatchet job that would be done on him in Rex magazine. His manager would be livid. But his manager didn't have to stand here on display as Evan was, faced with the prospects of stripping out of his clothes and then driving this senseless young woman to orgasm so that one more of her childish fantasies could be fulfilled.

Then desperation inspired him. "You know, Christine," Evan explained cautiously, "I'm worried about Eddie. It's not my style to take advantage of another man's woman. It wouldn't be right."

Christine stared at Evan, dumbfounded.

"I can only imagine how much he treasures you and I wouldn't want to be any part of spoiling that for him. I know I wouldn't want another man moving in on my girl when she was far away from me."

Christine was beside herself. If she tried to protest, it would be like admitting that Eddie didn't 'treasure' her.

"I'd better go," Evan went on, "before we get into some kind of trouble that we can't get out of. But it was a real pleasure to meet you, Christine. I hope you have a safe trip home."

Without so much as a good-bye from her, Evan left Christine sitting naked on her bed.

In the elevator going down to the lobby, he signed an autograph for an excited female tourist. Then he tipped the parking valet generously before jumping into his black Mercedes and speeding toward home, alone.

*   *   *

Dorianne's cashmere skirt, her suit jacket, and her expensive silk under things were strewn across her living room carpeting. She was completely naked except for her shiny black spiked-heeled shoes. Kent had insisted she put them back on after he'd stripped her out of the shimmering black stockings.

Being totally naked except for her pretty shoes made Dorianne feel even more naked, for some reason. It delighted her.

She allowed Kent to lead her by the hand to the bedroom, stopping once in the hall so that Kent could go down on his knees between her long legs again. He licked and sucked her down there, holding her slippery lips spread to more readily torment her clitoris, while she steadied herself against the cool wall. When he stood, he kissed her full on the mouth, letting her taste herself on his lips, his tongue. Then he put a firm hand on the back of her head, guiding her down to her knees to please him with her mouth in return.

When other men did this to her, Dorianne always pushed their hands aside, uncomfortable with the idea of pleasuring anybody with her mouth when she wasn't in the mood. And she was rarely in the mood. But with Kent, it had always been different. Everything about his body excited her.

She went down to her knees willingly in the hall. She kissed and licked the length of his cock before taking him all the way in. She didn't mind his fingers grasping lightly at her hair as he guided his thick hard-on in and out of her mouth, gently, at first, then more insistently as his pleasure increased. With Kent, she didn't object to anything. She welcomed all the different forms his pleasure could take.

Kent was back to his old self now. He didn't seem fifty years old. Maybe he wasn't in the best shape he'd ever been in, but his lust for Dorianne was as powerful as it had ever been. His sense of command, his ability to lead her and to stay in control of her while he guided her through the lovemaking hadn't diminished a bit.

When they were in Dorianne's bedroom, he told her to bend over the end of the bed for him—to spread her legs apart for him.

"Wider than that," he said.

Dorianne did as he asked. She spread her legs wider and bent over the edge of the bed for him, going all the way down to her elbows, even though she quickly discovered that the impossibly high heels she wore made this a longer trip down than usual and that her full, round ass felt even more on display.

Kent got down between her legs to watch his fingers slide in and out of her soaking hole. Slowly, thoroughly. He took his time with Dorianne as he watched her entire vulva become more and more engorged. Then he pulled his fingers out of her, spread her lips open wider and teased her clitoris with the very tip of his tongue.

Those familiar, delightful whimpers she'd always made once again filled the room.

Then, at last, when Dorianne was so aroused with lust that she was thrusting her bottom out wickedly with every stroke of his probing tongue, Kent righted himself and mounted her, his thick cock sliding in deep.

"Oh god," Dorianne groaned, feeling as if it had been a lifetime since she'd felt Kent inside her.

As he pushed up into her all the way, she felt her tight hole opening around him, accommodating his size, his length. "That feels so good," she cried softly.

As he'd done with his fingers, Kent worked his cock in and out of Dorianne slowly—at first until he was certain she was ready for something more demanding. Listening to her sweet cries, her occasional deep groans, Kent steadily picked up his rhythm with her until he was pounding into Dorianne's hole so hard and so deep, she had to grasp tight to the blankets to keep her balance in those tall high heels.

"Oh god," she was crying out, losing all sense of herself. "Yes, oh yes."

She pushed her hole out to him, to meet his powerful thrusts and show him she could take it, that she wanted to feel it hard.

"Scoot up onto the bed," Kent told her. "Get your legs up under yourself."

Dorianne did as he asked, knowing that she was completely exposed to him now, her hole vulnerable to his repeated pounding, but she didn't care. She craved his force. She offered herself too him eagerly, spreading her thighs wide.

.   Kent positioned himself between her legs again, grabbed hold of her slender waist and resumed his merciless rhythm. Up into her hole he plunged, all the way up, over and over—her sweet, helpless cries, pulling his cock in deep.

Dorianne was in ecstasy, coming on his cock as he fucked her, taking the relentless pounding with joy as she came, remembering what it felt like to be in love again, finally, after so many years of convincing herself she could live okay without it.

CHAPTER THREE

The Los Angeles night was balmy and clear. Evan Crane sat alone on the terrace off his bedroom in his house way up in the Hollywood Hills. He stared idly down at the city lights and smoked a cigarette.

What a waste, he thought. He'd given up an entire day and most of an evening to that interview and now it would be a miracle if a flattering story came out of it.

Not that he needed to be flattered, but a hatchet job in a magazine as trendy as *Rex* meant that the tabloids would jump all over it. Endlessly re-printing the most damaging quotes and, of course, printing them totally out of context. It had a trickle down effect, too, that could get very tiresome. Once the tabloids got a hold of bad press, the misquoted information would turn up in interview after interview for years to come.

Nothing was as unflattering in an interview than seeming defensive about something in the past, even if that something had been a pack of lies in the first place. Evan would certainly have his work cut out for him for the next several years if the *Rex* interview was a bust.

It was already after midnight but Evan decided it would be best to call John Ebbins, his manager, and warn him about what might be lurking on the horizon. Evan flipped open his cell phone and hit the speed dial.

When John answered, it was obvious Evan had woken him from a sound sleep. It took John a minute to even figure out who he was talking to.

"Evan, it's after two. What is it?"

"I just wanted to let you know how the interview with the reporter from *Rex* magazine went today."

"This can't possibly be good…"

"No, it's not. It went okay up until the end. But then I refused to sleep with her—"

"Evan," John cut in. "You've got to be joking. You can't sleep with journalists. It's too damn risky. And you have the nerve to ask me why the press is always labeling you a womanizer."

"What are you trying to say, John? That I'm not supposed to want to have sex with a good-looking woman, even if she's a writer?"

"Was this woman from *Rex* good-looking? Who was it?"

"Christine Miles."

"Oh not *Christine*, Evan. She's a regular rumor factory all on her own."

"Well, she was cute enough, but then she looked to be about twelve with her clothes off. At first, when she came on to me, I went along with it. But when it came down to actually doing it with her, I couldn't go through with it. I didn't exactly leave her in 'coitus interruptus.' But it was close enough."

"Jesus, Evan. I can't believe this. Haven't you ever heard that phrase about Hell having no fury like a woman scorned? And Christine Miles, of all people. She has a mouth on her that won't quit."

"Well, what do I know? I figured she was just some opportunistic kid from London."

It went silent on the other end of the phone and Evan could hear John lighting a cigarette. John was fully awake now.

"This is going to require some damage control. Let's put our thinking caps on, Evan. The article for *Rex* won't be going to press for about three months and not many U.S. newsstands are going to be carrying it anyway. We might be able to confine the damage to the U.K. And as a safeguard, we can generate all kinds of beneficial stories for you here in the States in that amount of time. After all, you'll be doing the shoot for *Blast* in the meantime. We just have to figure out the angle on this."

Evan succumbed to that sense of hopelessness that always overtook him at times like this, when it was late and he was feeling tired and depressed.

"Sometimes I wish there was a way I could just get it all out," he lamented. "Tell the real story of my life, get the facts straight once and for all. Stop all the gossip, all the crap they sling at me all the time. Have my say for a change, you know? Like it would matter though," he added in defeat. "I know that's never going to happen."

"You know, Evan, you might have something there. We could do a book, a memoir. I'm sure we could get you a colossal deal. Then you could have your say and have something big to promote at the same time."

"A book? That's insane, John. How am I supposed to write a book? I can barely focus long enough to write a postcard."

"We get someone to ghost it for you. Or do one of those " as told to

' jobs . Get a top-notch writer to do the actual work. Someone hot, you know; further increase the potential interest."

"Someone like Christine Miles, for instance?"

"No, but we could think of someone who'd be a little more supportive. You know, someone who would be on our team. There's bound to be someone out there who's perfect."

Evan agreed to at least give it some thought. "I'll sleep on it," he said. "Sorry I woke you with all this, John. I hope you don't have too much trouble getting back to sleep."

"Forget about it, Evan. That's what I'm here for."

Evan clicked his cell phone closed and stared distractedly at the night.

A book about his life was a lousy idea, Evan thought. No way did he really want all the details of his life becoming further fodder for the unpredictable public. Mostly he didn't want to have to talk about his childhood, about his father, or about his mother's many marriages to men who had always disrupted Evan's life. And god knows Evan didn't want to put down on paper what it had felt like when his mother was dying. Or how horribly unfinished everything had seemed since she'd died.

And who on earth could he possibly tell any of this stuff to? These were the kinds of things it was hard talking about to a close friend, how could he tell it to a stranger? A writer, no less—the type of person Evan found the least trustworthy. Too adversarial, every last one of them.

Except Dorianne, of course. She hadn't had some secret agenda going on. She'd just wanted to write the best story she could.

Suddenly Evan's thoughts sprang to attention. Why not, he wondered. Dorianne Constance could be the perfect person for a project like this. She built a career on putting movie stars in the best possible light.

Evan dialed John Ebbins again. This time, John answered on the first ring.

"What is it, Evan? I knew it would be you."

"Dorianne Constance, John. What do you think of that?"

"She'd cost us a fortune."

"But it would be worth every penny."

"Let's see what we can do in the morning. I'll call some people. See what kind of money we might be talking about. Find out what we could even offer her. Try to get some sleep now, Evan, okay? Your career isn't over yet."

*   *   *

The early morning was rainy and cold as the gray dawn crept in low over the Manhattan sky. Dorianne had hardly slept a wink. Her face in the bathroom mirror looked puffy and tired, as if she had cried all night, and that's exactly what had happened. What little sleep she'd managed to get had been filled with restless dreams about Kent.

As she'd been half-expecting, she regretted having had sex with him. It had been like opening Pandora's Box. After they'd finished making love, Kent had informed her that he couldn't spend the night with her. That in fact, he had to leave quickly to attend a cocktail party—that he was late already. He didn't bother to invite Dorianne to come along with him. He showered and got dressed, he kissed her, and he left. Once more, she felt used.

But now that she'd experienced being intimate with Kent again, she was forced to admit to herself just how much she'd actually missed having him in her life. And now she was faced with the very real possibility of having to let him go forever. Because even though Kent's wife was no longer in the picture, Dorianne wasn't going to take a backseat to his career again. In a way, she thought, Kent might as well still be married to Katherine, if he was just going to go off to parties and leave her feeling used and exposed like that.

The schedule for the day ahead of her was full. She would need to be at her desk late into the evening if she were going to make up for the time she'd lost spending so many hours with Kent the day before. But her mind was too scattered to focus. How would she get any work done?

Dorianne sat in her favorite chair, looking out the window at her view of the Hudson River and drank a cup of coffee. The river that usually flowed by so beautiful and blue was now only reflecting the drab, gray sky.

When her telephone rang, she didn't know how long she'd been sitting there motionless, staring out the window. Her half-drunk coffee was cold.

"Hello?" she said wearily.

"I'm sorry, Miss Constance, did I wake you?"

"No. Who is this?"

"This is John Ebbins. I'm Evan Crane's manager, calling from L.A. It sounds like I might have caught you at a bad time."

Evan Crane's manager? It took Dorianne a moment to figure out who Evan Crane was. When it finally sunk in, she was mystified. Why would Evan Crane's manager be calling her?

"This certainly is a coincidence, Mr. Ebbins."

"Please, call me 'John.'"

"Okay—John."

"And why is it a coincidence?"

"An old friend and I were just talking about Evan Crane at lunch yesterday."

"Well, I hope you had nothing but good things to say."

"That would depend on what side of the table you were on."

"I see," John laughed. "I won't touch that one. Let me tell you why I'm calling."

"Please do."

"Evan and I have a little proposition for you."

"A proposition?" Dorianne repeated skeptically. "And what might that proposition be?"

"Harrisberg, Barker & Bliss have offered Evan a seven-figure advance on his autobiography."

"That's very impressive," Dorianne replied. "And what does that have to do with me?"

"Well, Evan maintains that he can't focus long enough to write a postcard."

"Seems odd that if he felt that way, he would go after a book deal to write his memoirs. You can't seriously be getting ready to ask me what I think you're going to ask me. I'm not a ghost writer or a hired gun."

"Think of it more as a collaboration. Evan very much wants to be a part of this project. He wouldn't be simply turning it over to you, Miss Constance. He would be counting on you to help him really express himself. And you wouldn't be ghosting it; I want that to be clear. Your name would be on the cover, if that's what you want. I know we want that. And we're willing to negotiate a share of the advance plus royalties. What do say, do you want to think about it?"

"I don't know, Mr. Ebbins."

"Please, it's John."

"I have a full plate as it is. This is right out of left field. I've never done anything like this before."

"Just look at it like it's a really long interview with Evan that pays really well. I'm sure you can do it with your eyes closed."

John laughed uneasily, setting Dorianne's already worn nerves on edge.

"And what's "pays really well" mean in terms of actual dollars?"

"It's negotiable."

"That's not much of an answer."

"Listen, I'll tell you what. Are you going to be around today? I can have Evan call you himself and the two of you can discuss it. Would that be better for you?"

"I'm really booked solid today, John."

"It won't take more than a few minutes. Please, Dorianne, it means a lot to Evan. You're one of the few writers he actually respects. It's a tough industry, you know that."

"Yes, I know that."

"What do you say? Can he at least call you?"

Dorianne sighed. She wondered if she'd really get any work done today or not. Maybe she would simply sit and stare out the window until night fell. "Okay," she reluctantly agreed. "You can have Mr. Crane call me. I'll be here."

"*Fabulous*," John replied emphatically, sounding as if he'd already clinched the deal. "Evan is going to be very happy to speak with you."

"Well, I'll be very happy to speak to him, too, I'm sure."

It was no more than ten minutes before Dorianne's phone rang again. It can't be Evan Crane already, she thought.

She picked up the phone warily. Half-prepared for an all-out snow job. "Hello?" she said.

"Dory, honey, it's me, Kent. I hope I didn't wake you."

Dorianne's entire body eased a sigh of relief. Kent hadn't forgotten about her. Maybe she had overreacted last night.

"Good morning, Kent," she said in a genuinely friendly tone. "No, you didn't wake me. I've been up since dawn. You know what?"

"What?"

"I just got a call from Evan Crane's manager in L.A. Isn't that a coincidence?"

Kent's voice perked up. "Evan Crane's manager? What was he calling you for? Something percolating out there in Hollywood?"

Dorianne loved to hear Kent's voice sounding so chipper and enthusiastic. Just like old times; whenever work was involved, or a hot story seemed imminent, Kent was on the scent of it like a bloodhound.

"Something's percolating, all right. Evan got offered a seven-figure deal from Harrisberg, Barker & Bliss for his memoirs and they want me to write it."

"*No*," Kent laughed. "You can't be serious. That's incredible."

"Oh, I'm serious. Evan Crane is going to be calling me today to 'negotiate' the money side of the offer."

"They're letting *Crane* do the negotiating? Are they nuts?"

"Probably."

"You know, Dory, if the money's right, this could be a good project for you. You could spend some time out in L.A., in the sunshine, at the beach. It would be a nice change of pace for you. I don't think you ever leave New York. Granted, you have a beautiful apartment now, but you're like a hermit over there."

The notion of leaving New York and spending any length of time in Los Angeles hadn't even dawned on Dorianne yet. She didn't like the thought of it—especially not now.

"Kent, I couldn't go away and leave you," she confessed foolishly.

"Hey, whoa, wait a minute, Dory. Don't you dare pass up a good opportunity solely because of me. If you don't want the job, that's one thing. But I won't have you stuck here in New York all winter on my account, passing up a shot at some big bucks.

Not to mention the Hollywood parties and premieres."

Dorianne felt her heart breaking all over again. Kent didn't really want her, otherwise, wouldn't he beg her to stay? Maybe it was just simple exhaustion going to work at her, but she couldn't disguise her grief. "But Kent I *want* to be here with you."

"They have phones in L.A., you know, and we could do email. We wouldn't really be separated."

"But it's not the same," Dorianne said quietly. "I haven't been able to be with you for ten years. And now that you're back here, I don't think I'm ready to be on the other side of the continent from you."

"I appreciate that," Kent replied, "but this is a once in a lifetime chance for most writers. I'm not going to let you toss it aside without giving it some real, serious thought. You need to examine it from all sides. Don't you think that makes more sense than dismissing it out of hand?"

"I suppose so," she agreed reluctantly. Then she tried her best to sound like the professional she'd been up until yesterday. "You're right, as usual, Kent," she admitted. "I need to behave like a grown up, look out for my career. I'm not a little girl anymore. I have responsibilities. I'm a grown woman."

"You sure are, honey," Kent sighed. "Boy, are you grown."

When Dorianne hung up the phone, she thought she could feel Kent's hands all over her. But it made her feel like crying. Something in his voice had been pulling away from her, pushing her to L.A.

*   *   *

It was after three in the afternoon, New York time, when Evan Crane finally called. Dorianne had drifted to sleep on her living room couch.

"Hello?" she answered sleepily.

"Dorianne? This is Evan Crane. Did I wake you?"

"Well, Evan Crane. It's been a long time." Dorianne struggled to rouse herself from sleep. "I guess maybe you did wake me. It looks like I fell asleep on the couch."

"I'm sorry," Evan said. "Should I call you later?"

"No, no, really. This is fine. I just had a rough night last night and I'm really exhausted."

"I hope it was nothing serious."

Without even realizing she was doing it, Dorianne confided to Evan. "An old flame of mine turned up out of nowhere and it threw me for a loop. Oh—you know him; Kent Cryer."

"Kent Cryer? You two split up?"

"Years ago. You may recall he was married. He just turned up out of nowhere, told me he was single again, apologized to me about everything, and then walked all over my heart. Well, I guess that's simplifying it a lot."

"I know how that is," Evan said. "In a way, that happened with me and my mother. We were only sporadically close throughout my whole life and then suddenly she turned up out of the blue and wanted to make amends for everything. Only she had cancer. It was rough."

"I guess that's part of dying," Dorianne offered. "Wanting to make amends."

"Would you rather I called you back at a better time? You must be going through a lot right now."

"No, Evan, really. It's okay. So you've got yourself a book deal, have you? Want to tell me about it?"

"It's not really a deal yet. My manager put out some feelers and the first response we got was a pretty astounding offer from

Harrisberg, Barker & Bliss. They gave us an offer within an hour actually, but I didn't want to pursue anything definite without having a writer on board that I really trusted. I couldn't undertake something like this on my own. In fact, this was more John's idea than mine, initially."

"Are you sure you want to go through with it then?"

"If I'm working with someone I can stand for more than five minutes a day then, yes, I want to go through with it."

"You know, Evan, I have to be frank. This isn't the kind of work I do. It would be a huge commitment of time and energy for me. Not just to write it, but to promote it, as well."

"But the money they're offering is great and I'm willing to split it fifty-fifty with you. Right down the middle; advance, royalties, all of it."

Dorianne was skeptical. "Fifty-fifty, Evan? That's insane. Why would you do something like that?"

"Because I already have more money than I can spend in this lifetime, Dorianne. And I'm booked solid with film deals for the next two years. I wouldn't be doing this for the money."

Dorianne was still incredulous, but she was intrigued. "Why are you doing it then?"

"To have my say," Evan confessed. "In the long run, I know it probably won't matter a bit, but it would give me a chance to express myself. Tell my side of things."

"What do you mean by 'things'?"

"Life. You know, things like that."

"I don't suppose you're planning on moving to New York for this project?"

"No, but we'll put you up here. We'll cover all the expenses. You can stay wherever you want. How about a bungalow at Casa Hollywood? You could probably stand that for awhile, couldn't you, Dorianne?"

Dorianne laughed. "Yes, I think I could stand it. For a little while, anyway."

"You could always move in with me if you wanted to," he offered. "I have a huge house in the hills all to myself."

"I don't know about that, Evan. I'm sure you would want your privacy. I know your social life is pretty active."

"And how would you know that? Don't tell me you believe what they print in the movie magazines? You of all people!"

Dorianne laughed again. "Sometimes I do."

"Well, okay. But don't believe *all* of it. I might have an active social life, but I don't bring it home with me. My privacy is something I'm rabid about."

"Well, then I wouldn't want to intrude. Evan, listen, let me think about it."

"Sure. How about twenty-four hours?"

"*Twenty-four hours?* That's not very much time. What's the big rush?"

"There's no rush, really. I just want to know. I'm impatient. Take twenty-five hours, if you have to. It's a sweet deal for you, Dorianne. All expenses paid, an advance of one million five, and a four percent royalty until it goes out of print."

Dorianne was astonished. *"What?"*

"I told you I'd go fifty-fifty with you, all down the line."

"Jesus, Evan. That's some serious money."

"It's a serious offer."

"Well, I know, but—wow. I had no idea."

"Give it some thought and call me, Dorianne. Soon. It was really nice talking with you again, you know that?"

"Thanks, Evan. It was nice talking to you, too. Thanks for calling. I promise I'll call you as soon as I've had a little time to think. Better give me your number, or would you prefer I talk to your manager about this?"

"No, you can call me anytime, Dorianne. I mean that. Whether you want the job or not."

CHAPTER FOUR

Central Park in the fall looks just like it does in the movies, Dorianne thought.

The breathtaking hues of the changing leaves were everywhere in abundance. Young lovers strolled hand in hand along the paths. And the elderly men and women, with perhaps too much time on their hands, dotted the park benches, remembering autumn yesterdays that had probably swept past in the wink of an eye.

Dorianne always found it strangely amusing, how her impressions of real life could still be so profoundly influenced by images from the movies, even though she'd been exposed to every aspect of filmmaking during the past ten years of working for *Babylon*. She was well aware of how the 'magic' was created on movie sets and sound stages, and in editing rooms with the help of elaborate computer programs. Yet Hollywood's idea of Central Park in the fall was in a sense more real to Dorianne than the actual park was.

Whenever she found herself marveling at the beauty of the trees, the sloping greens, the boats on the lake, the fountains; she'd think to herself approvingly, *'this is just like in the movies.'* As if the celluloid images of the past gave authenticity to the reality of here and now.

One thing about the so-called magic of Hollywood, though, that her career had changed drastically for Dorainne was her perception of the people who starred in the films. It was true what Kent had said at lunch the other day. People didn't make it to the top in Hollywood by being nice. Not that every star she'd encountered over the years had been ruthless or over-sexed, they did all tend to share a steely determination to succeed no matter what the sacrifice or cost. Many of them were shockingly vain and constantly insecure about how they measured up to their peers.

There were full-time publicity machines that cranked out manufactured personalities for every movie star, depending on the type of picture that star was promoting at any given time. Dorianne sometimes saw entire chunks of a star's past disappear from the public's perception. And it wasn't by accident. It was because it contradicted the star's persona in a movie they were trying to promote at the time. It was a tightly orchestrated strategy on behalf of the publicity machine. It didn't matter how genuine or down-to-earth a star seemed. Dorianne knew from her countless experiences of interviewing the stars in person, that there wasn't one who'd escaped at least some aspect of the 'manufactured personality.'

What would it be like, she wondered, spending so much time with a hugely successful star like Evan Crane? Even though she had genuinely liked him the one and only time their paths had crossed, it had been many years ago. Evan Crane was hardly as successful then as he was now. Certain aspects of his persona were surely complete fabrications by now. Would he be difficult to be around?

And what about all those lurid stories about his womanizing? There was more than likely a germ of truth at the bottom of those tabloid stories. What concerned her more, though, were the stories that might be *more* lurid that had maybe been doggedly squelched by the many people who protected Evan Crane's career. Dorianne knew that every major star had at least a handful of those kinds of stories. After a certain level of staggering success had been achieved, as in the case of an Evan Crane, a star always went through a period of excess, when reality careened out of control.

Dorianne sat down distractedly on a park bench and searched her thoughts for anything she could recall that had caused so much as a blip on the screen of Evan Crane's career.

There was something about a sex party at a beach house in Maui once, she remembered. She was almost positive that had involved Evan Crane. The story had disappeared overnight, which was usually a sign that someone was being protected.

But why would I care about any of this, she wondered. Why do I feel so suspicious of Evan's offer?

Because the offer is too good, she answered herself. Something must be up, she figured, and she was afraid of tarnishing her hard-won reputation of integrity and taste.

On the phone, Kent had referred to this preoccupation with Dorianne's reputation as just her way of being an "old stick in the mud." And he had only been half-joking.

"You've got to lighten up a little, honey," he'd said. "Look at the amount of money they're offering you. Most people never earn that much money in a lifetime, let alone for one assignment. You might be taking yourself a little too seriously here.

You're only thirty, honey. You should be living the *hell* out of life."

"But writing a book is a huge commitment," she offered on her own behalf.

"I know that, but let's face it, part of the compensation for this particular commitment is an all-expenses paid, five-star stay in Hollywood and personal access to one of its A-list stars. Frankly, I think you'd be nuts not to jump at it. What will you be missing here in New York—the lousy winter, the ice and filthy slush in the streets? It's not as if winter in New York were just one long tracking shot of Central Park dusted with snow at dusk and the warmly lit Plaza Hotel sitting serenely in the background."

Dorianne smiled to herself now, thinking about what Kent had said.

There it is again, she thought—my hopeless idealism. Even Kent remembers me well enough to know that I'm always living a separate life in my head that's straight out of the movies.

She tried to picture herself actually doing it, living her life in Los Angeles, in one of those famous bungalows at Casa Hollywood. She would spend her mornings in one of those fluffy white robes, ordering room service, while typing away on her laptop, finishing up any deadlines that she was already committed to. Then her afternoons and evenings would be spent with Evan Crane; interviewing him, watching him, taking notes. She imagined herself wearing designer sunglasses and expensive evening gowns.

Would it be so bad, she wondered, spending all that time with Evan Crane? He was at the peak of his career now. And Dorianne had to admit, Evan was good looking.

"Almost *too* good looking," she said out loud, startling herself.

Kent was right, she realized. This was an offer of a lifetime and she would be nuts not to at least *try* it. Kent would still be around when she returned, and she'd already managed to survive ten years without him. And what could Evan Crane be after that would be so damaging to her reputation? So what if he'd bedded a lot of females in the past? He was obviously offering Dorianne an actual job, helping him to write his memoirs. It's not as though a man who was as famous as Evan had to offer someone like Dorianne a million and a half plus royalties just to fly out to L.A. and sleep with him.

"Good lord, if that isn't flattering myself, what is?"

Dorianne looked around quickly to see if anyone had noticed her talking to herself and then she lightened up considerably. She made up her mind to put in a call to Evan as soon as she went back to her apartment. Barring any unforeseen details that might come to light after talking to Evan again, Dorianne was prepared to accept his offer.

*   *   *

It was, as always, a bright sunny morning on the avenues and boulevards of West Hollywood. The traffic was thick with cars in a hurry to get someplace. High above it all in the hills, Evan was already awake and drinking a cup of coffee on his terrace, quietly overlooking the criss-crossing madness far below. The last few nights, he'd been having trouble sleeping. Compared to his usual habit of sleeping late, this morning he could almost qualify as an early bird.

He lit his first cigarette of the day and inhaled, but it wasn't satisfying. He surprised himself by stubbing it out.

Why did everything seem so disenchanting lately, he wondered. Was it one of those mid-life crisis things, sneaking up on him early? He was only thirty-five, but he was starting to feel ancient.

Being interviewed by a jaded twenty-three year old journalist like Christine Miles doesn't help, he decided.

Evan tried to remember what he'd been like at twenty-three but all he could remember doing was working. It seemed as if all he *ever* did was work. He had all the outer trappings of wealth; a couple of expensive cars, a mansion in the Hollywood Hills, a beautiful beach house on Maui, and plenty of money to eat whatever he wanted to eat and travel wherever he wanted to go. Yet aside from the caretakers in his two homes, his Personal Manager, and his accountant, Evan had no one significant in his life. People came and went, but none of them could qualify as a constant friend.

Evan hadn't been aware of ever wanting anyone in his life who would be too permanent. In fact, he was well aware of having gone out of his way to keep his life free of entanglements that might complicate his work schedule, or bog him down during his rise to fame. He enjoyed waking up when he wanted to, staying out as late as he wanted to, picking up and traveling somewhere when the spirit moved him, and partying with whoever seemed interesting at the moment.

He didn't even like to be encumbered with possessions. He bought expensive things mostly to give away as gifts to co-stars or other business associates. He read voraciously, but rarely even held on to his favorite books. He had eclectic tastes in music, but as often as his CDs piled up, one by one the stack disappeared as he traveled from place to place for business or pleasure.

Nothing was constant in his life and it never had been, as far back as Evan could remember. Beginning with his mother's first divorce and then the death of Evan's father when Evan was barely four. And continuing with man after man who'd come into his mother's life and try half-heartedly to be a father to Evan.

Each new stepfather brought a new house to live in that Evan pretended to call home, a new school filled with new kids who were never Evan's friends for very long, and sometimes even a new city or state.

By watching his mother, a very young Evan had surmised that 'true love' only resulted in children who then needed to be provided for no matter what the personal cost to the mother; children who were created by one man and then thrust on to other men who might be willing, at least for awhile, to be the financial providers.

When Evan grew to be a little older, he began to discern that men were willing to be the providers for another man's child for as long as the mother remained sexually appealing. When the constant lovemaking died down, the fighting started. Soon enough after that, it would be time for a new stepfather.

Evan had been drawn to acting—at first to the drama department at school, then to local theaters and finally to low budget television commercials—because pretending to be someone else was an irresistible lure for Evan's imagination. His home life was so distasteful and empty to Evan that he already lived his life mostly in his head anyway. It wasn't much of a stretch for him to extend his flight from reality to include acting out parts in plays.

After landing a spot in his first television commercial, though, when he was only seventeen, it became immediately apparent to him that there was plenty of money out there to be made in a way that he thoroughly enjoyed. After his first paycheck came from the television commercial, it didn't take too much pleading on Evan's part to persuade his mother to let him drop out of school and pursue a professional acting career full-time.

Once he had a handful of local commercials under his belt,

Evan had been able to land a good agent who secured spots for him in top-paying national commercials and then Evan was essentially on his way. Even though it had taken seven years' worth of feature films before Evan finally broke through to the big time, it had been seven years of *consistent* work, which was more than most actors ever achieved.

Evan didn't kid himself. He knew most of his success had been based on not only his good looks, but on how photogenic he was; an ability to act was almost secondary. But that didn't mean that Evan hadn't tried his best. He'd gotten an acting coach and taken private acting lessons, elocution lessons, deportment lessons— anything that would enhance his presence on screen.

All of it had worked to make Evan a hugely attractive star. Yet when he'd signed on to do *Catastrophe in the Valley* with second billing to the legendary Robert Trask, Trask had refused to speak to Evan except when it was only absolutely necessary to the filming. It was clear Trask considered himself a 'serious actor' and Evan merely an empty-headed pretty boy who couldn't act his way out of a paper bag.

Life on that set had been hellish for Evan. It was a 'serious' picture and few of his fellow cast members had taken Evan's presence in the film seriously. But he came through it smelling like a rose to the public. The success of *Catastrophe* had garnered Evan millions and millions of dollars.

There it is again, Evan realized. My personal relationships are practically non-existent, and still my career escalates.

Then his phone rang.

It was Evan's private home number. Since there were so few people in Evan's private life, he never hesitated to answer his phone. It was bound to be someone he didn't mind talking to.

"Evan? It's Dorianne Constance. Just as the phone was ringing,

I realized it might be a little early out there for you. I hope I didn't wake you."

"No, Dorianne, not at all. This time *I'm* the one who couldn't sleep. I'm already up and having coffee. I'm glad to hear from you. I hope you have some great news for me."

"I think I do, Evan. I gave it a lot of thought and I've decided I'd like to accept your offer. I'm going to have my agent work out the details with your manager and the publisher. Unless there are any new developments you wanted to tell me about?"

"What do you mean?"

"Well, you had said when we spoke last time that you hadn't continued your negotiations with the publisher because you wanted the writer on board first. I was just wondering if there had been any other discussions I might need to know about."

"No, nothing. I was just waiting to hear from you."

"Evan, can I ask you something?"

"Sure, Dorianne, what is it?"

"Why this sudden compulsion to tell your life story? I mean, didn't you tell me it was more your manager's idea? Are you sure you want to go through with this?"

"Yes, I'm sure. Especially now that you're on board. It was John who put the idea into play, but I've actually been toying with the idea of telling my story for a while. And now it seems like the timing is right."

"Well, it's certainly going to be a new adventure for me. I don't usually spend too much time in L.A. I'm a New York City kind of gal."

"I know you are, Dory, but something tells me we're going to have a lot of fun with this. I'm really looking forward to seeing you again."

"Thanks, Evan. I appreciate that. I'm looking forward to it, too."

*   *   *

When she hung up the phone, Dorianne was struck by how genuine Evan Crane had sounded. As if he really were looking forward to seeing her—as a person. And the fact that he'd called her 'Dory;' most people regarded her as too professional to call by a nickname. She was never called Dory by anyone but Kent or her parents. There was something very endearing about that.

Dorianne spent the rest of the day watching videos of Evan's movies; movies that she hadn't paid much attention to in the past. She was struck by how handsome he'd become. That he'd matured gracefully into a very good-looking man. The kid she'd met ten years ago was long gone.

Trust Not the Innocents, from only a year before, had a famous sex scene in it that took Dorianne's breath away.

She knew that most of the A-list stars used body doubles for their more explicit nude scenes, but it was common knowledge that Evan had chosen not to do that during his sex scene with Norma Pearl. Everything on screen in *The Innocents* was the real Evan Crane, enhanced with make-up and a bit of computer touch-ups. Other than that, though, Evan was hiding nothing and Dorianne was spellbound by his animal magnetism. This was a side of Evan Crane she'd never considered before. She'd always thought of him as how he'd been that one and only time they'd met; an eager-to-please, hopeful twenty-five year old with a lot of dreams. Now he was clearly a man with passion.

Dorianne found herself unable to resist rewinding the video several times to watch the sex scene again and again. She understood now what all the hoopla had been about. It was quite an erotic scene. Evan did have a tendency to seem one-dimensional and awkward on screen, but not this time. He had given it all he had.

Uh-oh, she thought, as she felt herself becoming aroused by the images of Evan making love to the actress Norma Pearl, over and over again. I hadn't counted on this.

Dorianne forced herself to switch off the VCR.

But later that night, when she was lying awake thinking about Kent, wondering where—if anywhere—they were headed as a couple, images of Evan naked on film, making vigorous love to Norma Pearl resurfaced in her mind.

At first, she tried hard to disregard it. She focused her thoughts instead on how incredible it had felt to make love again with Kent after all these years. But there was no denying that Kent was fifty years old now, and Dorianne only thirty. She couldn't help but regard Evan—a man more her age—as more physically attractive. He was still in the prime of life. He was probably spending a fortune keeping himself physically fit, to stay at the top of his game.

She methodically redirected her thoughts back to Kent. And in the privacy of her dark bedroom, alone in her bed, she let herself relive her brief hours of making love with him.

How exquisite it had felt to be at his mercy, bending over for him again, surrendering herself, spreading her thighs wide and offering herself up to him as she'd done in the old days. Feeling herself filling with his cock; being forcefully penetrated by him over and over. The pleasure it had given her was almost unspeakable. How his hands gripped tightly to her waist, her hips, as if she might try to get away from him, or how those same masculine hands had felt, eagerly groping her ample breasts.

Dorianne's fingers deftly stroked her clitoris, fueling the images; igniting the fire again between her legs. She was lost in her reverie, remembering Kent's mouth on her. How greedily he'd sucked at her down there, making her swollen and wet. His tongue mercilessly probing up into the hood of her stiff clitoris, his fingers keeping her spread wide as she succumbed to the constant flicks of that relentless tongue.

She had come in Kent's mouth, and it had felt as exciting as she remembered it feeling when it had happened the first time, back when she was still in college. When having a man's mouth explore her between her legs had been a new sensation. Kent had been the first man patient enough and experienced enough to keep at her down there, licking her and sucking her, until he'd brought her to orgasm.

Kent had been a 'first' for her in many ways. He'd been the first man to tell her to bend over for him, to go at her from behind; her white panties down around her knees and her skirt shoved up high.

Now she was more interested in wearing silky stockings and black lace, but Dorianne had found it just as thrilling as she ever had, giving in to Kent's powerful masculinity. On the surface, he wasn't as dynamic as he'd used to seem to her. But in bed, Dorianne thought that he was even better than before.

Or maybe it was that she herself had changed. She'd grown. She was more comfortable now with what she wanted from sex, with what she needed to feel with a man.

Dorianne's fingers rubbed more insistently at her clitoris. It felt acutely sensitive and very responsive tonight. She ached to have Kent on top of her, stretching her open, filling her to capacity as his cock drove in hard and deep.

With her other hand, she tugged lightly at her nipple. Twisting it, squeezing it, pulling it; flooding her whole body with that insatiable desire.

In her mind, she was underneath Kent again. He'd hiked her

long legs up over his shoulders as he sometimes would. He was plunging in hard, with determination. No man had ever been able to open her hole like he did and then fill it to the point where she ached deliciously with each thrust.

Dorianne increased the pressure on her clitoris. She tugged harder on her nipple. She was going to come. The pictures filling her head became chaotic; the images as swollen with desire as her body felt.

First, she was underneath Kent, holding her legs open for him, offering herself completely to his merciless force.

Then he was behind her and she was as immodest as she could be; her bottom raised up to him, spread wide, while he pressed her open even wider and plunged into her relentlessly, making her cry out.

She straddled his face in the next moment, as he lay flat on his back then, her aching clitoris hovering over his mouth as she held her swollen lips apart for him, keeping the stiff, tender flesh of her clit as vulnerable as it could be to his persistent tongue.

Then to her complete amazement, as the orgasm rocketed through her, Dorianne pictured herself under Evan Crane. It was *her* naked, eager body being ravaged by his lust in *Trust Not the Innocents*. She and Evan Crane were locked in passion, her legs around his waist tight. His lean, muscular body pressing down on her as his erection filled her to capacity and pounded into her. And just as Evan had done to Norma Pearl in the movies, he kissed Dorianne's mouth. It was a kiss that mashed their tongues together, that devoured her. His determined grunts collided with her cries while they kissed. Then he came in her hard, extending her no mercy. And she came and came and came.

Dorianne slowly surfaced from her amorous reverie, feeling spent. She stared up at the dark ceiling and tried to collect herself.

This trip to Los Angeles is going to be a problem, she thought as she gradually drifted off to sleep. What have I gotten myself into?

CHAPTER FIVE

It seemed to Dorianne that the next few weeks flew by in a heartbeat. She was busy trying to catch up on as much work as possible before she had to leave for L.A. and begin the intimidating task of starting a new book.

She'd managed to speak to Kent every day on the phone, but they'd only met once in person in the three weeks it had been since they'd first gotten back together.

Kent had stopped by Dorianne's apartment early one evening unannounced and they had made love. It was the slow and lingering kind of lovemaking, Kent taking his time with her, easing her into several positions without making her feel rushed, bringing her to orgasm three times.

He'd made an effort to stay as late as he could that evening, but still he hadn't spent the night with her as Dorianne had hoped he would. She'd lain awake that night, wondering why it was that she felt used. Kent enjoyed her body almost aggressively, true.

He took pleasure in her but he gave her pleasure in return. He'd stayed as late as he could that night and he'd been calling her everyday. She was the one who was too busy to spend much time with anybody. What more was she expecting? Why did she still feel that something wasn't right between them?

Should he be begging me not to go to L.A.? she wondered. Is that what I'm really expecting?

Still the days had gone by and now Dorianne's trip to Los Angeles was imminent. She was in a midtown diner, waiting to have an early breakfast meeting with her agent who was running late.

It was November now, cold and gray. Dorianne watched the early rush hour traffic inching by outside the window of the diner. On the table in front of her, she had the advance proofs of the next issue of *Babylon* to inspect. Again she had the cover story, an interview with Vera Randolph, the new British sensation.

As Dorianne idly watched a traffic light turn from green to red, she saw him. She saw Kent approaching the corner. She was certain it was him. It was his coat blowing in the wind, his aging face braced tightly against the chill. And it was his arm around another woman out on the busy early morning street.

As the traffic light changed, they headed straight toward the diner, this man and woman. In a mere second, Dorianne would know positively if it was Kent.

A gust of cold November wind blew in the open door and Dorianne's heart sank. There was no mistaking this man whose face, whose entire body she knew by heart. It was Kent and he was with another woman, a smiling redhead, a woman who appeared to be more than just a casual friend. Clearly, this was the reason why Dorianne had felt things weren't right between them.

She didn't have the stomach to face it, though. Not here, not so publicly. She wanted to run out of the diner instead, but it would only attract attention to her and force the situation on Kent.

Besides, she realized, her agent would be expecting to find her there. She couldn't be so childish as to run away.

Kent and the other woman slid into an empty booth at the front of the diner, choosing to sit side by side, like lovers, instead of facing each other, as friends or business associates did. They were oblivious to Dorianne's presence as she self-consciously slid lower in her seat several booths away.

Then Dorianne watched them kiss and her heart shattered. It was not a quick peck on the cheek. It was a lingering kiss, mouth to mouth. Dorianne thought they had that bedroom look, as if it had been the best they could manage, forcing themselves out into the cold world of the morning rush hour when the heat of their bodies entangling intimately in the same bed all night was still all over them.

Dorianne did her best to block them out by trying to focus her attention on the issue of Babylon that sat on the table in front of her. She was too distracted to proof her interview with Vera Randolph. She stared blindly at the other pages instead. The useless pages, the pages she didn't need to proof and didn't care about.

What was she going to do, she wondered frantically. She would have to confront Kent with this before she left for L.A. How would he possibly explain it? If this was a woman he'd wanted Dorianne to know about, he would have told her.

Dorianne saw her world falling to pieces all over again. How could she have been such a gullible fool for Kent—once more, after all these years?

Then Dorianne's eye happened upon a small color photo of Evan Crane. He was once again written up in a side item in *Babylon*:

Was that Handsome Evan Crane our sources spied with the very blonde, very British Christine Miles at the Hotel Beverly recently? If she's so hung up on Eddie Bailey, bass player for the Space Lillies, then why was she fawning all over Crane in the Paradise Lounge? And was he really escorting her to her room because he was a gentleman and she'd clearly enjoyed one too many cocktails, or was he a cad, getting chummy with another chum's bird when she'd had too much to drink? Our sources say they disappeared behind closed doors and Crane wasn't seen leaving until the wee hours. Is it finally love, Evan? Our sources are dying to know!

For some inexplicable reason, Dorianne felt a sudden blazing contempt for 'Handsome' Evan Crane, although she didn't understand why. It wasn't as though Evan owed her any loyalty. They were only going to be working together. He could date whomever he pleased.

Perhaps she'd expected him to have better taste than that—Christine Miles!

Another blast of cold wind came through the open door of the diner as Dorianne's agent, Bethany, came inside.

"Why, Bethany Taylor, hello!"

Dorianne heard Kent's voice plain as day. She saw Bethany stop at Kent's booth and shake hands with him and the other woman. Bethany was wearing her usual plaid cloth coat and her short gray hair was windblown. The three chatted amicably and then Dorianne saw Bethany glance around the diner, clearly looking for her.

Kent saw Dorianne first, though. And it was evident by the expression on his face that she was an unwelcome surprise.

Dorianne's pulse skyrocketed, her anger climbing up her throat, as she watched Bethany and Kent come over to her booth.

"Dorianne," Kent said awkwardly, a fake smile plastered across his guilty face. "What a pleasant surprise. Imagine, you sitting here all this time and I didn't know. Bethany just told me you two are having a meeting before you leave for L.A."

Bethany took off her coat and slid into the booth, blissfully ignorant of what was really taking place.

"I haven't seen Kent Cryer in years," she chided Dorianne. "Why didn't you tell me he was back in town?"

"It slipped my mind," Dorianne said flatly, tears straining to come to the surface of her eyes, but Dorianne fought them back ferociously. She refused to humiliate herself any further for the lying, cheating Kent Cryer.

Kent shook Bethany's hand. "Great seeing you again, Bethany. I won't keep you two from your meeting."

Then he reached for Dorianne's hand and held it a moment longer than he had to. "Why don't I give you a call later, Dory? I'd love to speak with you before you leave town."

"Why don't you, Kent," Dorianne replied, making every effort to sound civilized for Bethany's sake.

"I will," Kent said. "I promise." Then he turned and walked back to his table.

Within moments, Dorianne watched him help his lady friend into her coat and briskly escort her out of the diner, leaving the waiter standing blankly in the aisle with two full cups of coffee in his hands.

WHEN HEARTS COLLIDE

CHAPTER SIX

The cab driver set Dorianne's luggage on the curb outside the terminal at JFK and within moments, a porter was loading them onto a cart and whisking them off to the check-in.

Her all-expenses-paid trip to Los Angeles was beginning now and she was traveling first class.

Dorianne pushed through the revolving door, into the terminal and once again her cell phone started ringing. She checked the number of the incoming call and, sure enough, it was Kent. He was relentless. Dorianne knew that eventually she would have to take his call. He seemed determined to follow her, at least by way of her cell phone, all the way to California.

She clicked the phone open. "Hello?" she said.

"Finally! Damn you, Dorianne, why are you doing this to me? Why won't you give me a chance to explain?"

"Because you had three weeks to explain. Three weeks to be honest, to do the right thing, and instead you chose to be secretive and sneak around all over again, Kent."

"For god's sake, I was hardly sneaking around."

"Well, you weren't very upfront with me about what was going on in your life, either."

Dorianne studied the schedule for departing flights and noted her gate while she listened guardedly to Kent's defensive attack. She tried to keep an emotional distance from the sound of his desperate words. She wouldn't let him get the best of her again, ever. Her mind was made up that she was through.

"Dorianne, she was just a friend!"

"Come on, Kent you've had two whole days. Couldn't you have dreamed up something better than that? A long lost sister or something? Wasn't there a movie once about a wife unexpectedly returning after seven years of being lost at sea?"

"Dorianne, you don't have to be sarcastic."

"Well, it's the simplest way I know of to hide my disgust. Look at you. You're a grown man, Kent. You're fifty years old and you still can't come up with something more original than lying and sneaking around."

"I told you, I was not sneaking around! We were just dating, you and I. We were getting reacquainted."

"That may be. Maybe I jumped the gun about you and me. But I get the distinct impression that the woman you brought into the diner with you would probably feel cheated on if she knew about what you've been doing in my apartment with me, on my couch and in my bed, before rushing off to cocktail parties with *her*. To me, that qualifies as lying and sneaking around."

Dorianne stopped in front of a busy newsstand on the way to her gate and a British tabloid caught her attention.

"You're not being fair, Dorianne," Kent was insisting.

A color photo was featured on the tabloid's front page, made to appear as if torn down the middle. It was a photo of journalist Christine Miles and bass player Eddie Bailey, separated by a jagged computer-generated tear. A headline taunted: "Is it Splitsville for Love Birds after Christine's Sordid LA Tryst with Hollywood Star Crane?"

"You're being so stubborn, Dorianne. This isn't like you."

"No, it's not like me. You're right, Kent. I'm usually a pushover."

"That's not what I mean and you know it."

In smaller print, the headline continued: "Rex gives Miles the sack after drunken romp in LA."

"Kent, be honest. That's exactly what you mean. You expect me to take everything you dish out, but I'm not a kid anymore."

Dorianne set her money on the counter and stuffed the tabloid into her carry-on bag.

"It was really fun being with you again after all these years," she continued, " but, frankly, a roll in the hay I can get anywhere. I'm not interested. I have to go now. I have to catch my plane."

"Dorianne, don't do this."

"Have a good life, Kent," she said and she clicked off her phone.

*   *   *

High in the air, above a layer of clouds, somewhere out over the Midwest, Dorianne took the British tabloid from her carry-on bag and turned to the story about Christine Miles.

It was a full-page spread, with a large black and white photo of Christine and Eddie Bailey out on the town somewhere—apparently in happier days. They were dressed like twins almost; like a couple of bohemian gypsies. Arms around each other, looking as if they were barely old enough to be out of high school, they were smiling happily for the paparazzi.

Farther down the page, there was a much smaller photo, blurry and in color, of Evan Crane and Christine, standing together outside the Hotel Beverly's front entrance in Los Angeles. It was obvious to Dorianne that the pair had no idea they were being photographed.

Not being a fan of either the Space Lillies or Christine Miles, there wasn't much in the article that held Dorianne's interest. Until she reached the unpleasant paragraphs toward the end that concerned Evan Crane being the alleged cause of the split between Christine and Eddie Bailey:

"I wish I could say he was a gentleman," Miles said of Crane, "but that would be a stretch by any definition of the word."

Miles maintains Crane plied her with liquor, helped her find her way to her hotel room at LA's famous Hotel Beverly, and then put some rather unsavory moves on her, which, being a little star struck, she felt helpless to fend off.

Speaking to our reporters via telephone, Miles elaborated: "I used to be Crane's biggest fan, I'm not ashamed to say it.I think he used that against me and led me on. He thought I was an easy mark. He knew I was involved with someone else but it didn't seem to faze him. His ego is huge."

Miles went on to say, "He smoked all my cigarettes, too. And frankly, he wasn't any great shakes in the bed department."

Ouch! At press time, Mr. Crane wasn't available for comment.

Dorianne stuffed the tabloid into the pocket of the seat back in front of her. She felt disgusted by the whole sordid affair. She'd heard that Christine Miles had a reputation for being emotionally unbalanced. *Rex* magazine had probably let her go because someone at the top couldn't stand working around the histrionics any longer. After all, plenty of journalists all over the world had a history of drinking with abandon while on assignments and hadn't been fired because of it.

Or maybe it was a simple case of PR. It sure sounded as if Eddie Bailey had dumped Christine. Without a pop star on her arm, Christine would be useless for the publicity machine, so why would *Rex* want to put up with her?

But what about Evan's role in all this?

Dorianne lowered the window shade next to her seat.

If there were any truth to what Christine had said about Evan, then it was a contemptible way to behave.

She slipped the black sleeping mask over her eyes and, for now, tried not to think about all the Evan Cranes or Kent Cryers out there in the world. She would sleep it all away instead, at least until her plane descended onto the runway in Los Angeles. Then, ready or not, she would be on her next assignment: unveiling the *real* Evan Crane and presenting him to the world; up close and in the best possible light.

But what about her own integrity, she wondered. What if the final result, the book that would have her name on its cover—what if it was just like everything else that came out of Hollywood; dressed-up and smiling, but still a pack of lies?

CHAPTER SEVEN

When her plane touched down at LAX, a driver was waiting for Dorianne at the gate. As he'd promised, Evan had hired a limousine to take her to her hotel. The driver, an oversized, muscle-bound white man with a discreet ponytail, while dressed formally in a chauffeur's uniform, looked as if he had another life working as someone's bodyguard, or a bouncer for an after hours club.

"Mr. Crane thought it would be better to wait in the car," he said casually. "You know, sometimes the photographers lurking around here can really slow things down. They can make the simple things like claiming luggage very complicated."

"Mr. Crane is waiting out in the car?" Dorianne was pleasantly surprised. "I thought he was planning to meet me at my hotel later."

"No, ma'am. He's out in the car."

Dorianne followed the driver to the baggage claim area and tried to picture what that looked like; Evan, one of the more famous movie stars in the English speaking world, hiding in plain sight, in broad daylight, sitting alone in the back seat of a darkened car. She wondered how often famous people were right under the noses of the 'regular' world.

When she and the driver stepped out of the terminal, the intensity of the sun stabbed Dorianne's eyes. It was a peculiar sensation that she experienced every time she came to LA; the incredible brightness of the sun. It was hard to believe it was the same sun that shone down on New York City every day. The towering skyscrapers and high rise buildings that stood crammed together on every block of Manhattan always kept the sun's rays at a filtered distance. In Los Angeles, there was nothing to block out the pervasive light.

The driver had parked the limo illegally and, as they approached the car, Dorianne saw that there was already a traffic ticket stuck in its windshield, but this didn't seem to faze the driver.

When he opened the passenger door to help Dorianne inside, she became immediately aware of strangers stopping to stare at her. Then, as if it were her fault that she wasn't famous, they walked on in a noticeable huff, as if to say that she had some nerve, getting into the back seat of a black limousine without being a movie star.

"Dory, hello."

Evan Crane, every gorgeous inch of him, sat forward in the back seat of the limo and extended his hand to Dorianne.

"It's been a very long time," he added with a dazzling smile. He wore a black tee shirt and a pair of black jeans, which, simple as they seemed, had probably cost him about five hundred dollars. He looked nothing less than casually stunning.

Dorianne took his offered hand and slid in next to him. She wasn't usually bowled over by celebrities, but Evan's sheer presence in the back seat of that car overwhelmed her. She was blushing.

"It was really nice of you to come out here to meet me," she said, her voice suddenly sounding like an anxious ten-year-old.

"I hope you didn't have to wait long."

Evan shrugged. "I'm used to it. Most of my career involves sitting around and waiting."

Again, he flashed her his dazzling movie star smile and Dorianne wondered how genuine it was. It's a very impressive smile, regardless, she thought.

The driver started the car and began the long trek toward Sunset Boulevard in West Hollywood, avoiding the freeways, taking the more scenic routes to their destination.

"John Ebbins has a rental car waiting for you at your hotel," Evan said. "If there's anything you need that we've overlooked, just let me know and I'll tell John, okay?"

"Okay, Evan. I will."

Dorianne knew she had a nervous grin plastered across her face. This is crazy, she thought to herself. Why can't I just make simple conversation? This is only Evan Crane. The same person I knew a million years ago. But he seems so mature now, so incredibly handsome. It's intimidating.

"You look fantastic, you know that?" Evan said. "You don't even seem like the same person I met however many years ago. You're so, I don't know, *grown up*. It's kind of intimidating."

Dorianne laughed—a little too self-consciously. "I was thinking the very same thing about you, Evan."

"Really?"

"Yes, really."

They were silent for a few awkward moments. Dorianne looked out the window, at the bungalows and the one-story shops; the palm trees and the ubiquitous blue sky. She felt the palms of her hands beginning to sweat. The uneasy silence somehow felt like her fault.

"So, how are things?" she finally said.

"Things are okay," Evan replied.

"I saw that thing in the tabloid," she offered without thinking. "You know, Christine Miles."

Evan's demeanor changed noticeably. "Yeah, well. It could have been worse."

"What does *that* mean?" she asked, a little alarmed. Then she caught herself. "Maybe it's none of my business," she said.

"No, that's okay. Let's just say it's better for me that Miss Miles no longer works for Rex."

The particular way he phrased the statement made Dorianne wonder if Evan had had anything to do with Christine getting fired. She decided to steer clear of the topic for now. If he had been involved, she didn't want to know about it yet. And if the things Christine was telling the tabloids were true, Dorianne wanted to stay blissfully ignorant of the fact for as long as she could. She wanted to be on Evan's side. She already recognized the signs in herself; she wanted Evan to be infallible. She looked away from him again, this time with the distinct impression that she was going to get too emotionally involved with this job, this man. He was too damn good looking.

*   *   *

When the limo pulled up to the front entrance of the infamous Casa Hollywood hotel, it was Evan who exited the limo first and helped Dorianne out of the car.

Dorianne had the impression she could hear the distinct sound of cameras clicking and whirring for every step they took into and through the lobby, yet she hadn't seen a single photographer anywhere.

As was usually the case when Dorianne was in Los Angeles, she felt conspicuously overdressed. She dressed like the conservative New Yorker she was—black high heels, a tailored black suit and a discreet black handbag. While everyone around her dressed more as

Evan Crane was dressed; casual, as if they might pop out to the beach at any moment and call it a day.

"It's nice to have someone else stared at for a change," Evan said quietly.

"Excuse me?"

"Everyone's looking at you, Dory. Don't tell me you haven't noticed."

"It's because I'm so overdressed."

"No," he assured her. "It's because you look sensational."

"How can we help you today, Mr. Crane?"

The desk clerk was almost painfully cheerful. Another marked difference, Dorianne noticed, between LA and New York.

"I reserved a bungalow for Dorianne Constance," Evan replied.

"Of course, you did, Mr. Crane. And we have that bungalow ready and waiting."

A smiling bellman appeared from out of nowhere as another snappy bellman came through the front entrance with Dorianne's bags.

As they followed the bellmen to her bungalow, Dorianne felt excited, almost giddy, for the first time in a long while. She had been to Casa Hollywood several times in the past, but she'd never indulged in a bungalow. She's always stayed in a regular, more readily affordable room. And now, walking alongside Evan Crane, through the thick tropical foliage that crowded the private flag stone footpath that led to the private bungalows, she was being treated like absolute royalty by the cheeriest hotel staff she had ever encountered.

Dorianne's bungalow had three main rooms, a living area with a kitchenette, a bedroom with a small but very private patio adjoining it, and a bathroom that seemed to have come straight out of an old Hollywood glamour movie. The bungalow had the same Mediterranean feel that most of Los Angeles had adopted in the early twenties. She found the rooms charming; utterly different from how she was accustomed to living in Manhattan.

The bellmen hadn't been gone for sixty seconds before Dorianne's phone was ringing.

"Miss Constance," the operator said. "You had a call from New York about an hour ago."

"I did?"

"Yes. A Mr. Kent Cryer called. He left his number."

Dorianne was dismayed. She instinctively turned away from Evan as she spoke into the phone. "Thank you, operator. I have the number," she said and hung up.

Then the bungalow was quiet. The surrounding foliage blocked out any sounds of life from the other bungalows or the busy boulevard not far from the hotel's front gate. It seemed to Dorianne as if she and Evan were miles away from anywhere, she was so used to Manhattan's constant noise.

"Thank you, Evan," she said, feeling at a loss for something to say. "The accommodations are really charming."

As a way of replying, Evan simply smiled.

"Well, I suppose I should unpack now," she went on, that same nervousness welling up in her again. It was like she'd felt in the car; she was overwhelmed by his mere presence. She started to get a clearer understanding of why Evan had become such a successful movie star. Even while he had a history of being an uneven performer, he had charisma in spades.

"Would you like me to swing by later and take you to dinner?" he asked.

"I'd like that a lot, Evan. But I'm still on New York time. I hope you don't mind eating early."

"I don't mind. Give me a call when you're ready. I don't live far from here, you know. Just up the hill."

"Thanks, Evan."

"You don't have to keep thanking me, Dory. I'm the one who's grateful that you took this job. It means a lot to me to be able to work with you again."

Dorianne wondered why he would feel that way about her, a woman he'd only worked with for a handful of hours so many years ago. Maybe he was just being polite, she decided, as she watched him walk out of sight on the footpath heading back to the main building of the hotel.

*   *   *

When Evan called for Dorianne at her bungalow early that evening, he was driving his own Mercedes. The limousine and driver were gone. It was just the two of them alone together in the front seat of Evan's car, with a breathtaking sunset out in front of them on the boulevard.

Dorianne's chestnut curls were pulled back slightly from her face and Evan thought that in the waning light, Dorianne's big dark eyes glistened with life. She seemed to him to be a very happy person, contented.

"How are things working out with Kent Cryer?" he asked suddenly.

"I'm through with him. That's how things worked out with Kent Cryer."

"Oops. That was a quick story."

Dorianne laughed. "I guess so. But at least I only wasted a few weeks on him this time. I didn't throw away a couple more years. I've already wasted ten years on that fool, hoping he and I would get back together again. But he hasn't changed a bit. He was just using me and wasting my time. You know, for a smart girl, I've been really stupid about love."

"I can't believe you'd ever do anything stupid, Dory."

"And I can't believe I just unloaded on you about Kent! That was probably more than you wanted to know."

"That's okay," he said. "I asked."

"But you didn't bring me out here to hear my sad saga about Kent Cryer. I'm the one who's supposed to be asking *you* those kinds of questions."

"But I've never even met Kent Cryer."

"Very funny, Evan."

He pulled the car onto a side street and then into the back parking lot of a quiet restaurant. "Late at night, you can't even get close to this place," he said, "it's so crowded. But I've discovered that the food here is actually pretty good. Usually, everyone's too busy drinking and pretending not to be impressed with each other to even notice the food."

It sounded a lot like the Hollywood Dorianne had been exposed to many times in the past, on her various assignments for *Babylon.*

"Do you spend a lot of your nights drinking and pretending not to be impressed with people, Evan?"

"Is this the beginning of those questions you were threatening to ask me?"

Evan turned off the motor and took the key out of the ignition. They sat in the quiet car and smiled at each other.

"Oh boy," Dorianne sighed.

"What?"

"I just got the distinct impression you're not going to make my job an easy one."

"Why do you say that?"

"Because that was an evasive reply if I ever heard one."

"Listen," Evan said. "Why don't we agree to start working tomorrow? Let's just take tonight to get to know each other again. No pressure, no stress, no work. Just a little fun between friends.

Does that sound okay to you, Dory?"

"Actually, it sounds great."

As they walked together toward the restaurant, she said, "Do you really consider us friends? Or is that just something you're saying to be polite?"

"Of course, I consider us friends. We're *simpatico*, you know? I've always felt that with us, haven't you? We may not know each other yet, but we have a rapport, right? We always have."

"Thanks, Evan. That's a nice thing to say."

"I told you before," he said, putting his arm around her shoulders, "you don't have to thank me. I'm the one who's grateful to you."

He gave her a quick hug, but his arm lingered there, his skin against her bare shoulders. They had never touched like this before and Dorianne felt the unmistakable spark of chemistry between them. She wondered if he felt it, too; if that's what he'd meant by simpatico.

Or maybe it was only Dorianne's romantic imagination. Perhaps Evan took this kind of thing in stride. He had that reputation for being physical, for being a womanizer, didn't he? After all, hadn't he seduced Christine Miles after an interview?

Evan gave Dorianne another quick hug. "Hey," he said. "What's going on?"

"What do you mean?"

"You're a million miles away."

Dorianne shrugged and politely extricated herself from under Evan's arm. "I'm just trying not to be a fool," she replied.

Evan held the door open for her and Dorianne thought that for a fleeting moment, he looked hurt.

"I'm sorry," she offered. "I'm just a little worn out from traveling today."

"That's okay," he assured her, feeling that wall of privacy going up inside him, pushing her away.

*   *   *

Dinner went off without a hitch. Only two women managed to impose on their privacy with requests for Evan's autograph and another woman asked if Evan might pose for a snapshot with her eight-year-old daughter.

Evan was polite and obliging of all their requests, flashing his enigmatic movie star smile with gracious ease.

Dorianne was impressed with Evan's ability to make nervous fans feel comfortable around him and she guessed that his fans went away from Evan liking him even more; crystallizing that fleeting moment with him in their hearts and minds forever.

"It's really generous of you to behave like that with your fans, Evan," she said, as they lingered over their desserts. "I'm impressed that you can make it seem so easy."

"It is easy."

"If it's so easy, then why doesn't everybody do it? I've been out in public with a number of actors who don't even try to disguise their contempt for fans intruding on their privacy."

"It used to be hard in the beginning, but I look at it this way," he explained. "I'm a public personality now. There are no two ways about it. When I'm out in public there's no such thing as my privacy. But I need 'my public' to keep working. When I want something to be kept private, there's a way to be low key and discreet and keep it private—mainly, by not airing it out in public."

Dorianne wanted to say 'then what about Christine Miles?' but she bit her tongue. She didn't know why she was becoming so obsessed with it anyway.

"Of course, when I'm involved with somebody," he went on, "in an intimate relationship, that is, it can get difficult. Intrusive, maddening. I mean the photographers, mostly. They pop up everywhere."

Dorianne studied him in the flattering half-light of the candlelit room. He seemed younger now, boyish almost. It seemed incongruous that he could be the same man accused of so many seemingly heartless indiscretions with women.

"I know we promised we wouldn't work tonight," she said. "But I want to ask you something."

Evan looked at her guardedly. "What is it, Dory?"

"Everyone's always talking about you being in love with this one or that one, yet you never seem to be with any one woman for very long. Just how many significant relationships with the opposite sex have their been in your life?"

"Not many," he replied.

She waited for him to elaborate, but he stared at her in silence.

"All right, I get it," she finally conceded. "We're not working tonight, right?"

"Right. We're putting the rest of the world on hold and just getting to know each other."

"But that's part of getting to know each other, isn't it? Finding out about old flames?"

"No," Evan corrected her. "That's a journalist going for the jugular, Dory, and you know it. I'm surprised at you."

His disappointment in her seemed genuine and Dorianne was glad for the dimly lit room. She hoped it made her embarrassment less noticeable.

"I'm sorry, Evan," she said. "I really was just curious. And I don't think it was the journalist in me talking."

"I'm sorry, too," he said. "Maybe I'm more nervous about this project than I realized. It's a lot to take on. Telling the story of my life, trying to dig out some words of wisdom without coming off as a complete ego maniac."

Dorianne saw the bigger picture and felt she understood.

"Or feeling too exposed?" she asked.

"That, too. When you're famous, the jury is always passing judgment on you somewhere in the privacy and comfort of their own homes. Faceless strangers, you know, who don't have to take the rap for their hostility against me publicly; who don't know the difference sometimes between the seduction of movies that are making people rich, and the frustration of dreams that they've let die somewhere that had nothing to do with me."

*   *   *

Evan escorted Dorianne back to her hotel after dinner and everything about the place seemed transformed.

Casa Hollywood had an infamous cocktail lounge that was starting to overflow with trendy and boisterous patrons. Everyone seemed to notice Evan Crane the minute he stepped into the hotel lobby. The air hummed with a tangible electricity. His mere presence seemed to set people buzzing with a feigned air of their own importance.

"Notice me, notice me," they seemed to be saying with a smug despair.

The corridor that led to the footpath was now manned by hotel security. Evan was allowed to pass without a word. Dorianne had to show her room key to prove she belonged there.

"The privacy of our guests is our top priority," the security guard stated mechanically.

But Dorianne had plenty of memories of staying in the less glamorous areas of the hotel where the privacy of the guests never seemed to be much of an issue. Still, when she and Evan left the noisy hotel behind them and were alone on the footpath that led to the bungalows, she discovered, to her delight, that nighttime had transformed the private world they were entering into a magical place.

The tropical foliage was strung with tiny multi-colored lanterns and the gentle sound of a waterfall seemed to emanate from somewhere within the trees. The air smelled vaguely of citrus and cinnamon— an aroma Dorianne hadn't noticed in the daytime.

"It's all piped in," Evan explained. "The sounds, the smells. It's the only thing Hollywood knows how to do, create illusions."

"Illusions or not, it makes me want to sit out on my patio and have a drink. Would you like to stay for a little while, Evan?"

They were in front of Dorianne's bungalow now. "Maybe for a few minutes," he said. "I wouldn't want to crowd you."

"You're hardly crowding me," Dorianne smiled. "I'm totally alone here."

Inside the bungalow, Dorianne's phone was flashing. Another message. She knew it had to be Kent. She would retrieve it later.

The mini bar was stocked with everything from champagne to chocolates. Evan chose a bottle of imported beer. Dorianne opened a small bottle of red wine.

Out on the patio, the night was still enchanted. Dorianne didn't care if every bit of it was fake.

"I've done a fair amount of traveling," she said. "Yet why is that I feel I never left New York until now?"

Evan pulled a chair close to Dorianne and sat down. "I don't know. I miss New York sometimes. I liked living there."

"Do you think you'd ever move back?"

"I think about it from time to time. I might."

"Really? You'd move back to Manhattan and leave paradise?"

Evan laughed. "I don't consider this paradise. In fact, I have a house on Maui that's much closer to paradise than this. They don't have to pipe in the smells or the sounds. And instead of tiny Christmas lights covered in paper lanterns, we have the sky full of stars. I should take you there someday, Dory. I think you'd like it. I used to invite people to stay there with me all the time, but it got out of control. People get crazy and take advantage. Now I usually just fly out there by myself when I want to escape from it all."

Without thinking, she said, "I remember an item getting pulled from *Babylon* once about someone having some sort of sex party in a beach house on Maui, was that you?"

Evan fell silent again, then sighed. "Well, I've had sex before, if that's what you're asking. And I've had it in my house in Hawaii—Dorianne, why do you keep bringing up this tabloid stuff?"

"I don't know, Evan. I'm sorry. I usually don't pay attention to gossip. I don't know why I'm doing it. I guess it's because these are the only things I know about you."

"But that's not me. That's what I'm trying to get a break from." Evan took Dorianne's hand in his affectionately. "That's why I hired you, remember? That's why we're going to be working together. Plus, I'm at a disadvantage here. I don't know any lurid tabloid stuff about you."

Dorianne liked the feel of her hand held in his. But she wondered if she ought to feel patronized—she didn't think Evan would hold hands with a male journalist. But she couldn't deny it. She liked the nearness of Evan. "Okay," she promised. "No more lurid tabloid stuff. Except—"

"Except what?"

"Nothing. Never mind."

"Tell me."

"No, you're just going to get mad at me. Let's drop it."

Evan looked into Dorianne's eyes. The night was silent except for the delicate sounds of a fake waterfall somewhere in the distance. He smiled at her. "Okay," he agreed quietly. "We'll drop it. You know what?" he added.

"What?" she asked, her eyes looking steadily into his. It almost seemed like he was going to kiss her.

"I have to go now," he said. "It's late. Thanks for the beer."

Dorianne was disappointed. She tried to disguise it. "Okay," she said quietly. "Give me a call tomorrow when you want to get started."

"I will," he said, still holding her hand in his. "Do you want to work at my place? There's plenty of room there. No distractions. It's just me and the caretaker."

Dorianne wanted to ask Evan to stay; to keep holding her hand, to kiss her, to come to bed with her. "Your place sounds good," she said. "I'll wait for your call."

She followed Evan back through the bungalow to the front door. He still held her hand. Dorianne felt certain he was going to kiss her, like he did to the girls in the movies. It was in his body language. It was filling the room.

Evan paused at her door before opening it. "Dorianne Constance," he said strangely, as if to hear the sound of it. "It's been good seeing you again. It really has."

"I feel the same way," she said. She knew that if she were in a movie, this would be her close-up, this would be the big kiss.

"I'll see you tomorrow then," he said, letting go of her hand and letting himself out instead. There was no kissing. He didn't even come close.

Dorianne watched him walk away—the handsome, unpredictable movie star. He was behaving like a true enigma and she wondered what was happening to her.

I think I'm falling in love, she realized. What a terrible idea.

* * *

Evan let himself in to his dark, quiet house. Henry, the caretaker, had separate living quarters slightly up the hill, past the pool. Evan was alone and he needed it—the space. He was distracted, preoccupied.

That woman is unbelievable, he thought to himself. God she's gorgeous. I've got to get her into bed with me at least once. I've got to get her to say yes.

He felt his way into the dark kitchen, switched on a light and then grabbed another bottle of beer from his refrigerator.

He knew what John Ebbins would say, he could hear it inside his brain. "Evan, when are you going to quit doing that? This whole idea of sleeping with journalists is too damn risky."

But wait until John gets a load of Dorianne Constance now, Evan thought on his way upstairs to his bedroom. What a knockout she is. How could any man resist wanting to get naked with a woman like her?

Evan was amazed that he'd been able to keep himself from kissing her. To have simply said goodnight and walked away from her had felt insane to him. Her mouth had obviously wanted to be kissed.

But this project meant a lot to Evan. For once, he was trying to take his manager's advice by keeping things strictly professional with Dorianne.

Evan switched on his bedroom light, set down his beer and fished in his pocket for a cigarette. He hadn't felt like smoking all day. Now, he felt as if he couldn't light his cigarette quick enough. He inhaled deeply and swung open the door to his terrace.

Jesus, Hollywood looks beautiful from here, he realized. And he looked in the direction of the boulevard far below, searching for the glow of lights that he was certain staked out Casa Hollywood's grounds. Somewhere down there, she was probably getting into her bed. Alone.

Evan wondered if it really was over between Dory and Kent Cryer. She'd sure sounded like it was over. At least, if something did ever happen between him and Dorianne, he couldn't be accused of moving in on another man's girl.

"Woman," Evan said, correcting himself out loud. "That woman is all woman."

Evan smoked his cigarette with emphatic deliberation. He was getting a killer hard-on inside his jeans. His cock had been threatening to spring to attention all evening.

And now he'd invited her into his home—where there were no distractions, he'd said.

"None, if you don't count her *incredible ass*," he practically shouted.

How would he keep his hands off her, keep his hands from touching her all over? He wanted her body up close to his; naked and excited, writhing all over him. Something about her seemed like she would be receptive to that.

Evan went back inside for his beer. His cock ached something fierce. He was going to have to do something about it. He headed toward his bathroom.

He'd spent a fortune making it a veritable pleasure palace in there but he rarely pleasured anyone in it but himself.

He switched on the light and flushed his cigarette down the toilet. There he was, in all his bachelor glory, reflected in the enormous mirror over the twin sinks. He stripped off his clothes, his hard cock springing free, and then he stepped into the sanctity of his enormous shower, his favorite place on earth; his escape from everything ordinary in the world.

Evan turned on the faucets and the hot water gushed down and out over the blue mosaic tiles on all sides, like a serious waterfall, a world of water. Nothing like the light plashing sounds they piped in outside of Dorianne's bungalow.

Evan sat on one of the several stone ledges recessed in the shower wall. As the force of the water cascaded down over him, he leaned back into it and jerked himself off.

He tried to picture Dorianne naked right there in the shower with him; everyone of her inviting curves, glistening wet.

He wondered what her breasts were going to look like. He knew her tits were real. He was certain of it. He could tell by the natural way they'd moved as she moved—when he was watching her that evening, stealing glances at all her glorious inches when he hoped she wasn't looking.

He wondered if her nipples were the tiny, stiff, pink kind that some women had, or the fat-mommy kind that other women had; the hard kind that cried out for hard sucking. He wondered if she was the type of woman who got off on her own tits.

He pictured her impaled on top of him, writhing luridly on his hard cock, while her gorgeous tits bounced down free. He wanted to watch her play with those breasts, really torment them, while his cock pushed up into her as deep as he could get it to go.

Oh, it would be an incredible view, he thought, jerking himself furiously in the gushing water. He wanted his mouth all over those tits. He wanted to bite down hard on her delectable ass, too. He wanted to devour her with his lust.

Damn. Why hadn't he at least kissed her this evening and broken the ice? Then he would have known for sure if the lady was willing. He could always tell from the pressure of a woman's kiss how far they were likely to go in bed; how uninhibited they were likely to be in the throes of passion.

Evan wanted to see Dorianne really let go. He wanted to see her stripped bare, holding herself open for him, displaying the soaking-swollen-with-desire goods that she kept so carefully concealed inside those perfect little black dresses.

Jesus, New York women had *so many* little black dresses...

Evan jerked himself to a fevered pitch now and he was going to come. His mind was bursting with the lusty sight of Dorianne holding herself open just for him, spreading herself wide and begging him to fuck her, to fuck her hard, to make her come, to make her scream, to cream all over her, up inside of her, to fill her holes until the cum was spurting out of her everywhere. Fuck me, she would cry. Fuck me, god, fuck me. Don't stop fucking me. Fuck…

It was a quick frenzy of lust, but Evan felt spent. The traces of his orgasm had already been whisked away by the force of the gushing water and rushed swirling down the drain.

He was tired but thinking clearly again. And he wondered now if Dorianne was the kind of woman who liked talking dirty when she was making love. Somehow Evan found it highly unlikely that a woman as civilized as Dorianne seemed to be, could even utter a dirty word.

* * *

Though she was exhausted, her body still on New York time, Dorianne wanted to stay out on her little patio in the balmy night air and finish the small bottle of wine.

How incredible it all was. How many times had she been to L.A. in the past—to this very hotel, in fact—and felt that she couldn't get back to New York fast enough? And now she wanted it to last forever.

She looked up in the direction of where she thought Evan's house must be, somewhere up above her in the hills. She was excited about seeing his home, seeing how Evan lived. And she was glad they would be working there instead of in her bungalow. For Dorianne, Evan's overwhelming presence had a way of making a room seem smaller. She was afraid of what might happen in the confines of her very private little bungalow. To be alone with him, so close to her bedroom, would probably be too much temptation for her to withstand. And they had too much work ahead of them to let things between them get complicated.

Dorianne finished her wine and decided that she'd better call it a night. She went inside and once again saw her phone flashing. She had no desire to hear Kent's voice, let alone hear what he had to say. She'd let the message go until morning.

When she was at last in bed, she thought again about Evan's house. She wondered what he was doing now, alone up there.

But he hadn't said he would be alone, she realized suddenly. In fact, he hadn't even said he was going home. Maybe he had a late date. Maybe he was out on the town, carousing with some starlet in some trendy nightclub. Maybe Dorianne was the furthest thing from his mind.

She was going to have to get a grip on herself. The last thing she should be considering was falling in love with Evan Crane.

Still, she couldn't help wondering what it would be like to make love with him. He sure seemed to know his way around women when he made love to them in the movies, and even the feel of her hand in his this evening had made her want to melt.

Why hadn't he kissed her, she wondered. It had seemed like such a sure thing, she would have bet money on its happening. Her lips were ready for his lips. She had really wanted him to kiss her. Had he sensed that when he'd turned away?

Dorianne idly stroked her breast through the thin material of her silky nightgown, feeling her sensitive nipple respond to the light graze of her fingertips brushing across it. But before she could pursue the feeling any further, Dorianne was fast asleep.

CHAPTER EIGHT

The following morning, Evan woke early. He'd jerked off again before falling asleep the night before and now he awoke to another rock hard erection. This one, he wanted to leave alone. He needed his strength.

In the event the lady is willing later, he told himself.

He thought about coffee instead. He threw on a pair of boxers and headed downstairs to the kitchen.

The plan that his hard-on would go away all on its own didn't seem to be making much progress. Evan went into the kitchen and Henry was pouring himself a cup of coffee.

"You're up early," Henry remarked. "And I mean that in more ways than one."

"Very funny," Evan replied. "Listen, Henry, I need you to do me a favor."

"Boss, you pay me good, but not that good. Those kind of favors you gotta get somewhere else."

"Okay, give me a break. Henry, I met this woman—"

"That much is obvious."

Henry handed Evan a cup of coffee.

"I need you to do something nice for dinner tonight. Maybe even for lunch—let's say, a late lunch. I don't think I'm going to be able to hold out until dinner."

Evan took his cup of coffee and sat down at the kitchen table.

Henry leaned against the counter. "When you say 'nice' what exactly do you have in mind?"

Evan gave it some thought. "I guess raw oysters and champagne are a little too obvious, huh?"

"For a late lunch? It would depend on the girl, boss. And whether or not you're planning on having lunch served next to the bed."

Evan smiled. "She's not that kind of girl."

"Maybe we should think 'subtle' then," Henry suggested. "So who's the girl?"

"A writer from New York. The woman who's working on the book with me, Dorianne Constance. I knew her once a million years ago. She did my first interview for *Babylon* magazine when I did *The Devil Gets His Way*. But she's different now—not that I didn't like her before. It was just different."

"I haven't heard you talk like this since Norma."

"Forget about Norma, Henry. This girl is nothing like Norma. This girl has class."

"There are still some circles where folks think that Norma Pearl has a little class."

"You know as well as I do, that's because they don't really know Norma Pearl," Evan said with contempt. "Or maybe they do; she does have a little class—very little."

Henry steered clear of the topic of Norma. He had a feeling

Norma's name would never be brought up in the house again and that was okay with him. In fact, it was a relief. Evan's affair with her had flared up quickly while on location, burned white hot, and then exploded with the heat of an atomic bomb when the news of Norma's engagement to some British producer was announced in the papers.

It was right there at the kitchen table, Henry was thinking. Evan was going on all lovey-dovey about Norma over breakfast, when they both heard Norma's engagement announced on the morning news. Evan had gone ballistic. He hadn't really been the same since.

"She was more than some opportunistic tramp," Henry said aloud. "She was a megalomaniac, that one was."

Evan seemed startled. "What are you talking about?"

"I'm talking about Norma."

"I told you to forget about Norma, Henry. Let's think about lunch. Hey, what time is it?" Evan wanted to know. "Maybe I should give Dory a call now. We could get to work early. That way I don't have to spend all morning being totally distracted by my overly active imagination. I could have the real thing distracting me."

*   *   *

Dorianne jumped when the phone rang. She was certain it was Kent calling from New York. It was too early for Evan to even be out of bed.

Maybe I'd better answer it anyway, she decided. And get this annoying thing with Kent over with. She wanted him to quit calling her.

"Good morning, Dory," the voice on the phone said. "This is Evan. I hope I didn't wake you."

"No, you didn't wake me. I'm still on New York time. But what's your excuse? What are you doing up so early?"

"I told you I'd call you when I was ready to work."

"Wow, I'm impressed."

"What can I say, Dory? I'm motivated."

"Well, good. Me, too."

"Do you want me to come get you?"

"You mean now?"

"Sure."

"Well, I have the rental car, you know. You can give me directions and I can drive up there."

"I'll come get you," he insisted. "When can you be ready?"

"I hate for you to go out of your way. I have the car—"

"It's not out of my way. And if we work late, I don't want you driving down through the hills in the dark when you don't know your way. I was thinking you might want to stay for dinner—work through dinner, I mean. You know, have it here with me."

"I hadn't really thought that far ahead." Dorianne was lying through her teeth.

It sounds like I'm going to be seduced, she thought with glee. He's worrying about dinner and it's only nine o'clock in the morning.

"I'll stay as long as it takes," she assured him. "I can't wait to get started, you know. I'm very interested to hear what you have to say, Evan. About your life, I mean. If we have to work late, then having dinner up there would be great."

"Okay, good," Evan said. "I'll be down to get you in a few."

She's willing, he was thinking. And he hurried to get his clothes on.

$*$ $*$ $*$

Dorianne hadn't expected Evan's house in the hills to be practically at the top.

"You have a spectacular view," she said. "But I guess you already know that."

"Wait'll you see it at night, Dory. I was noticing it again just yesterday when I got home, how beautiful everything looks from here. I spend so many hours staring out at it, but I'm usually too wrapped up in my thoughts to notice what I'm looking at, you know?"

"I do that, too," she said. "I have a great view of the Hudson river at home that I love to sit and stare at. Of course, it's nothing like this."

Dorianne was impressed. She'd been expecting some sort of elaborate 'movie star' ode to wealth and, structurally, this house was it. Unexpected vaulted ceilings that created a feeling of sanctity within an orgy of art nouveau detailing. Ornate, curving walls that subtly led one room into several other rooms, ending in a kitchen suddenly so modern Dorianne wasn't sure she'd know how to boil an egg in it. Enormous windows looked out on both the Hollywood of vanities that mortals created and the more spectacular beauty of the eternal things, the things that would last long after Hollywood's celluloid monuments had disintegrated into forgotten dreams. And yet she was struck by how strangely empty the complicated house seemed.

"You're not much of a collector, are you Evan?"

"No. I travel a lot. I lose things. I give things away."

"It's a beautiful house, Evan, but it's kind of hard to imagine that you live here."

"I know what you mean. I spend most of my time upstairs in my room. Up there, it's very lived in. Later on, if you feel like it, I'll give you the grand tour."

For now, Evan led her into a room that he always thought of as 'the study.' It was furnished like a study; it had two walls lined with shelves that would have been perfect for his collection of books if only he'd managed to save any of them. It got very little direct sunlight, so it was almost always dark and cool.

Dorianne took her tape recorder out of her bag and set it on the table methodically, along with a stack of blank tapes. She took out a small pad of paper to make notes, then she sat down next to the table in a luxurious leather club chair.

"No," Evan said. "You can't sit there, not like that. You look too formal, like this is going to be a therapy session or something."

Dorianne wondered if Evan had ever been in therapy, but she decided now wouldn't be the best time to ask.

"Well, where should we sit where you'll feel the most comfortable?"

Evan gave it some thought. He wanted to say 'upstairs in my room' but he decided that might be pushing it, even for him.

"Well, just sit closer to me," he said. "Here on the couch."

Dorianne collected her things and dumped them instead on the couch. Then she sat down and faced him.

This was what she did best, putting movie stars at ease. Leading them into revealing themselves as painlessly as possible. Keeping them on topic if they were the garrulous type, or coaxing them out of their shells if they were more inclined to be hostile to prying journalists.

Once again, Evan was wearing a simple black tee shirt and a pair of black jeans.

Dorianne had anticipated this and had purposely dressed to mirror him, to create familiarity. Today she wore a simple black pullover and a pair of black slacks.

"You must have been a beautiful baby," she said, smiling warmly, sounding genuine. It was something she said a lot— most movie stars liked to feel that they'd been beautiful since the moment God had presented them to the world; as if beauty itself had been their destiny. But oddly enough, Dorianne meant it this time.

"I mean it," she said. "You're a very good looking man."

"'Handsome' Evan Crane," he replied, with more than a little distaste.

"Okay," Dorianne said. "I'll stay away from that for now. Should we try again?"

"Sorry. Sure."

"Do you want to just chat for awhile before we get going, or should I go ahead and turn on the tape recorder?"

Evan wanted to lean across the couch and bridge the gap between them. He wanted to lie on top of her and kiss her mouth. He wanted to get her upstairs in his bed. Yet having her here in front of him, in the flesh again, in broad daylight, was intimidating. The woman he had ravished with such ease in his imagination last night, now seemed too professional to be approachable. "Let's chat," he said.

"All right."

Evan took the pad of paper, the tapes, and Dorianne's tape recorder and set them on the coffee table in front of them. "I'm sorry," he said. "I just feel better having them a little farther away."

Dorianne figured she was coming on too strong, but she didn't know of any other way to work. She had created a schedule for the amount of ground she'd hoped to cover each day, and she was in the habit of sticking to her schedules, meeting her deadlines without the frazzled craziness many journalists went through. She was methodical and organized and—

—she felt that the dynamics in the room had decidedly shifted. Now there was nothing in the space between her and Evan on the couch; nothing but him looking at her. It suddenly felt intimidating.

She started to feel exposed. Without the work to focus on, she feared the very intimate nature of her thoughts would be harder to conceal. She needed her work to shield her.

"You've been famous for ten years already, Evan," she began. "Certain facts about your life have been consumed by the public over and over again and they're as ordinary as breakfast cereal now. I want to find a new way into those facts, uncover the lesser-known facts that surrounded the incidents of your life. Create a story that's still true to you, but with vibrancy, too. Does this sound like a good approach?"

Evan regarded Dorianne peculiarly and she wondered if he was listening to her.

"You still want to do the book, Evan, don't you? You're not having second thoughts, are you?"

"Not at all," he said. "I still want to do it."

"You seem a little distracted."

"I am."

"You are?"

"I am."

Dorianne wasn't sure she wanted to know what it was Evan found so distracting. She was afraid of finding out that it might not be her. Maybe something had happened during the night that she couldn't possibly be aware of. Still, she couldn't help but notice that the energy between them was changing. The air seemed charged, electrified, as it had felt out on her patio the night before. And Evan's presence, so near to her on the couch, was once again making her feel overwhelmed. It was something in the way he was looking at her as she tried to conceal the thoughts that were in her head.

I'm not the kind of woman who gets involved with movie stars, she wanted to say. I'm too intelligent for that. I have my work to do, she told herself. My work comes first.

Instead, she said, "Is there something on your mind, Evan?"

He gave it some thought. How should he respond? It was a simple question. It was the only question he needed, really, to open the door wide and see if she walked through it.

One simple question was hanging in the air between them, as they sat alone together on the couch, where nothing else in the world existed.

"You're a very beautiful woman," he said, without realizing that the words had even come out of his mouth.

Dorianne's heart was beating faster.

Don't fall for it, she told herself. How could he possibly mean it, when he's been with every famous beauty in the English-speaking world?

Her mind was crowded with memories of every press photo she'd ever seen of Evan Crane at movie premieres, award ceremonies, film festivals; never appearing twice with the same glamorous woman on his arm.

"I mean it, Dory," he went on, suddenly finding the words easier to say. "I can't stop thinking about you."

He wants to get laid, she thought. Maybe he tried to get lucky last night and the lady had spurned him. Why else would he be coming on to me so early in the morning? We haven't even had lunch yet. I'm convenient, she thought.

"Thank you," she said.

"I told you yesterday to stop thanking me. You don't have to thank me, Dory."

Evan reached across that great divide of space between them on the couch and he took her hand in his.

I got this far last night, he told himself. There's nothing intimidating about this. This is not new territory. I can hold the woman's hand.

Dorianne looked at her hand held in Evan's. It was broad daylight now. She could see things clearly, through her own eyes, and not filtered through the romantic imaginings of her idealistic brain. Not clouded by some tropical hotel paradise built by set designers who were between pictures.

She hadn't realized Evan had such large, masculine hands. The sight of them aroused her.

I knew this was coming—she reminded herself—this seduction. I could feel it in his voice on the phone this morning. It had excited me then. Why am I trying to talk myself out of it now?

"We have so much work ahead of us," she said, still looking at his hands.

"There's nothing but time," he replied.

Even Christine Miles had been given her shot at an interview with Evan before she'd been pounced on by him, Dorianne thought. Then she tried hard not to picture the rest of it; Evan and Christine Miles naked together, tumbling wildly in the anonymity of some lavish bed—in an expensive suite, most likely—of the Hotel Beverly. Meaningless, drunken sex, going through the motions— that's not what I want.

Then she thought: he's not very discriminating, is he? I mean Christine Miles and I are as different as night and day.

"We have nothing but time," he repeated. "We have all afternoon, all evening. There's always enough time for work, Dory."

"I know," she said.

Then she found her mind filling with those salacious celluloid images of Evan naked with Norma Pearl, the scenes in the video that Dorianne had rewound a hundred times at home, until she'd felt herself being absorbed by the images, her own lonely lust becoming part of the videotape somehow. In real life, she had heard the rumors. They'd run rampant at the magazine; that Norma and

Evan had screwed their brains out on the set of *Trust Not the Innocents*. That the smoldering duo had to be pried out of Norma's trailer in order to shoot their scenes. And that was why their onscreen sex together had seemed so blistering hot—because they were actually *doing* it; for the camera, the crew, the director. The pair couldn't get near each other without behaving like a couple of wildcats in heat—

—but those were just rumors, Dorianne cautioned herself. That's not the real world. Just more lurid tabloid stuff, fueled by envy. 'That's not me,' Evan had insisted last night.

"Who are you, Evan?" she asked.

Evan pulled her closer to him on the couch. He felt the door swinging open. She was coming inside.

"That's what I hired you to find out," he said.

"Me, personally?" she asked, as she was effortlessly pulled into his arms.

"You, personally," he said, kissing her finally on the mouth. The mouth that he'd suspected would be very willing to be kissed.

As her lips parted, Evan felt the passion in Dorianne's kiss, searing hot, even while her hands were making a noble effort to push him away. And if her mouth weren't locked onto his own so tight, those little moans she was making would probably turn into words, little protests about how much work there was to be done. But now the resistance was draining out of her and her arms were wrapping around him, pulling him closer to her. She was returning his kiss with her whole body. There was nothing left in her that was pushing him away. And the moans that he felt in her kisses had shifted somehow. They were no longer protests, they were invitations. They had crossed that great divide.

She smelled pretty, he thought. Her soft hair brushed against his face. She felt substantial in his arms. Not just the soft mounds of her breasts crushed up against his chest, but all of her, her curves, the feel of her round ass in his hands as he pulled her more completely on top of him and they lay outstretched on the couch, bodies writhing now, kissing like a couple of teenagers.

He wanted to slip his hands up under her shirt. He wanted to slide his hands down inside her pants. But he was too busy keeping up with the intensity of her kiss. His cock was hard inside his jeans and the weight of her squirming body on top of it was making him crazy. Yet something told him not to rush her.

This one will run fast if I make one false move, he thought.

And they had all the time in the world...

There was a light tapping on the door of the study. It was Henry.

"Evan," he said. "You in there? John Ebbins is on the phone."

Dorianne and Evan stopped writhing, stopped kissing; they lay motionless on top of each other.   "Tell him I'll call him back," Evan called out. "I'm busy."

There was the sound of Henry's footsteps disappearing down the hall.

Evan heard John's words of caution in his head, not to turn everything into sex, not to jeopardize the project.

He looked up into Dorianne's eyes, her soft hair hung down, framing her pretty face. "I guess we're supposed to be working," he said quietly, trying not to break the spell. Still he hoped that she would take the lead, take control, be professional, be the one to steer them back on track and get them off of this detour he'd taken them down.

At first, she didn't say anything. She just stared down into his eyes, breathing a little unevenly, looking as if she still needed to be kissed.

Then her eyes closed slightly, and Evan saw that look come over her. She sighed. When her eyes opened, she had pulled herself together.

"I guess you're right," she agreed softly. And she scooted off him. She sat up. She made a half-hearted attempt to straighten her mussed up hair.

They sat side by side on the couch and said nothing. Dorianne loaded the tape recorder and set up the small microphone. She didn't turn it on. She looked at Evan uneasily and when he returned her curious gaze, she couldn't take the intensity of his beautiful brown eyes. He was obviously still aroused. She felt as if he were looking at her through centuries of human passion, a flicker from beyond life that said, 'we lived before and we knew each other well there.' She was being pulled back in.

She dropped her eyes, hoping to break the spell, but that was no good either because now she was looking at his crotch. He had an unmistakable erection inside his jeans. It looked enormous. It looked uncomfortable. Then she wasn't sure where to look.

"Where do you want to start?" he asked.

He was trying so hard to behave himself and she didn't want to be the one to send them reeling back into lust. But this was ridiculous. She couldn't focus. How was she supposed to work when Evan Crane was sitting right next to her with what appeared to be a very impressive hard-on?

"I don't suppose it's time for a lunch break yet?" she asked weakly.

Evan laughed. He pulled her back into his arms and she collapsed against him in delight.

"I feel so crazy," she said.

He looked into her eyes.

"I want to make love," she confessed.

"You mean now?" he asked.

"Yes," she said.

"You're sure?"

She said, "Yes."

"Do you want to go upstairs?"

Dorianne's belly fluttered at the thought of it. Something about his room seemed vaguely terrifying, but more in the sense of riding the fast curves of a dangerous roller coaster flying out over the water. It seemed thrilling. She said, "Sure, let's go to your room."

Evan took Dorianne's hand and led her quietly up the grand staircase to his world at the top of the stairs.

She followed close behind him, trying not to make a sound. Feeling as if the mysterious caretaker Henry, whom she still hadn't met, was somehow the embodiment of every authority figure she'd ever known. From her parents, to her publisher, to her agent— even to her high school principal, and her stern father figure/ex-lover Kent Cryer. Anyone who could find her out and be disappointed in her for her lack of good judgment, for her weakness. For the indiscretion she was about to surrender to; the lust she could feel herself plunging into when she knew she was supposed to be working. She was under contract. They had given her a lot of money already and, frankly, she didn't want to have to give it back.

There seemed to be a number of unoccupied rooms on the second floor, but Evan took her directly into his own room and closed the door.

"You're right," she said. "This room feels lived in."

It was a large master suite with a rough-hewn beamed ceiling. There was an inviting terrace beyond a set of French doors, laid with Mediterranean style terra cotta tiles, hedged in on three sides by well-trimmed greenery.

The room itself was dominated by an unmade king-sized bed, and an expensive entertainment center along one wall. There were framed photos here and there, of family and friends, and a few obvious highlights from Evan's professional career. There were several books piled in small stacks on the bedside tables. And there were clothes strewn over one of the large, upholstered chairs.

The room was mostly white and deep blue, with hints of forest green throughout, giving the room a warm feeling. On a coffee table, a half-smoked cigarette was stubbed out in a large ceramic ashtray and a lighter in the shape of a topless woman in a grass skirt stood next to it. "Aloha!" she was probably saying. Dorianne wondered if it was a souvenir from Evan's beach house on Maui.

Evan had removed his black tee shirt. At that moment, Dorianne decided to give in all the way. She was forced to admit it, she couldn't help herself, for it was true; he was only partially undressed, and it was already obvious that Evan Crane was 'the sexiest man alive.' Or at the very least the sexiest man she had ever been this close to.

She pulled her own shirt off over her head and then stepped out of her slacks. She was standing in front of him in only her bra and panties. Her hard nipples were clearly discernible through the sheer fabric of her bra.

"I don't know why I always imagined that when a girl made love to a movie star, she was always dressed to the nines," Dorianne joked shyly.

"Movie stars don't exist, Dory, and you know it. It's the image machine that exists. Outside of that, I'm just a man."

Evan pulled her close to him. Dorianne wrapped her arms around him. She wondered if they would kiss again, if they were going to behave as lovers did, or if this was just going to be sex; a quick, wild ride that would be over before she knew it.

Evan moved to unhook her bra and then he removed it. Was that the answer to her question? When her ample breasts were hanging full and free, Evan didn't kiss her lips, he grabbed her breasts in handfuls and leaned down to kiss them instead, twisting the stiff sensitive nipples repeatedly before sucking them into his mouth.

"I knew you were going to have gorgeous tits, Dory. I just knew it." Without once taking his hands from her breasts, he signaled her to follow him to the unmade bed, where he lay down amid the tangle of blankets and sheets and urged her to lie on top of him, her soft, luscious tits hanging down in his face.

Evan sucked Dorianne's nipples determinedly, long and hard, barely coming up for air. Keeping her breasts held firm in his large, masculine hands while she straddled him.

Dorianne couldn't recall her nipples ever getting such thorough attention. The sensation was making her lose control. Her panties were already soaking as she ground herself against Evan's jeans. She could feel him hard again and ready underneath her.

"Don't you want to at least unzip your pants?" she offered.

"Not yet," he managed to answer. Then he pulled her whole body up to his face. "I want to make sure you're ready for me first," he explained, as he pushed aside the crotch of her panties.

She liked his answer and lowered herself on his mouth.

Immediately, his tongue went to work on her, zeroing in on her clitoris as he clutched her ass firmly, keeping her where he wanted her. His tongue pushed deep into the stiff, tiny hood of her clit and tormented it insistently. She was writhing hard on his mouth as he held her in place over his tongue. She could do nothing but let the pleasure swell in her, building in her tiny clitoris until the pleasure felt like a huge, aching wave. Then she held her lips open for him as she hovered over his face, helping him to keep his tongue planted firmly on its target.

Moments before she thought she would come, Evan pushed Dorianne off him.

"Turn over for me," he told her, finally unzipping his jeans and shoving them down his legs.

It was the position she liked best and she assumed it eagerly. She was on all fours now on Evan's bed, with Evan in complete control.

He stripped her soaking panties down her thighs, leaving them around her knees, and he mounted her from behind. His thick erection felt enormous as it worked its way deep into Dorianne's slick hole. Dorianne cried out from the exquisite intrusion.

Evan grabbed tight to her hips and found his rhythm in her right away. Pulling out smoothly and then pushing in hard, until he had opened Dorianne so completely that she was taking the full length of him in no time and crying out sweetly with each new plunge.

She clutched at the bed to steady herself. Her raised bottom shaking fiercely against his repeated poundings. The stiff tips of her tender nipples brushed excitedly against the blankets with each new thrust and Dorianne felt insatiable. Her lust was overtaking her. She positioned her knees even farther apart, ensuring that her engorged clitoris was an easy target for his tight balls as they slapped against her.

Any moment she was going to come.

"Oh god," she cried out, feeling his cock growing even thicker, harder, as he drove it into her over and over with renewed fury. He was coming. Dorianne was certain of it even before she heard him cry out.

She ground herself against him, bucking her hips on the impaling shaft because he was in her so deep. She felt the probing head of his cock wedged up inside her womb somewhere. She rubbed her clitoris hard against his tight balls then because they were jammed right up against her mound. And that was all she needed. She came an instant later; a long, shuddering wave that intensified when Evan grabbed hold of her hips more firmly and helped her rub herself against his balls until every ripple of her orgasm had dissipated.

"That felt good," he sighed when he was sure she was finished. He uncoupled from her and collapsed on the bed.

Dorianne felt a little foolish. She still had her panties down around her knees. She kicked them the rest of the way off but then didn't know if she should lie down beside Evan in his bed, or give him a little space. Who were they to each other now? Lovers? Co-workers? A couple of impulsive people who had just had sex?

She sat at the edge of his bed and looked at him. He had a flawless physique. He was a little thin but other than that, Dorianne thought he looked even better lying naked in bed than he did in the movies. And every movie star she had ever met (albeit, fully-clothed) had always looked more attractive to her on screen.

"What's up?" he said.

"Nothing," she said.

"I think I know what that look means," he said. "You want to get back to work, don't you?"

"Well, don't you?" she asked.

He didn't answer right away. He was thinking how pretty she looked. He wanted her to stay naked for a while. He wanted to keep looking at her. He wanted to make love to her again and then maybe have lunch.

"What are you thinking about?" she asked.

"Taking a shower."

"Maybe I should get dressed then and give you a little space."

"I meant with you, Dory. Don't you want to take a shower?"

She actually hadn't thought that far. But now she understood:

he wasn't finished yet. She felt herself getting aroused all over again, wondering what he had in mind.

*   *   *

"I've never seen anything quite like this," Dorianne said quietly—almost piously. She felt that she had walked into a sacred place. It was hard to believe it was simply Evan's bathroom. "Most of my apartment could fit into this bathroom, you know."

"It's kind of special, isn't it? I spend a lot of time escaping from the world in here. Wait 'til you see the shower."

Evan found himself not so much showing off, as taking delight in Dorianne's obvious wonder. He opened the faucets full force, sending the waterfalls rushing down and she seemed awestruck. "Come on," he encouraged her. "Let's get in."

She stepped gingerly onto the blue mosaic tiles and quickly discovered that the tiles were covered with transparent rubber treads. She was on secure footing. But she felt overwhelmed by her own senses. A fine mist came down from overhead, where recessed lighting in the ceiling flattered her hopelessly pale skin. Behind the rushing waterfalls, walls of frosted acrylic encased tropical trees and plants.

"All plastic," Evan assured her. "But who can tell from this side?"

"I'm surprised you don't have birds and fish in here," she said in shock. "I feel like we're on some secluded island somewhere."

Evan wanted to say, "Wait until I take you with me to the house on Maui. I'm going to show you some incredible things." But it seemed presumptuous, that whatever was happening between them would last. It never did. Instead, he took her in his arms and kissed her, pulling her naked body impossibly close.

At last, she was thinking. He's kissing me again.

It made her feel that they were lovers.

"You have a great ass, Dory," he said in her ear, grabbing a firm handful of her rear end.

She resisted the temptation to say 'thank you.' Instead she said, "You have a great ass yourself, Evan Crane." And she grabbed a good portion of his very muscular behind.

He smiled self-consciously and it seemed as if he actually blushed.

He's not so intimidating like this, Dorianne thought. He's real. It's true, what he said before; he's a man.

She took his stiffening cock in her hand and stroked it while she kissed him again. His cock responded instantly to her touch, thickening to its full size. She squatted down then, and took it in her mouth. She sucked him fervently as the water gushed down around them on all sides. Why was it that whenever she was alone with him, it felt like paradise? It was a blowjob in a shower. Still she felt as if she were under a spell and couldn't get enough of his cock in her mouth. She sucked it longingly. Her tongue giving careful attention to every ridge and swelling vein as her mouth moved over the whole length of it. Up and down.

He steadied himself by holding gently to her hair. And as much as she moved her mouth up and down the length of him, he also worked his cock in and out of her mouth. They were in sync and it seemed that he could come like this. Easily.

He looked down at her and watched her pretty mouth working, working all over his thick cock. He felt her delicate hand caressing his balls. She was glistening wet now, the water splashing and spraying all over her body. Her breasts looked sensational, swaying like they did with every perfect movement of her head. Her pink nipples were stiff. He wanted those tits again, passionately.

He wanted to squeeze them, to come all over them, devour them. He wasn't sure *what* he wanted—

—"I think I'm going to come," he sputtered, surprising himself.

Dorianne had already tasted him beginning to ejaculate. She was just as surprised as he was; most men didn't come in her mouth. She never felt she was very good at it. But she stroked him quickly with her hand, kept at him, letting him come deep in her throat.

It sounded exquisite, the little cries he made, as if his orgasm were snaking up through him like irresistible fire; like it pained him every inch of the way, but like he wanted it just the same.

Ecstasy, Dorianne thought.

And she had brought it out of him.

In a matter of moments, it was all over and he helped her to her feet.

*   *   *

Dorianne was wearing one of Evan's robes, her hair dripping wet down her back. Evan had pulled on a pair of shorts. Both barefoot, they came into the kitchen and it was then that Dorianne met Henry.

He regarded them curiously. He looked out the window in the direction of the swimming pool. Then he decided to keep his mouth shut.

"Henry, this is Dorianne. Dory, this is Henry, my caretaker around here and a good friend."

"Hello," Henry said. "Nice to meet you. You're the woman about the book, aren't you?"

"I guess I am," she said shyly.

"Well, how's it going?"

Evan cut in. "What can we get around here for lunch, Henry?

We're starved."

"Anything you want, guys. We probably have it. I went shopping."

Henry eyed Dorianne and Evan again. "Can I ask you why you're all wet?" he finally said.

"No," Evan replied. "We just want a little lunch. Make us something surprising, Henry, and bring it to us upstairs." Then he turned to Dorianne. "How does that sound to you?"

"Like we aren't going to get much work done," she answered quietly.

*   *   *

Dinner was merely an extension of lunch; an incredible assortment of food that wasn't hot and wasn't cold, it was simply perfect. And there was wine. Henry came and went, but they never left Evan's room.

For Dorianne, it was all a blur. She'd never had that much sex with anyone in a single day. She'd heard that people—lovers—did things like that, indulged in their abandon. But she never gave much credence to hedonism. Why would people want to do that, she'd wondered; lose all those hours of productivity?

Even now, it sat somewhere in the pit of her stomach and made her uneasy; the fact that they'd gotten no work done on the book. Still, she couldn't deny that the view of the city at night from Evan's terrace was spectacular. It was a crystal clear night with a slight chill in the air. They were dressed, finally. Evan was having a cigarette.

"I'll have Henry drive us to the hotel," he said. "I think I've had too much wine."

"Okay," Dorianne said, already getting used to the ubiquitous Henry.

"This is when it usually happens," Evan said cryptically. He draped an arm around her shoulders and looked out at the night. "Just when you're a million miles away from anything on earth, surrounded by that feeling of having made some incredible love, when everything seems so right with the world—and then somewhere out there, a photographer with a telephoto lens is robbing you of that moment. Stealing it from you without your even knowing it. And then something you never dreamed could exist outside of you, winds up on some stranger's kitchen table in the guise of 'entertainment news.' That part's the hardest part of this life to get used to."

"Like what happened with Christine Miles," Dorianne said without thinking.

Evan looked at her, confused at first. Then he seemed amused. "What are you talking about? Why would I ever feel that way about Christine Miles?"

"That picture of you and Christine in front of the Hotel Beverly. It's in an upcoming issue of *Babylon*."

Evan looked at her blankly. "Really? There's a picture of us?" Then he shrugged it off. "Well, that's not what I'm talking about. I mean, when I've been 'with' somebody, you know? Intimately. Like we've been all day. And then it winds up in the papers somehow."

Evan looked into Dorianne's eyes peculiarly, as if he was trying to read something in her face. He had that look, like he was going to kiss her again. Then it dawned on him, what Dorianne must have meant, and he was taken aback.

"You don't mean that crap Christine is babbling about in London? Dory come on. That's a pack of lies. Christine has a serious problem. She screws too many famous guys—but I wasn't one of them. I didn't have sex with her."

"Oh," Dorianne said casually, trying to disguise her relief, wondering if she should believe him. "I wonder why that guy Bailey is dumping her then."

Evan said, "I heard that a couple nights after she interviewed me, she supposedly got really trashed at the Essex Club. A couple of British bands were playing there that night. They say she went off with two of the guys from one of the bands and, you know, did them both at once in her hotel room. But those guys weren't famous enough, apparently. I guess if Christine is going to get dumped by Eddie Bailey, she'd rather have people think it was over something a little more glamorous, more newsworthy, than what seems to have happened. Who knows? It could all be a rumor. I only know that I didn't have sex with her—although I came close."

Dorianne found his final remark a little unsettling. But she tried not to pry; she tried to hide how she was feeling. Why should she be so jealous about Evan and other women anyway? It wasn't like her to be jealous, or to be so gullible about gossip. She needed to get a grip on herself. It wouldn't be smart to let Evan think that she was falling in love with him. Besides, maybe she wasn't. Maybe it was just a crush, a phase, something that would pass when they got used to being around each other.

"Should we get going?" Evan asked, stubbing out his cigarette. "It's getting late and I know you want to get an early start tomorrow. I'll try to make up for the time we lost today, I promise."

*   *   *

Evan walked Dorianne into Casa Hollywood's lobby and the usual thing happened; people began behaving strangely. Dorianne wondered if this was going to happen every single night. It did have a way of draining a person's energy—trying to act as if she weren't aware of how other people were acting. Most people looked at her with scorn, as if she had committed a glaring *faux pas* by standing so close to Evan Crane without being famous herself. Other people acted as if she wasn't even there.

Once again, the security guard, a different one this time, made Dorianne show her room key while Evan was allowed to pass through to the bungalows with a nod of the guard's head.

When they were on the footpath toward Dorianne's bungalow, with the tiny paper lanterns surrounding their heads and the sounds of the waterfall playing somewhere inside the trees, she smiled. "You know," she confessed, "none of this is quite so impressive, now that I've been in your shower."

Evan laughed. "I liked having you in my shower."

When they reached Dorianne's door, he took her in his arms and kissed her goodnight. "Tomorrow, we'll behave," he said.

"I know," she replied.

"Will you do me a favor?" he asked.

"What?"

"Let's not talk about this, okay? I mean, to other people. I don't want how I'm feeling right now to get trampled on by idiots. Or wind up all over the pages of *Babylon*. I'm not ready."

Dorianne felt a little offended. "I'm not going to tell anyone at the magazine, Evan. I would never do that."

"Thanks," he said. "I had a really great time with you."

He kissed her goodnight a second time and Dorianne was struck by what he was really saying. He was feeling something that mattered to him. Something that involved her, that he didn't want trivialized.

Dorianne said goodnight, and when she let herself into her bungalow, her cell phone was beeping and her room phone was blinking.

Kent, she thought with despair. When is he going to leave me alone?

CHAPTER NINE

The following morning, very early, Evan sent Henry to pick up Dorianne and bring her up to the house. Dorianne was beginning to wonder why they'd bothered to rent her a car.

"It was very nice of you to come get me so early," she said.

"Not a problem," Henry replied, and they sped off into the quiet hills at an unsettling pace.

When Dorianne had arrived at Evan's house, he was waiting for her with a cup of coffee. He was wearing a bright white tee shirt and a pair of blue jeans. He looked happy and relaxed.

"We're working in the living room today," he announced.

Dorianne followed him into one of the more architecturally surprising rooms in the house. It was the room where the vaulted ceilings were most pronounced. A fireplace was the centerpiece of the room and its hearth, an elaborately carved edifice of solid concrete, extended clear to the high ceiling. One of the living room walls was a multi-paned window with French doors set into it.

The doors were open wide and the view was primarily of the swimming pool and its surrounding garden—although a jungle might have been a better word for it. In the distance, just visible up the hill, sat the modest guesthouse where Henry lived.

The living room was furnished with over-sized leather couches and club chairs, and an eclectic mix of art deco and art nouveau sidepieces. The room, as wide open as it was, was less suffocating than the study had seemed, and certainly less intimate than Evan's room, where the king-sized bed couldn't help but be the focal point of attention.

"We should work well in here," Evan explained. "Fewer distractions."

Henry brought Dorianne a cup of coffee and then left by the French doors and headed up to his own quarters.

"Did you sleep okay?" Evan asked.

"I slept great," Dorianne replied. "Like a log," she said, leaving out the part where she woke twice from fitful dreams only to discover her body was still thoroughly aroused from having been so sexually active with Evan. She'd had two orgasms during the night and then another before getting out of bed only an hour ago.

"Me, too," Evan said. "I slept great." He leaned over and kissed her quickly on the mouth.

They sat opposite each other in comfortable chairs and Dorianne set up the little microphone between them.

"Let's start with something simple," she suggested. "Let's talk about some of the things in your life that have made you really happy."

Evan's defenses were down and he talked easily for two hours about the high points of his career, about his early relationship with Lisa Wilson, the actress who was now engaged to the guitar player Paul Rydell, from the band F-Stop 4. Evan even recalled a few memories from his childhood that he could say with certainty were happy ones. Then he mentioned his first interview with Dorianne, in support of *The Devil Gets His Way*. At that point, he moved over to where Dorianne was sitting and he sat on the arm of her chair.

"So tell me," he said, turning the tables on her. "What was it like having sex with the famous Kent Cryer?"

At first, Dorianne thought he was only kidding her.

"No, I want to know," he pressed her. "You were in love with him. I'm not sure I've ever been in love. I was wondering what it felt like. How did you recognize it? As love, I mean. Was the sex spectacular?"

Dorianne wasn't sure where he was going with this, but just the word 'sex' coming out of Evan's mouth made her want to get naked with him again right away.

We have to work, she reminded herself.

"The sex was good, Evan," she said. "But in hindsight, I think I was in love with the sex. Not the man."

"Interesting answer," he said. "You know what?"

"What?"

"I have to go out tonight. I have to attend a party for business reasons. I want you to come with me, Dory. Be my date."

"I don't have a thing to wear."

"Don't be a coward. I'm sure you have the perfect little black dress. In fact, I've already seen it on you—at dinner the other night."

"But it isn't clean."

"What's the matter with you?" he demanded, sliding down into the seat with her. "Don't you like me anymore?"

Dorianne wanted to say, 'Of course I like you; I'm in love with you.' Instead, she replied, not untruthfully, "I don't know if I have the energy to be out with you in such a public place, Evan. It would be a lot easier if it were a place where nobody knew you, although I can't imagine where a place like that might be."

"You make it sound like I have a bad reputation."

Dorianne smiled. His body was pressed up against hers in the leather club chair. She had a feeling they were done working for a while. "You're too famous," she said quietly. "How do you stand it?"

"I'm used to it. There are a lot of things about it that I love. Other things are not so lovely." He ran a hand through her hair, brushing it back from her face. "You, on the other hand, are quite lovely." He kissed her on the mouth and she returned his kiss. Then he began to unbutton her shirt. "Come with me tonight," he said. "I'm obligated, I have to go. But I don't want to go without you."

Dorianne was already in a swoon. She was eager to make love with Evan again.

Evan had her shirt completely unbuttoned and he sucked her already hard nipples through her sheer bra.

"Shouldn't we turn off the tape recorder?" she asked breathlessly. "It's still running."

Evan tugged down the cups of her bra until her tits popped out, exposed. His mouth sucked in one of her naked nipples and his tongue tormented it.

Dorianne caught her breath sharply. Her nipples were still tender and aroused from having received so much attention the day before. Her nipple responded immediately to the flicking, licking, the swirling caresses of his tongue. She moaned repeatedly, quickly succumbing to utter lust, surpassing how she had felt with him already.

Evan reached for her hand and guided it to his crotch so she could feel the hard-on he had for her inside his jeans. "It misses you," he said in her ear. "It needs to be in you again. Right here, right now. What do you say? Are you going to let it come out and play, or are you going to work me like a dog today?"

"Evan, the tape recorder," she whispered.

"Forget about that for a minute and answer me. Doesn't your pussy want my cock? It sure wanted it yesterday, remember? Your pussy took me all the way in, over and over and over."

"I know, I remember."

"You do?"

"Yes."

"Do you remember asking me to fuck you very, very hard, and not to worry if we didn't get any work done, ever, as long as I kept fucking you?"

"No," she answered with a little laugh.

"No? Then maybe I dreamed that part," he confessed. "But it sounds like something you might do, doesn't it? You can be very accommodating when you want to be, Dory."

"I know," she said.

"Come to the party with me," he said.

"Okay," she surrendered at last. "I'll come. But first we have to get some more work done."

Evan agreed that it would be a prudent thing to do and then he resumed sucking her nipples and pushing her into ecstasy. With a little help from Dorianne, he tugged her black stretch pants and then her lacy panties down her thighs, so that his fingers could be up inside her while he sucked her nipples, and occasionally taunted her clitoris with fleeting caresses.

When he was sure that she was past the point of caring; when the intensity of her moans and urgency of her sighs signaled to him how aroused she'd become, he said, "Should we get back to work now, or do you want me to switch off the tape recorder?"

*   *   *

It was the first time Dorianne had ever been so thoroughly explored, probed, and penetrated while sitting in a chair. Although part of the time she was bending over it and some of the time she was leaning into the arm of it. And for a while, her back was flat against the seat of the chair, her knees up to her shoulders and her ankles around Evan's neck while his huge cock filled her relentlessly. Over and over, he shoved it up into her, giving it to her hard because she was finally asking for that.

"Fuck me hard," she was crying breathlessly, holding tight to him. "Fuck me. God."

They were so locked in each other's passion, in giving and receiving the lust that each of them was consumed with, that it never occurred to them to get out of the chair, to seek a more comfortable place for their lovemaking, even though the living room was well-appointed with furniture and consisted of more square footage than Dorianne's entire apartment had.

Sex for them had quickly become like a drug. The more they engaged in it, the more they needed to have it.

What's happening to me, Dorianne wondered, as they were once again engaged in intercourse in Evan's magnificent shower, and then she went down to her knees again and took his erection into her mouth. I can't seem to stop this, she realized. I can't seem to get enough of him.

And yet she never once asked him to stop. She climbed on top of him while he sat on one of the stone recesses cut into the shower wall. She lowered herself—her engorged, swollen hole—down on Evan's thick shaft. She ground herself down on him until he couldn't be in her hole any deeper. She lifted one of her breasts to his mouth and encouraged him to suck hard on the tender nipple, the water gushing down all over them as they writhed together in sheer lust.

At one point, they stopped and foraged down in the kitchen for something that passed for lunch. Then they were back at it, back in Evan's room, far from the tape recorder and all of Dorianne's notes that sat on a coffee table in Evan's living room.

They didn't stop for good until it was time to drive Dorianne back to her hotel so that she could get ready for the party Evan was taking her to. And even then, they were pressed for time and Dorianne had to hurry while Evan waited for her, dressed and impeccably groomed, in the living room of her bungalow.

When Dorianne was putting the finishing touches on her make-up, her room phone rang.

"Aren't you going to get that?" Evan called out to her.

"No," she said. "It's probably Kent again. He's been calling me like crazy."

Evan stared at the ringing phone and wondered what it was exactly that Kent Cryer had done to Dorianne to make her have such a change of heart. He found himself hoping that it had been something significant and irreversible. Not because he wanted Dorianne to be hurt, but because he wanted Dorianne to be his.

The room phone finally stopped ringing but soon enough, somewhere in the room the sound of Dorianne's cell phone started ringing.

"Does he always do this?" Evan called out.

Dorianne came into the living room, looking conservative but stunning. "Always," she said. "It's like he's chasing me with bells. It makes me crazy. It's hard to believe I spent so many nights waiting for phone calls from him that never came. And now I can't get far enough away from them. I wish he would stop."

*　　*　　*

The party was held at a swanky spot in Beverly Hills called Bertold's Bistro; a faux-euro lounge, known primarily for its red velvet rope that kept undesirables forever on the outside. Inside, it was crawling with photographers who'd been specifically welcomed to the occasion, since publicity for the affair was considered a must. Photo-ops were plentiful and Dorianne felt more conspicuous than ever.

It was an elaborate engagement party for the only daughter of the executive producer of Evan's next film—a film that would soon be going into production and consuming all of Evan's time; a big budget action picture, tentatively titled *Blast*.

Evan introduced her to everyone who inquired, by saying she was "Dorianne Constance, the writer from *Babylon* magazine. We're doing a book together."

But everyone sized her up suspiciously, as if they assumed that the book was just a subterfuge and that she and Evan were sleeping together.

Dorianne had never had her picture taken so many times in one evening. She never considered herself very photogenic. Every time she saw the burst of light from a camera's flash, she noticeably cringed, while everyone else around her seemed either to bask in the attention or be oblivious to it.

To Evan's credit, he tried to shield her as much as possible from any unwelcome intrusions. But the party was less a chance for him to relax and enjoy himself, than it was another aspect of his career, his work; just another obligation to his fame that he needed to pay attention to. The chances of disappearing into a dark corner together were non-existent. He had to present himself as open and accommodating in order to start out his next picture on the right side of the executive producer.

They had been at the party for nearly an hour, when havoc struck the evening in the guise of a newly blonde Norma Pearl. She entered the room in a gust of camera flashes, looking dangerously over-sexed, sizzling hot in a tight, silver sequined gown, and about as short-fused as a firecracker. She made a beeline for Evan's table, followed closely by several photographers.

Two of the country's top stars in one place; co-stars from one of the top-grossing films of the year before; a veritable god and goddess who were rumored to have made very good use of the same bed while on location. The cameras went crazy for them and Dorianne was in awe. She'd never seen so much chaos explode so quickly and then disappear so suddenly. When the photographers had gotten the shot they were after, they were off to attend to someone else's arrival. But Norma Pearl wasn't in a hurry to go anywhere.

"Nice of you to call and congratulate me on my engagement, Evan," she said icily. "Or maybe 'eviscerate me for it' is a better way of putting it."

"I'm only sorry your engagement was so short-lived," Evan replied flatly. "It must have been humiliating to get dumped as publicly as you were. And after you'd been considerate enough to make your ass so available to that weasel."

Dorianne was quietly appalled by the ugly tone of their exchange. She couldn't understand how rumors of an affair between the two stars could ever have surfaced. They evidently despised each other.

Maybe Evan was a much better actor than Dorianne had given him credit for. After all, in *Trust Not the Innocents*, there seemed to be genuine sexual chemistry between him and Norma on screen. Yet, in 'real life,' nothing of the sort was happening.

It was clear that Norma was livid and Evan was doing his best to act as if he didn't even know she existed. He certainly didn't invite her to sit at their table.

"So, is this your latest bimbo, Evan?" Norma spat, indicating Dorianne.

Dorianne was too aghast to be offended.

"No, this is Miss Constance, from *Babylon* magazine, Norma. She's not a bimbo; she's a writer. You're the only bimbo I've had the pleasure of knowing—or should I say of 'having'? Not that having you was that much of a pleasure."

"Oh that's rich. Is that your version of who had who? Does it help you sleep better? You know, Evan, you may have a bigger paycheck than mine, but it wasn't always that way. You've screwed everything that moves to sit where you're sitting today and you know it. You're no better than me."

"Maybe we'd better go, Evan," Dorianne suggested quietly.

A small crowd was obviously eavesdropping on the nasty exchange and it wasn't going to look very flattering in the tabloids.

"No, there's no reason to leave," Evan said calmly. "Soon enough, a pair of expensive trousers will come into her field of vision and she'll go chasing after it with no help from us."

Dorianne was grateful when an assistant to the executive producer, not wanting bad publicity of any sort, appeared out of nowhere to escort Norma Pearl to a less volatile corner of the party.

But even after Norma had gone, Dorianne was visibly shaken. Not so much by what had been said, as by what had been revealed. "Did you really sleep with her?" she asked quietly, hoping nobody was overhearing her.

"That isn't half of what I did with her," Evan replied between clenched teeth. "I actually asked that tramp to marry me. What an asshole I was."

Dorianne felt stung. She felt betrayed, even though she knew there were no logical grounds for feeling that way. Evan didn't owe her fidelity of any sort, past or present. Really what she was feeling was old-fashioned jealousy.

"I thought Lisa Wilson was the only girl you were ever engaged to," she said, hoping she didn't sound as defensive as she felt.

"Why would you think that?" Evan replied.

"Well, because that's what you were talking about this morning, being engaged."

"But you were the one who asked me to talk about 'happy things,' remember?" he said, a little too sarcastically. "There was nothing pleasant about my relations with Norma Pearl. Tomorrow, if you'd like me to expound on my unhappy memories, I'll be glad to chew your ear off."

"Okay, Evan. Maybe we should talk about something else for now. This is going nowhere fast."

Evan apologized and tried to regain his equilibrium, but it was obvious to Dorianne that, despite his collected exterior, he was still seething underneath.

The next hour was grueling. Dorianne tried hard to pull Evan out of his shell, to make conversation. But the best he could manage in return were monosyllables. Finally, they decided that two hours of being on display for the press was enough goodwill and they left the party.

"Let's take the long way home," Evan suggested as they got into his car. "You want to ride around for awhile? Get away from everyone?"

"It's fine with me, Evan." Dorianne was relieved. He didn't seem in a hurry to get away from her. "I don't have anywhere to be tomorrow except with you."

"You know, I was thinking back there. Maybe we should try working in your bungalow for a change, instead of at the house. How would you feel about that? Maybe it'll be less distracting and we'll actually get some work done."

Dorianne was doubtful but she agreed to give it a try.

They drove along Wilshire, heading toward the ocean.

"One of these days," Evan said, "we're going to head north until we hit the old highway 1 and we'll just keep driving until night falls. Would you like to do that?"

"You seem to have escaping on your mind tonight."

"That's not much of an answer."

"I didn't realize it was a real question. I thought you were just sort of thinking out loud."

"No, it was a real question. I'd like to run away with you for a little while. You're very easy to be with. Dory, listen," he said. "I'm sorry about what happened at the party. If I'd been thinking clearly today, I would have realized that I would probably run in to Norma tonight and I wouldn't have invited you. You didn't need to see that. But I wasn't thinking clearly. When I'm with you, I don't think clearly."

"That's a compliment, right?"

"I suppose so, but don't start thanking me again."

"Okay. I'll just return it by saying I'm having the same trouble, Evan."

"You are?"

"God, yes. Normally, I work like a crazy person; nothing can keep me from sticking to my schedule, keeping my eye on a deadline. I know we have a lot of leeway here, because we've just started. Yet I can't seem to think about anything but..."

"But what? Finish what you were going to say. Or should I finish the thought for you? You can't think of anything but having sex all the time."

There it was again, the word 'sex' coming out of Evan's mouth. It was all Dorianne needed to hear. She could feel herself getting stirred up again. "It's so unlike me, Evan," she said. "I know you're probably used to it, living like this; having so much sex."

"What's that supposed to mean? You think I'm like this all the time?"

"I don't know what to think," she replied truthfully. "At first, I thought there was something between you and Christine Miles. That turned out to be a lie. It never occurred to me you'd really had an affair with Norma Pearl, and now I find out that you wanted to marry her. So it makes me think the other rumors I'd heard, about you and Norma together on that movie—"

"—Okay," Evan cut in. "That was an isolated situation. I'm not like that all the time. With Norma and me, it was, well, like what you said about Kent. You realized you were more in love with the sex than with the man. But I found out about Norma the hard way. I heard it on the news. She accepted a marriage proposal from someone else while she was still sleeping with me."

"Jesus."

"I'm starting to think I'm just like my mother when it comes to marriage and judging character. She didn't know how to pick a guy with staying power; a guy who would stick around after the initial thrill was gone. My mother was married four times, and she was divorced again right before she died. To me, that was a very sad statement for her to make. That she'd rather succumb to cancer alone in a nursing home, than to leave this world married to someone who had disappointed her. I don't know if I'm ever really going to get married, Dorianne, but if I do, I sure don't want to be like my mother was—making such useless choices. And to think I came close to doing just that, to marrying a woman who's totally self-centered and deranged. Well, maybe I didn't really come close. Who knows," Evan said thoughtfully, "maybe Norma was never seriously considering my proposal. But the fact that I even asked her, what was I thinking? Who did I think she was?"

"She was whoever she wanted you to see, Evan. It happens. People are deceptive. You're lucky you found out about her in time, even if you had to find out the hard way. That's like what happened with Kent and me a few days before I came here. I was in a diner waiting to have breakfast with my agent, and Kent walked in with his arm around another woman. It was early enough in the morning to assume they'd been together all night. And they sure didn't seem like they'd just recently met. That was all I needed to see. I knew I'd been a fool for Kent again. Even though I was so sure I had my head on straight about him."

"I'm sorry," Evan said. "I'm sorry that had to happen to you. You're a sweet person, Dory. You didn't deserve that. But it sure makes my life less complicated."

"What do you mean by that?"

"I'm having a hard enough time keeping my hands off you as it is," he said. "I can't imagine how much more distracting it would be, trying to work with you if you were unavailable."

She wasn't sure what he was saying, if there was anything more to it than just that, that he couldn't keep his hands off her. But it suddenly made Dorianne feel very grateful that it was over forever between her and Kent.

"Maybe I've said too much," Evan asked. "You're very quiet over there."

They had reached a stretch of highway that was deserted, with the vast darkness of the ocean stretching out to eternity along one side and the brooding hills up above them on the other. Dorianne had no idea how far from the city they'd driven. She'd paid no attention to the world passing by them.

Evan pulled off the highway onto a road heading into the hills. His headlights immediately illuminated several 'Private Property' warnings. He pulled the car over and switched off the headlights. Then he turned off the ignition.

"What's going on over there," he said.

"I'm just thinking."

"Is it private, like this road we're hiding on? Or is it something you can share?"

"I didn't realize we were hiding."

"You have a strange way of answering questions," he said.

With the headlights off, the night surrounding them was incredibly dark.

"It's not private," she confessed. "I was just wondering about what you said."

"How glad I am that you're not with Kent?"

"Yes."

"How I can't keep my hands off you?"

"That, too."

"You don't have to worry about anything that might have gone on with me and Norma. Anything good I might have felt about her is long gone. There's no comparison between you and her, you know. You're classy. You're in a league of your own, Dory. You earned your success with your brain. Norma's a foul-mouthed piece of trash whose key to success has been her rear end. And she's had so much cosmetic surgery that, under all the glitz, she's starting to look like a freak. Hollywood does that to people."

Dorianne was silent. She didn't want to start bashing Norma Pearl, a woman she didn't even know.

"Well?" Evan said.

"Well, what?"

"Do you want to kiss for awhile?"

"You mean, now? Right here?"

"Sure."

"In the car?"

"Why not? I just want to kiss you, that's all. Have my arms around you for a little while before I take you home."

Dorianne considered the absolute darkness of the car, the road, the surrounding hills. "I don't know, Evan. I don't think I'm capable of just kissing you and leaving it at that."

"We have a stick shift between us to help us behave."

She knew all about stick shifts—and how inviting they made back seats seem.

"Just a kiss," Evan said. "If it progresses to something more than that, I promise we won't do anything that can't be done right here in the front seat with a stick shift between us, okay?"

The proposition intrigued her. Dorianne leaned over and kissed Evan on the mouth. She had hoped to kiss him quickly, to steer clear of any danger. She wasn't the kind of woman who did tawdry things in cars. But when her lips were on Evan's, when their lips parted and their tongues met, Evan held Dorianne's face in his hands, forcing their kiss to linger.

They kissed until Dorianne surrendered to the passion and threw her arms around Evan's neck.

When he wanted to caress her breasts, she didn't protest as he unzipped her little black dress, or when he lowered the top of it down to her waist. And she was the one to remove her bra so that her naked breasts could be his to explore.

She found it secretly thrilling, being topless in a dark car on somebody else's private property. And Evan had such a way with her tits. He made love to them as if he worshipped them. His hands squeezing her breasts together, his mouth devouring the full mounds of flesh—it was enough to make her lose all sense of propriety.

She unbuckled his belt and unzipped his fly.

And while Evan's tongue tormented her stiff nipples, her hand was down inside Evan's trousers, freeing his cock through the opening in his boxers.

She stroked his hard-on vigorously while he sucked on her tits— until she couldn't stand the torment of her own desire. She leaned over and sucked the full length of his erection into her mouth.

Evan groaned. He leaned back in the seat and watched her head move seductively up and down on his aching shaft. He felt the wet heat of her mouth enveloping him. Her tongue licked at the tender underside of his flesh and swirled over the taught head of his cock. And all the while her hand pumped rhythmically at the base of it, while her slick mouth kept moving, moving; up and down; his hard cock going in and out.

She had repositioned herself so that she was on her knees on the car seat. She was leaning over the stick shift, her naked breasts hanging down as her mouth rode his shaft without stopping. Her flesh was so white he could see the outline of her perfectly in the dark car. He wondered what her ass would look like; white, and raised like it was—if only she didn't have that dress concealing it.

He reached over and tugged the hem of her dress up over the firm, fleshy hump of her ass and was delightfully surprised to discover she had only a thin black thong under that deceptively conservative little black dress. The thong cut neatly up between her delicious ass cheeks, separating them into two inviting mounds, the tops of her black stockings stopping at her thighs.

She looked terrifically naughty like this, her round white rump in the air, practically naked and so enticing, while her swaying breasts brushed against his thigh with every downward swoop of her hot mouth.

He had promised they would only do what could be managed with a stick shift between them in the front seat. Still he had to have a better view of that ass. And he wanted his tongue in her hole. He wanted to hear the little cries she made when his tongue poked up into the tiny hood of her clitoris, too, and licked at the tender spot without mercy.

He wondered if she would go that far. She probably would.

"Turn around," he said hoarsely, his voice too filled with lust to speak clearly. "I want that white ass of yours in my face."

"Oh god," she groaned, feeling deliciously dirty when he talked like that. She would do anything he asked her to.

She turned around in the seat and presented her full behind to him, upturned and eager. He pulled aside the thong to access her completely and she felt his hot tongue lap across her exposed, swelling lips. It poked into her wet hole next and, in and out, it fucked her. His fingers spread the base of the hole wider; his tongue fucked her more deeply; over and over, in and out. Then it slid out of her hole and down the parted lips until it found her aching clitoris, vulnerable and waiting.

He licked the stiff point of flesh relentlessly while her moans and sweet cries filled the car. He sucked it in between his lips, tugging it gently.

After several minutes of having his face buried in the folds of her slick, swollen lips, he knew he was going to have to mount her. He couldn't help himself.

"Evan, what are you doing?" she cried.

"Just move down a little this way," he said, easing her knees over the stick shift so that her body awkwardly straddled it. Then, with his trousers and boxers down around his thighs, he mounted her, leaning closely over her, so as not to bang his head on the low ceiling of the car.

"Oh, Jesus," she gasped, when the thick length of his cock

ploughed into her vagina. Thrusting away at her, pumping hard, opening the tight passage of her pussy completely until he had filled her hot hole with his cock.

She held tight to the car seat as he found his rhythm. She could tell by his intensity, that he was going to come fast.

"Jesus," she cried out, her voice sounding desperate as the power of his thrusts increased.

But he could tell by the way she arched her ass up higher, letting him get in her even deeper, that she was crying out from sheer lust, not pain.

Poised over the stick shift, she tried to steady her weight on her knees, which trembled, now that most of Evan's body weight was on top of her, too. Her upper body was pressed flat against the car seat, the cool leather growing warm under her bare breasts.

She felt so dirty like this, like an animal in heat; her clothes shoved this way and that, to ensure he had clear access to her choicest female parts. And yet she did it willingly; she would stay the whole night in his car and service him with her sex, if that's what he asked her to do. She wanted to keep him close to her. She wanted him always inside her, filling her. She wanted him groping her, probing her—if that's what pleased him. Her body was his because she loved him. Loved him!

It was shocking to hear her mind admit it, and to feel her heart corroborate it. She loved him; she was in love with him—the notoriously unavailable movie star, Evan Crane. The man whose grunts and cries were filling the car now, too, mingling with her own, as his lust climaxed inside her in several hard bursts.

Her fingers were down between her legs, rubbing her clitoris relentlessly, as her orgasm followed closely behind his. Her hips convulsed, her thighs shook, the force of her climax was that extreme.

"Oh god," she whimpered, "god. I'm coming, I'm coming," she cried.

He was panting on top of her, jerking against her in the final spurts of his lust.

And then, suddenly, the car was silent again. Silent and quite dark.

They uncoupled gingerly, re-positioning themselves on either side of the stick shift; straightening their clothes, their hair.

"You'd think we were teenagers," he said finally, starting the engine, "with no place to go but the car. While I have a huge house in the hills all to myself and you have an empty bungalow only a few miles from there."

"Evan," she said, feeling stunned and a little needy. "Will you spend the night with me?"

He reached over and pulled her head close to his and kissed her quickly on the mouth. "Of course I will," he said quietly. "Thanks for asking me."

*   *   *

In the privacy of Dorianne's bungalow they showered and ordered room service. When the food arrived, it was only passable but they were both famished so it didn't matter. They ate their food as they made love, as if it were an orgy.

It didn't take long for them to find their way to Dorianne's bed. They climbed in together naked and lay entwined.

Dorianne felt fragile, a little foolish about how wantonly she had behaved in the car; giving her body over to him so unconditionally.

At least I didn't tell him I loved him, she reminded herself. I wasn't as foolish as all that.

"I'm sorry if I overdid it today," Evan said quietly, as if he were reading her mind. "I feel like I'm going to use you up, like I can't get enough of you. I'm sorry if I pushed you too far in the car."

"It's okay," she assured him. "I had fun. But I've never done anything like that in my life. For me, being wild has meant not doing it on the actual bed, you know?"

"I know. We don't always have to be wild. Do you think this craziness between us is going to wear off any time soon?"

"I don't know," she sighed. "But I'm glad your going as crazy as I am."

"I am," he said. And then they kissed.

It wasn't long before Evan was once again aroused. But they were quieter about it this time, more subdued. Evan got on top of her and Dorianne's legs parted to accept him.

They made love like that, sanely. With Dorianne's legs wrapped loosely around Evan's waist as his cock went in and out of her vagina slowly, with a steady purpose. And they kissed.

When it was time for Evan to come, Dorianne spread her legs wider, held tight to Evan's ass and let him get in her deep. When he'd finished, he lay on top of her a while.

"I'm so glad you came here," he said.

"Me, too," she replied.

"I knew we were going to get along," he continued. "I just knew it. But I hadn't expected this."

"Me, neither."

"How do you feel?" he wanted to know.

"What do mean?"

"I mean, well...I like you," he said, retreating decisively. Dorianne could hear it in the changing tone of his voice. "I really like you," he said.

"I like you, too," she replied.

It seemed a long while then, that they both lay there silently, lost in thought. Holding each other, neither awake nor sleeping, caught in the same half-aware dream.

CHAPTER TEN

The phone woke them at the crack of dawn. Dorianne was too startled from sleep to keep herself from answering it.

"Who do you think you are? Avoiding my calls for several days, and now *this*."

It was Kent. He was furious. But Dorianne didn't have a clue what he was talking about.

"What is it, Kent?" she said wearily, giving up any hope of shielding Evan from who the unwelcome caller was. Evan stirred next to her in the bed, awake.

"*What is it?* What do you mean, what is it? I'm talking about the Fritz & Conway column in this morning's paper! Not just the darling photo of you, Evan Crane and Norma Pearl looking like you're going to duke it out in eveningwear. But those precious lines about your 'ongoing affair' with me while I was still married and how it 'only recently ended' when you left me 'for Evan Crane and Hollywood'!! Thank you, Dorianne. We're all just pleased as punch around here. I can't tell you what you've done to my world this morning!"

Dorianne was speechless. "What are you talking about, Kent?"

He was livid. "Don't you read the papers?!"

"Kent, it's six o'clock in the morning here. I was sound asleep until two seconds ago."

"Well, do yourself a favor and get out of bed!"

Kent slammed down the phone.

Dorianne looked at Evan.

"What's the matter?" he said.

"I'm not sure," she replied, hanging up the phone. "But it sounds like there's something in the gossip pages this morning that's already ruined my day."

"What do you mean? Wasn't that Kent?"

"Yes, that was Kent and he was irate."

Dorianne felt sick to her stomach. She picked up the phone and called the front desk.

"This isn't making sense, Dory. What's going on?"

"Can I have the morning paper brought to my bungalow?" Dorianne asked the operator, who sounded unnervingly cheerful for six o'clock in the morning.

"Of course, Miss Constance. Right away."

Dorianne hung up the phone. "It's something in the paper," she tried to explain. "Kent says there's an item about all of us in the Fritz & Conway column. But I want to see it for myself."

"All of us? Who's all of us?"

"You, me, Norma, Kent—and indirectly, Kent's ex-wife, and his current red-headed love interest."

"Jesus. That's quite a crew."

The morning paper arrived within minutes and they were already out of bed. Dorianne handed the paper to Evan. "You look," she said to him. "I don't think I can stomach it yet. I'm going to order up some coffee—or maybe a fifth of something a lot stronger."

Evan sat down on the couch in the living room and turned to the Fritz & Conway column. There it was, large as life: a less than flattering photo of him, Dorianne, and Norma Pearl from the party the night before. Dorianne looked visibly startled, he himself looked brain dead, and Norma looked like she was ready to attack both of them with pointed fangs and sharp fingernails.

The headline was bad enough: IS THE WORLD'S MOST ELEGIBLE BACHELOR FALLING FOR A HOMEWRECKER? But the accompanying story was even worse:

Hank Somerstien's party last night at Bertold's Bistro held some unpleasant surprises for heartthrob Evan Crane. Apparently, Mr. Crane, the notorious bachelor who's always flying solo, is not so unattainable anymore. In fact, it looked like he had his hands full last night with **two** unhappy females: Actress Norma Pearl, his former co-star and off screen love interest, and his newest 'big deal' Dorianne Constance, journalist to the stars.

Our sources say Miss Pearl is heartbroken over losing Evan, the man she left British Producer David Wilcox for earlier this year. But a close friend of Miss Pearl's warned us, "Norma's not giving Evan up without a fight. She's devoted to him!"

Meanwhile, it looks like Miss Constance will do whatever it takes to 'get that interview' and to assure that it's up close & **very** personal. Sources say that she and Evan Crane have been making the scene together nightly in a private bungalow at Casa Hollywood. Other sources indicate that before swooping down on Crane, Miss Constance was the long time love inter-est of award-winning journalist Kent Cryer—but didn't he only **recently** get divorced? Folks, you do the math!

"She had an ongoing affair with Cryer throughout his marriage," our sources assure us. "In fact, she only ended the affair a few days ago, when she left him for Evan Crane and Hollywood."

Should Miss Constance join Home wreckers Anonymous?! Since she's come onto Evan Crane's domestic scene, even sexy siren Norma Pearl has gotten the boot. (And whatever happened to Christine Miles, we'd like to know. Evan you dirty dog!)

We're waiting with baited breath for the outcome of **this** romantic thriller! (YAWN)

Evan quietly closed the paper and set it aside. He lit a cigarette and toyed fleetingly with the vain hope of simply lying to her; telling Dorianne that Kent had overreacted, that it was nothing, that it would all blow over before lunch. If it had merely been another story about Evan and Norma, even though it was a pack of lies, it wouldn't have amounted to anything. It would have been just another testament to Norma's egomaniacal insanity. But this time, they'd decided to go after Dorianne.

"How bad is it, Evan?"

"Bad enough," he replied evasively.

"Really?"

"Well, I can see why Kent would be upset."

"You can? Should I read it, or is it just going to upset me?"

"I think you should read it," he said, handing her the paper. "But I also think it's going to upset you."

Reluctantly, Dorianne sank down into the sofa next to him. She opened the paper. She read the Fritz & Conway column and then threw the paper aside.

She was furious, heartbroken, humiliated—all of it at once.

"Who are these 'sources' they're quoting?" she wanted to know.

"Who are they? Obviously, it's someone who knows me enough to know what I'm doing, but not somebody who really knows me. To call me a home wrecker, after everything I suffered through with Kent? To say that I'm sleeping with you to get an interview? It's insulting. It's demeaning. Why would somebody say those things?"

"For the money," Evan said.

He'd been there hundreds of times before. Most of it he'd gotten used to. Gossip became meaningless after awhile, there was just so much of it. But when it came to the personal betrayals, when it came down to something hurtful being exposed for the sake of 'entertainment news' simply because somebody near him wanted to make a few bucks; that was a thing he'd never gotten used to. How could anyone?

This was the darker side of Evan's fame and he hated to see Dorianne victimized by it. The press had baited the waters with her in pursuit of Evan's more rabid fans, the ones who swooned at any mention of his name and spent too much money on meaningless gossip. Dorianne had been thrown to the sharks to create a sensation where there was none. To give the impression that Evan's 'dashing movie star' status—that his dream career, his prized bachelorhood, the 'sinful amount of money' he earned by making movies; that all of it was vaguely in jeopardy now because of Dorianne.

It had happened to other women he'd been paired with in the press. But those women had been public personalities, more accustomed to fending off the constant assault of invasive fans. Evan's fans wanted to see Evan stay single no matter what. It made him a more attractive leading man. It made him seem available to countless lonely women in their imaginary lives. His fans wanted to believe that any female Evan would be taken in by was somehow salacious and cheap, not good enough for him.

And the press fed into that fantasy because it sold papers.

It was just old-fashioned greed. And Dorianne didn't have a highly paid publicist working around the clock to keep unwanted rumors out of the tabloids. Now a secret that Dorianne had managed to keep private for ten years was in newspapers coast to coast. Her own parents, her closest friends, her business associates; they were probably already thinking of her as 'the home wrecker.'

"They do it for the money," Evan repeated. "You know that. You've worked for *Babylon* for how many years? But I know it doesn't make it any easier."

"Evan, what is that supposed to mean? Just because I work for *Babylon* doesn't mean I'm a gossipmonger. I don't tell lies. I don't spread rumors, or divulge personal secrets and betray people."

"I'm sorry, it came out wrong. I didn't mean it like that. God," he sighed in frustration. "Why did I take you to that party?"

"I don't know, Evan. Why did you?"

"Come on, Dory, let's not fight."

"I'm not fighting," she cried. "I'm just angry! My reputation matters a lot to me."

"I know it does."

"If I'd wanted Kent's wife to know about me I would have said something to her myself a long time ago."

"I know. But it's not like they're still married. It could have been worse."

Every comment Evan offered only fueled Dorianne's outrage.

"I know it could have been worse, Evan, I'm not stupid. But it's still bad enough. I've worked really hard to be taken seriously, to be trusted in this industry, and now I look like a perfect fool. Like some sort of 'movie star mad' vulture who'll sleep with anybody as long as they're unavailable."

"Dory, it's not that bad. It's just one item in a newspaper."

"That's syndicated all over the country."

"All right, Dory, you win. I don't know what to say to make it better."

"There isn't anything you *can* say. I was a fool to sleep with you, Evan. I'm supposed to be working, not screwing around all over Hollywood. You brought me out here to do a job. I'm supposed to be a professional and instead, I've been playing games with a player. I left myself wide open for this by sleeping with you."

It was Evan's turn to be outraged. Her attack was personal now and it stung.

"I didn't realize that screwing a movie star was beneath you, Dorianne. I'm sorry if I insulted your intellect or tarnished your career."

"Damn it, Evan. I didn't mean it like that."

"How else could you mean it?"

Dorianne fell silent. She knew Evan was right; how else could she have meant a remark like that if not to put him down? She realized that it was true—part of her was ashamed of sleeping with him because he was a movie star, he was rich and famous, and she was too smart to fall for that, wasn't she? He could have any woman he wanted. In fact, he'd had *all* of them it seemed, including her now. She was just as silly as all the others were, falling for Evan's good looks and charm. And who would next year's model be, after the book project was finished; when Dorianne became obsolete and was tossed aside for Evan's next 'big deal'?

"You were the one who wanted to keep it a secret," she reminded him. "The fact that we were sleeping together."

She was trying to defend her guilty conscience.

"It wasn't because I was *ashamed* of sleeping with you. It was because I wanted to protect you," he insisted. "To protect *us*, from *this* for as long as possible."

"I didn't realize there was an 'us,' Evan."

Again, she'd lashed out. She was drowning in self-doubt and didn't seem able to save herself.

"You can be a very insulting young woman, you know that?" Evan snapped. "You've been full of snide innuendo ever since you got here. I don't screw every woman who comes on to me. And I don't go to this extreme with women I don't care about."

Dorianne was determined to keep the upper hand. She wasn't going to be fooled again. It was naive to pretend that rich and famous men had hearts, no matter what they claimed. They were rich and famous for a reason. They didn't really care about people. Even Kent had admitted it: no one gets to the top by being nice.

"You're a player, Evan. Everyone knows it."

"I'm a *man*, Dory. I don't care what everybody knows or says," he went on. "So what if they call me a player? I'm still a man. I was hoping you'd figured that part out."

"A man is more than just a constant hard-on, Evan. A man is more than something that needs to get laid."

Dorianne had outdone herself with hatefulness.

The room fell aggressively silent.

Evan got up from the couch. He wanted to walk out on her, then and there. He wanted to teach her a lesson about who she was fooling with; who it was she was insulting. Thanks to his bank account, he was one of the most powerful men in Hollywood and he was well aware of it. Maybe he would show her the difference between how it felt to make love with a man and how it felt to get screwed.

Instead he took a deep breath.

She's hurt, he reminded himself. She's in over her head. She doesn't know how to handle this. She doesn't know what she's saying.

Someone from room service knocked at the bungalow door with Dorianne's order.

"I'll get it," Evan said quietly.

When he opened the door for the room service waiter, Evan realized too late that, under the present circumstances, answering Dorianne's door at this early hour of the morning, wearing only his trousers, wasn't the smartest thing to do.

"Good morning, Mr. Crane," the waiter said with a knowing gleam in his eye. "Miss Constance ordered breakfast for two?"

"Bring it in," Evan sighed. And he got out of the way of the rolling cart.

*   *   *

Dorianne stewed.

Her breakfast sat on the table in front of her and she poked at it listlessly with a fork, while the telephone rang and rang.

"If you don't answer it," Evan finally said. "I will. I'll put him in his place and get him to knock this off. He's harassing you, Dory, and it wasn't your fault."

Evan was dressed now, with half a mind to leave her alone for the day. To give her some space and give himself some room to breathe. Since the moment her plane had landed in L.A., it seemed like they'd been inseparable. During the hours when he hadn't actually been with her, he'd thought about her constantly. Maybe neither one of them was thinking straight.

"I don't see how this isn't *all* my fault," she said.

Evan was relieved that she was at least saying something; that she was speaking to him again.

"That's crazy. You're overreacting. In fact, this is all his fault, when you get right down to it. He should never have slept with you when he was married or committed to someone else in any way."

"I can't believe you're willing to defend me after all the nasty things I said to you."

Evan went over to where she sat. He looked down into her pretty face and he smoothed the worried lines from her forehead.

"You were nasty," he agreed. "But I'm on your side. This isn't the end of the world, Dorianne. It's ugly and we have to deal with it, but it's going to pass. I've been through too many things like this before. How you handle it or don't handle it makes all the difference. And it makes the next assault that much easier."

"The next one?"

"If we're going to be"—Evan searched his thoughts quickly for the safest way to put it—"working together all the time, then we're going to be seen together and people are going to talk. I'm the most eligible bachelor in Hollywood, remember?" He smiled down at her warmly, without malice. "People don't like change. They want me to stay just the way I am. I'm easier to classify that way."

The room phone began ringing again, startling them both.

"Should I answer that?" he asked.

Dorianne found the idea tempting. It was a little like playing with fire but it might put an end to Kent Cryer intruding on her day and night.

"Okay," she said.

Evan picked up the phone and spoke without emotion into the receiver. "Hello."

There was a pause. Then a man's voice said, "I was looking for Dorianne Constance's room. Did I dial the right number?"

"You did. But she can't come to the phone right now. Can I take a message for her?"

The man's voice grew indignant. "No, I'll call back later."

"She won't be here later. You should probably leave a message now."

An affront. "Who is this?" the voice wanted to know.

"Evan Crane. Who is this?"

There was silence on the line.

Dorianne watched Evan with a renewed sense of awe. Not because of what he was saying so much as the fact he was doing it at all. He was going to bat for her. It would be like Dorianne taking on Norma Pearl. Would she have the guts to do something like that? It would be admitting that she cared for Evan; cared enough to let his troubles become her troubles.

"Is there a message?" Evan repeated coolly into the receiver.

"Just tell her it's Kent." The voice sounded forcibly restrained, as if fighting its way out of a jaw that was clenched tight. "She'll know what it's about, Crane."

"I know what it's about, too, Cryer, and I think you should leave her alone now. She's had a bad morning. You didn't help matters by waking us at the crack of dawn, either. We got to bed late."

Dorianne was floored. *"Evan!"* she whispered urgently, but she was filled with glee. She didn't think she'd have had the nerve to do it on her own; to tell Kent she really was sleeping with Evan Crane.

"You're a son of a bitch, you know that, Crane?"

"You're not such a prize yourself, Cryer."

"Look what you're doing to her, you ass. You're ruining her reputation."

Evan was unflappable. "I had nothing to do with that. I haven't done anything to put her reputation in jeopardy. That ball was in your court a long time ago. I think you could have come up with a better way of playing it but that's how it stands. For now, she's decided to be my little home wrecker and that's all right with me. I don't have anything to hide. I'm sure she'll give you a call if she wants to go back to your way of playing it."

Evan hung up the phone.

Dorianne was dumbfounded. "I can't believe you said that."

"Did I overdo it?"

She looked at Evan and Evan looked at her.

"No," she heard herself saying. "Did you mean it?"

"Yeah," he said. "I did. I'm more than happy to have you wrecking my little home for as long as you want to."

"Evan!"

Dorianne laughed for the first time in weeks.

*   *   *

Dorianne turned off her cell phone and stuck it away in a drawer. She called the front desk and told them to hold her calls indefinitely.

"Of course, Miss Constance," the operator replied. Was that a hint of curious intrigue in her voice?

Dorianne didn't care. For now, let people think whatever they wanted. She was rich, she was free, and she was in love.

With a deadline looming, she thought.

But she would handle it. She would pace herself. She'd never missed a deadline yet. Today, they had all the time in the world. Tomorrow, she would bring out the tape recorder.

Neither of them had made much headway with the breakfasts Dorianne had ordered. The food sat on the table, picked over, cold and unappetizing. And suddenly they were starving. They decided to re-order. This time it was a champagne brunch.

Within the hour, the same waiter from room service arrived with another cart. With a look of casual indifference, as if he had seen it all before, he removed the uneaten breakfasts and replaced it with something more elegant, including a bottle of the hotel's best champagne. And it was still only nine o'clock in the morning.

Dorianne signed for the brunch, but Evan tipped the waiter generously on his way out the door.

"Thank you very much, Mr. Crane." The waiter acknowledged the generous tip with the obsequiousness customary to employees of five star establishments.

"You're welcome," Evan said.

"You know the front drive is crawling with paparazzi this morning," the waiter added under his breath. "They've staked out your car."

"I didn't know that," Evan replied. "Thanks for telling me."

"One good tip deserves another," the waiter assured him. Then he disappeared down the flagstone path, pushing the cart of their first, uneaten breakfasts in front of him.

"Well, that settles it," Evan announced. "We're going into seclusion today. Whoever wants a picture of us allegedly sneaking around together, is going to have to earn it the hard way."

Evan was grinning from ear to ear as he eased the tight cork out of the champagne bottle. There was only a slight popping sound and a breath of frosty air came out of the mouth of the bottle.

Dorianne didn't usually go in for champagne but this morning she felt like celebrating. There was something curiously liberating about having it in papers coast to coast. The weight was lifted. It wasn't a secret anymore—her illicit affair with Kent Cryer. Yes, it was over, and had been over for nearly a decade, but in a way she felt she was finally getting her recognition. Her days of being hidden away while he was out wining and dining his way to the top were done.

She would have preferred if it had come from Kent himself, in the manner of his having divorced Katherine for Dorianne years ago, of his own volition. But since it had never happened, this was the next best thing. She felt sorry for his new friend, the redhead, whoever she was. But it wasn't Dorianne's problem. She hadn't been at fault in that one.

Dorianne raised her glass for Evan as he poured her some champagne.

Evan poured his own and then raised his glass to hers. "Is it mean to toast to the end of Kent Cryer?"

"Maybe," she said. "But I don't care. Especially if it means we're really toasting to the beginning of something else—for each of us, separate or together."

"Okay, then," he agreed, "because you need to play it so safe: to each of us. And to Norma and Kent, may they live happily ever after without us."

"To Norma and Kent," Dorianne chimed.

She drank her champagne and she ate her breakfast with gusto. And she regarded Evan with renewed joy because things had changed now. She hadn't allowed herself to feel in love for such a very long time. She couldn't guess where it would lead—maybe to heartache, perhaps even to disgrace—but for now, she was going to let herself be happy even if it turned out that she'd fallen in love alone.

Evan swallowed his food down in a flash, but he lingered over the champagne. And the headline kept scrolling across his brain: Is the world's most eligible bachelor falling for a home wrecker? Not that he identified himself, or anyone else, with labels. Sometimes they were annoying. Mostly he found them amusing. He didn't consider himself the world's most eligible bachelor, and he didn't think of Dorianne as a home wrecker. But labels aside, was he falling for her? Is that what was happening to him; he was in love?

He studied Dorianne's pretty face and the graceful way she had of presenting herself. He thought of the passion with which she delved into what she enjoyed. Not just her work, but the way she ate her food and drank her wine; the way she made love. She always seemed so cool-headed, still he knew well enough by now that underneath the collected exterior, she was a woman brimming with fire.

Yes, he said to himself. I think that's what's happening here. I've fallen in love.

It was remarkable, how it felt as if he were in love for the first time.

Just like in the movies, he thought with a smile.

"What are you thinking about?" Dorianne wanted to know. "You have a peculiar look on your face."

"I'm thinking about you," he said. "You remind me of the movies."

"I do? Any particular movie? An erotic thriller, maybe, where the female turns out to be psycho?"

Evan laughed. "I sure hope not. I was thinking along the lines of something more romantic."

"A Christmas movie? The kind where two sheltered and lonely people manage to fall head over heels in love by Christmas Eve and the snow is falling?"

"Yes. Something like that."

They looked at each other across the table, over the empty dishes.

"What are you doing for Christmas, Dory? You flying back east?"

"I hadn't thought about it. What are you doing?"

"I usually spend Christmas in the house on Maui, if I'm between pictures and can get away. Would you like to come with me this year?"

"Christmas in Maui?" she said. And she thought wistfully of Central Park dusted with snow at sundown and the fountain in front of the Plaza Hotel done up in white lights. "I think I'd go anywhere with you, Evan," she told him quietly.

"You think so?" he asked her. "Are you aware that you qualify everything you say? I think you think too much, Dory. I think you're a lot like me in that way."

Dorianne picked up her glass of champagne and walked around to Evan's side of the table. "I don't want to think today," she told him. "I don't want to think and I don't want to work."

Evan didn't need to be told more than that. He could take a hint.

*   *   *

Dorianne went through the motions of relaxing, but the truth of it was that she couldn't stop thinking. The wheels in her mind kept turning. Who was it, she wondered, who had told Fritz & Conway about her affair with Kent? There weren't many people who'd known about it.

But then, she thought, people gossip. Maybe more people knew about it than she'd realized.

At the very least, there weren't many people who knew she'd started seeing Kent again, breaking it off with him officially only a few days ago. Even her agent hadn't known that. It seemed as if the only people who'd known about it were Kent and Evan.

Evan stood in front of the closet in Dorianne's bedroom. He was undressing and carefully hanging up his suit. He'd still been wearing his evening clothes from the party the night before.

Dorianne wondered if it could have possibly been Evan who'd said something to the press.

But why would he do something like that, she wondered.

That would be inviting trouble. That would be hurting me on purpose. There isn't any rational reason for him to do a thing like that. Unless, she thought, he wanted to make sure it was really over between Kent and me.

Evan turned around to find Dorianne staring at him strangely.

"What's going on over there? You okay?"

"Yes. I was just thinking."

Evan smiled a little ruefully. He picked up his glass of champagne, went over to Dorianne's bed and sat down. From there, he watched her undress. "I thought you didn't want to think today."

"I don't," she said. "You're right."

She slipped out of her tee shirt and pulled off her stretch pants. She sat down on the bed with Evan and instinctively searched his face, not sure of what answer she thought she would find there.

"What is it?" he said.

"I'm sorry," she confessed. "I just can't figure it out. Who was it who told them about my affair with Kent?"

"I don't know," he said. "But you should try to let it go. It'll make you crazy. Eventually the culprit will turn up."

Dorianne accepted his answer. He seemed innocent, genuine. *I'm on your side*, he'd said earlier.

Evan set aside his champagne glass. He wanted Dorianne in his arms. He tried not to think about what he was doing. Inviting her to spend Christmas with him on Maui. He hadn't brought a woman there since the days when he and Lisa Wilson were engaged. It was a long time ago during his wild years when they were both very young and grabbing Hollywood by the horns. Maui was where he and Lisa had gone after Lisa had won the Oscar for best actress. She was on top of the world in those days—young and vital and crazy, but in an appealing way.

She wasn't wearing the wildness too well now, though.

Running with musicians who didn't treat her with much respect. And one after another, her movies flopped at the box office. Her constant insecurity had begun to show in her face. The last time Evan had seen Lisa he thought that the anxiety had aged her. She was only twenty-eight, but she looked used up.

"You look good," he'd told her, even though it was breaking his heart to have to lie. "How's life treating you?"

"The usual," she'd said. "Why is it every man I meet these days has a substance abuse problem?"

"Life's hard on some people," Evan had replied. He didn't have the strength to go any deeper than that with her. Lisa was too far gone. She didn't have substance abuse problems herself, but she had self-esteem issues that were crippling her. It would be a miracle if she ever got her career back on track.

If Evan had gone ahead and married her, the marriage would probably be in tatters by now.

"Okay," Dorianne sighed. "Now what are you thinking about?"

"Christmas," he said.

"But it's not even Thanksgiving yet."

"It will be soon, and I like to leave for Maui during the first week of December, get as much time in as I can."

"You don't have a 'Christmas in Maui' look on your face."

"I don't?"

"No. It looks more serious than that."

"Come here," Evan said, grabbing her hand and pulling her over to him, taking her into his arms. "I'm going to find the switch that turns off your busy brain if I have to search every inch of your gorgeous body to do it."

"That could take hours," she warned him.

"I've got hours," he replied. And he kissed her to make her mouth stop talking, to keep the words away until he knew what he was doing. Until he could figure out why he was thinking it—that he wanted to take her to Maui and marry her. He hardly knew this woman. And he wasn't going to make the same mistakes his mother had made.

Dorianne returned his kiss, but she felt an apprehension in him. Or was it coming from her? Was she pulling away? She couldn't be sure but either way, it jolted her. It was a fissure in their perfect chemistry. It was the first time she felt as if the sexual passion between them could dissipate into something mechanical. Like it had with all the other men she'd tried to be serious about in her efforts to replace Kent. Would Evan Crane be just another one of her follies; another dead end? It hadn't occurred to her until this moment that it could be possible.

Through an unspoken, mutual distraction, they stopped kissing. They proceeded instead, without words, to the ordinariness of intercourse. Evan got on top of her and Dorianne's legs parted, but she was too distracted to be sufficiently ready for him and for the first time, the entry was uncomfortable.

Still, she laid there and let him keep going. She didn't want him to accuse her of thinking too much. She didn't want everything to fall apart. Not yet, not so soon, not when only a little while ago, he had seemed like her perfect destiny.

What had changed? Dorianne tried to reclaim it, that feeling of joy. She wasn't going to surrender so easily. So what if she was rich now? So what if her career was going places? What did it matter if she was heading toward her prime with every indication that she would be at the top of the heap? What would it matter if there was no love at the center of it? How could she keep from collapsing in on herself, if all there was in her world was a successful career?

And she didn't want the mere trappings of marriage. The idea of stability, or security; those things she could have had with ease, with more men than she could count. And it wasn't that she needed children to feel fulfilled. What she wanted was to be in love with a man—really in love—and feel loved in return. She wanted to be excited by life, by its mysteries and surprises. And she wanted someone to share it with—all that joy.

Dorianne held Evan close to her. He was finding his rhythm in her and her body was easing into the rhythm he created. She could feel herself opening more for him, accommodating him.

She asked herself, what if? What if he lost it all, his fame and fortune? What if he fell from grace and his reign at the top were finished? What if Evan Crane was just a man, with few prospects for another shot at a spectacular success? Would she still feel excited to have him in her arms?

Then it was as if he were reading her mind again. He looked into her eyes and he was right there; all of him. Whatever apprehension she had felt in him before was gone. He was looking into her face with that inimitable passion. He was making love to her with his whole body, with his being. Then he kissed her mouth like he meant it.

And Dorianne thought that it wouldn't matter how much money he made, how he earned his living, what his prospects were for continued fortune and fame; there was something in him, in those eyes, in the heart she could feel pounding against hers, that she wanted to be with regardless. That she would follow to the ends of the earth, if that was what was required of her.

This is just like in the movies, she thought. I feel like I've never been in love before.

She held tighter to Evan. And now her legs wrapped around his waist, pulling him even closer, allowing him to get in deep. Her vagina was wet and open and accepting him. She was feeling insatiable again, like she never wanted to stop fucking him, even if it meant her career all but withered and died from her lack of attention to it.

"Oh god," she whimpered softly, clinging to him as he increased his rhythm.

Evan challenged her without words, with only the power of his aroused body, to keep up with him, to match his intensity, to receive willingly what he wanted to give her, without conditions, without constraints.

It angered him that he was falling in love again. These were the times when he was most likely to disappoint himself. When the woman in his arms would recede from him, evaporate like a phantom, an apparition in the bewitching Hollywood twilight. He had been seduced by dreams too many times before. It was true; he was only human. He was just a man. He, too, had been a victim of all of Hollywood's promises, only to rise up and rise up and rise up because he was determined to succeed. Success could be measured by achievements and achievements were earned by hard work and consistency: get the job, show up, be there, do the work. Then do it all over again.

But what about love? That was a different story. No rules there. No blue prints. Just faith and trust. And the wildly unpredictable gamble of lust, where the odds of winning were never comfortable. Where a man was always tempted to hedge his bets, to hold back just when giving his all was most required.

That's what love was; a thing impossible to distinguish from lust until too much heartache was already at stake.

Then the plunge, but to where, happiness or despair? Are you in love alone, self-deluded and looking like a fool? Or have you at last found the perfect other, the one who makes waking life feel as effortless on the soul as dreaming?

Who could know beforehand what the outcome would be,

and what mere human could withstand lust's erotic pull?

As Dorianne's arms clung to him, as her legs clamped around him tight and she urged him to push ever deeper into her mysterious depths, his pace quickened. Evan felt himself lured by that very power, by her almost magnetic pull. His heart was plunging into the fray, close on the heels of his carnal desire. He felt he could risk it all this time and win.

"Turn over," he told her. "I want to take you from behind."

She did as he asked, willingly. She was on all fours for him. She helped him find her hole again and she guided him in so they could resume their frenetic rhythm without more than a moment's interruption.

She knew now what he was after. She knew his tendencies. When he took her from behind, he was going to be merciless. He would challenge her to surrender her deepest spot, to offer herself up to him—open and vulnerable and unhindered by timidity. He was going to fuck the hell out of her and she was going to love every minute of it. He was going to prove to her why no other man could ever take his place.

Dorianne's fingers gripped the mattress as she took on the force of Evan's pounding cock. But soon she was overtaken by his power. She was face down in the pillows, her knees spread uncomfortably wide and the small of her back arched up high. Her hands pushed hard against the headboard to keep herself from being shoved up against it, to ensure that the very depth of her engorged vagina was there to meet the full force of his thrusts.

"God!" she cried. "Oh god!"

He was holding tight to her hips, slamming feverishly into her snug hole, feeling her push open to accept his thick, aching, stone-hard cock with every plunge. His body was in a state of arousal that even he was overwhelmed by.

She looked so beautiful like this his eyes could hardly take it in. How open she was for him. Her full, round ass was on utter display in the broad daylight; nothing hidden, every secret between her legs, revealed. The slope of her perfect back was exquisite. And how she pushed hard against the head of the bed, to meet his power, to take him on his terms, to keep up with him. It made him want to fuck her even harder.

He watched his cock disappear in her, clear down to his balls. Then emerge quickly, slick and glistening with the undeniable proof of her equal arousal. Then back in again, it plunged. He felt hypnotized by it, by the constant, driving, thrilling motion. What it was about her body that was different from other women he'd been intimate with, he couldn't fathom. Whatever it was about her naked strength that he found so entrancing, was the very essence of the mystery of love itself. A thing as indisputable as it was indefinable.

"Oh god!" she cried again with even greater urgency. The force of his cock had conquered her. "Yes, yes, fuck me, yes," she sputtered.

The words were coming out of her in a rushing, babbling stream of sound.

Dorianne was in a fevered heat, panting hard. Working, working to keep up with his rhythm. Her body giving out as much as it was receiving. Trapped inside the escalating energy between them, her pleasure mounted like a giant wave. It felt ominous. She was an open receptor now to the full force of his cock and he wasn't letting up. He wasn't stopping. His cock felt thicker, harder, more intrusive by the moment. She was spread open for it as wide as she could get, and her vagina wasn't flinching. It was taking his full force all the way in. She was pushing back hard against every incoming thrust, until her body was so brimming with pleasure that she couldn't keep the wave from breaking.

And then it happened. An orgasm like none she'd ever experienced came gushing out of her, splashing out hot all over Evan's pounding cock. She was filled with a searing, exquisite ecstasy. The fluids spurting out anew from the force of each plunge he drove into her, soaking the sheets and the blankets.

Dorianne knew this was no ordinary orgasm—as if an orgasm could be termed an ordinary thing. Her body had never been pushed to this extreme, had never been driven to this much pleasure. The more she opened herself to the release of it, the more delirious she felt and the fluids splashed out of her again.

"Oh god," she wailed, her voice streaming out of her with a high-pitched intensity.

Evan, locked in a trance of his own delirium, watched in awe as Dorianne's come gushed out hot and slick and enveloped his cock. The urgent cries she made, her grunts and whimpers and wailing, the utter ecstasy she was obviously feeling, filled his ears and he couldn't keep his own climax at bay any longer. It surged up from his balls and shot out of him in short, successive bursts that kept on coming. Over and over, the liquid fire pulsed out of him like Vesuvius, and in turn, exploded into her. Until every reserve of passion he could summon from his soul had been expelled from his loins.

When the force of their orgasms had depleted each of them, they uncoupled and collapsed together on the bed.

"What happened?" Dorianne was the first to speak, but her voice came out sounding miniscule and weak. It was no match for the profound silence that sat on the room as if it were an entity of its own. "I've never felt anything like that."

Evan was exhausted. His heart was still pounding wildly. He agreed with her, but was slow to find the words while he was trying to catch his breath. They lay there together and said nothing more for several, reeling moments.

Finally, Evan said, "Wow."

And Dorianne said, "We sure made a mess of this bed."

And Evan said, "Yeah. We sure did." The bed was soaking.

Then they fell back into the silence.

*   *   *

Dorianne stepped out of the shower and studied her face in the bathroom mirror. She wondered if she looked any different. If she looked like a woman whose body had been transported by love to an uncharted place.

Evan came into the bathroom and looked at her looking at herself. "You're beautiful," he said. "Any mirror would say the same thing. And if it doesn't, you just come and ask me."

Dorianne smiled. She felt as if she positively glowed. "That's sweet, Evan. Thank you."

"You don't have to thank me," he reminded her. And then he smacked her naked behind playfully as he got into the shower himself.

"I don't want to stay here," she said. "I want to get out and see things, do something. Go to your house maybe, or take a drive somewhere. Go swimming, or get something incredible to eat. What do you think?"

"I don't know," Evan called out to her. "You just suggested about a hundred different things."

"Well, what appeals to you?"

"Taking you to my house and taking your clothes off."

Dorianne wondered if they'd make it as far as her front door before falling all over each other again. She threw on a tee shirt and went out to the living room to pour herself another glass of champagne. Her body felt unusually alive and receptive. She was still in awe of what she had managed to do—to come the way she had, with such force, such a total release.

What a morning, she thought.

She saw the newspaper lying where she had left it, in an angry heap on the couch. She felt it cluttering up her perfect happiness so she tossed it into the trash. In a way, she felt like she was tossing Kent in there with it. Along with Norma and Katherine and any of the other women whose names Dorianne didn't even know.

Evan came out of the bathroom wrapped in a towel. "Let's at least go to my place so I can change my clothes. I can't keep wearing that stupid suit."

"Okay," she said. "I'll get dressed now."

"You might as well. But I want to warn you."

"About what?" she asked.

"The parking lot is probably still crawling with photographers."

Dorianne didn't care. For once, she felt too beautiful to be concerned about anybody wanting to take her picture. And what more could they possibly print about her? The worst damage they could do to her had already been done.

*   *   *

Evan and Dorianne stepped out of Casa Hollywood's lobby into the bright sunshine as the valet drove up in Evan's black Mercedes. Then the pair was suddenly besieged by what seemed like a sea of photographers, but who were in fact only about five in number. Yet the five were aggressive and relentless.

"Hey, Crane, look this way," one of them shouted.

Another called Dorianne by name many times.

One of them called out, "Hey home wrecker, over here!"

And there were shouts of "Are there wedding bells?" and "Where's Norma?"

Mostly, they swooped in from all directions and hooted, "Evan! Evan! Over here, Evan!"

And there was the overwhelming sound of cameras clicking away.

In all, the pandemonium lasted only long enough for Evan and Dorianne to get into the car, but to Dorianne it had felt like a feeding frenzy in a shark pool. It didn't take long for the damage to be done and she felt frazzled by the uproar; by how personal, how invasive, it had felt even though she'd been expecting it.

They were in the car, speeding up into the hills.

"Sorry about that," Evan said. "I hope you won't mind having to get used to it."

"You're actually used to that?" She was incredulous. "How does a person get used to that?"

"You just do," he said. "You can't control it, and if you try to fight it, they make it even worse on you. Those weren't the kind of photographers who deal with people like Fritz & Conway. Those were the real cutthroat guys. The ones who sell everything they can get their hands on to the tabloids. It's best just to suffer them and move on as quickly as possible."

Dorianne wondered if her colleagues at *Babylon* ever utilized those types of photographers. She figured they probably did. She figured photographers like those made a respectable living off *Babylon* every year.

"I feel like I'm sleeping with the enemy," she said.

"What's that supposed to mean?"

"Not you," she answered vaguely. "I mean my job."

CHAPTER ELEVEN

The following morning, Evan slept late. He awoke alone in his king-sized bed and his first thought was of Dorianne. He missed her. He had asked her to stay with him the night before. In fact, he'd reminded her of his earlier offer to move in with him, only now he was saying it with an entirely new meaning. He didn't want to be apart from her and he wasn't afraid to admit it.

But Dorianne had declined on both counts. Saying that she needed a little more time, a little space to think things through.

They had had a memorable day and evening together and by the time Evan had driven her back to Casa Hollywood, it was quite late. Even the lounge was deserted. He'd walked her to her bungalow door and kissed her good night.

"I'll see you tomorrow," he'd said.

And she'd said, "I think I want to sleep late tomorrow. I'm worn out."

He'd said, "Okay, me, too. I'll sleep in tomorrow. Call me when you get up." And so Evan slept late and alone. When he awoke, it was the first gray, gloomy morning he could remember in a long while.

Rain, he thought.

And he wondered if it would blow over or last all day.

When he straggled down to the kitchen, Henry was sitting at the table, drinking his second cup of coffee.

Without much emotion, he said, "There's more crap about your lady friend in the morning paper."

"Really?" Evan wasn't surprised. "About me and her?"

"No," Henry told him. "It's about her and some other guy. He's claiming you stole her from him and that you're just using her the way you supposedly used that Brit-chick, Christine Miles."

"Oh, Jesus." Evan sighed in disgust and sat down with his cup of coffee. He opened the morning paper.

This time, the item was carried in Nancy Fribane's column. She was high-end gossip, carried in more newspapers coast to coast than the Fritz & Conway column.

Evan couldn't believe his eyes:

There's no stopping Hollywood heartthrob, handsome Evan Crane. According to journalist Kent Cryer—who won the Pulitzer a few years back for Diamond Crimes, his bestselling peek into the secret life of murdered Algerian-born filmmaker, Pierre Jean-Jacques—loverboy Crane is at it again. This time with Cryer's own love interest, Dorianne Constance, the hired gun on Crane's upcoming memoir from Harrisberg, Barker & Bliss, tentatively titled Hollywood Upstart.

"I'm sure he's quite charming," Cryer said coolly, "and I'm sure he uses it to his best advantage. But he uses his charm to take advantage, as far as I can see."

Cryer is accusing Crane of stealing his girl out from under him and of letting the tabloids get the best of Miss Constance.

"Dory and I never once slept together when I was married. Our affair didn't blossom until well after I'd left my wife in Paris. I was Dory's mentor. I was like a father to her. I gave her her first big break. I helped her launch her career and make a name for herself as a journalist, which, as you know, isn't easy."

A few weeks ago, you may recall that British journalist Christine Miles saw her relationship with bassist Eddie Bailey crash and burn over a similar amorous move by Crane.

"I don't blame Dory for being temporarily blinded by Hollywood, but I'm not going to take this sitting down. I intend to fight for her—before Crane dumps her like he dumps everyone else."

The gloves are out, readers. You heard it here first.

Evan closed the paper.

"What is all that nonsense?" Henry asked. "More of the usual?"

"You know what?" Evan replied. "I'm not really sure."

He got up from the table and went with his cup of coffee back to his room. He toyed with the idea of calling Dorianne, but he didn't want to risk waking her when he knew she wanted to sleep late.

I'll let her call me, he decided, and then I'll tell her. She's not going to like this latest installment any better than she liked yesterday's news. I'll let her sleep.

*   *   *

Several hours passed and the gloom barely lifted. The sun made a gallant effort to poke through the clouds, but eventually lost to all-out rain. It was early afternoon and still Evan waited, with no word yet from Dorianne.

He decided to call her bungalow. She had to be up by now.

He flipped open his cell phone and dialed her number from memory. But her phone rang and rang, until at last, the generic hotel voice mail retrieved his call.

Evan decided not to leave a message and hung up.

Half an hour later, thinking that perhaps she'd been in the shower, he tried again. But it yielded the same result. This time, he left a message.

"Dory, it's me. I'm up. Give me a call when you're in."

It was a simple message that revealed nothing about how he was truly feeling.

Where was she? As far as Evan knew, she had only casual acquaintances in Los Angeles. Certainly, she would have mentioned to him if she'd had an appointment to meet with someone.

Maybe I came on too strong last night, he decided. I should never have asked her to move in here. I should have asked her to spend the night and left it at that. Especially after she said no. I'm being a fool.

But Evan wanted to be near her, and his home could easily sleep a family of six without anyone feeling crowded. There was no reason to keep her hidden away in that bungalow if she would prefer the privacy of her own room in his enormous home.

Evan tried her bungalow phone one more time and again, he got no answer. Without admitting to himself what he was doing, Evan got dressed, grabbed his keys and headed down to the garage. He got in his car.

The rain beat down on his windshield as he made his way down the hill to Casa Hollywood. Evan told himself there was nothing out of line in what he was doing. He was simply checking in on a friend, on someone he was doing business with, really. Someone who should have been there, who wasn't answering her phone. In fact, it was simply the considerate thing to do.

He didn't want to tell himself that things had gone too far

the day before. Or that maybe he'd been too open with Dorianne and made himself vulnerable to her feminine whims. He didn't feel like she was using him, like he often felt about most women he came in contact with. But maybe she felt pressured. Maybe she was pulling back.

Evan turned his car over to the parking valet and walked straight through the hotel lobby and out to the flagstone path that led to the bungalows. The rain had let up, but only slightly. It had turned into a persistent and annoying mist.

When he reached Dorianne's bungalow, he knocked on her door several times and waited in vain for several minutes. She never came out. It didn't sound as if anyone was in there.

He checked his watch. It was two in the afternoon. Maybe she was having lunch in the hotel restaurant.

But why would she do that, he wondered. She loves room service.

And especially now, when strangers were starting to hound her because of him. She wasn't the kind of woman who would want to spend too much time alone in public.

Maybe she's not alone, he thought. And the thought disturbed him.

But wasn't it he who'd thought that maybe they needed a little time apart?

They had practically been inseparable since her plane had landed.

"But what about last night?" he asked himself out loud. "We had a little time apart last night."

When Evan realized he was talking to himself, he knew he was getting out of control. He turned around to go back home and wait. She'd call when she was ready to call.

Evan started down the flagstone path, heading back to the hotel lobby.

A bungalow door opened as he passed it, and to his shock, Dorianne stepped out, followed by an older man. A gray-haired man. An unhappy man. Neither one of them looked happy. In fact, Dorianne looked like she was seething with anger, just barely keeping her cool.

Evan stopped in his tracks. "Dory, what are you doing? I've been waiting all day for you."

"Evan," she gasped. She was visibly distraught.

The three of them stood staring at each other, momentarily speechless.

Evan looked to Dorianne, then at the man. Then back at Dorianne. "Dory, what's going on?"

"Evan, this is Kent," Dorianne practically spat out the introduction. "He just flew in this morning from New York. He's taken a bungalow right here at the hotel. He called me this morning from LAX and said he was on his way over. Naturally, I'd only picked up the phone because I'd thought it was you."

The longer she talked and the more she explained the situation, the angrier she became. Evan wanted to move to hold her, to comfort her somehow. Clearly, this was an unwelcome surprise for both of them. But as he took a step toward her, Kent took a step toward him, getting in between them, extending his hand with a brooding look on his ragged mug that betrayed his utter lack of civility.

"I'm Kent Cryer," he announced, as if he needed to introduce himself.

"I know who you are," Evan replied, refusing the extended hand. "But what I don't know is why you feel you have to torture her."

"I'm not torturing anybody," Kent insisted. "I just don't like unfinished business. And the business Dory and I have between us is none of *your* business, Crane."

Evan looked to Dorianne for even a hint of agreement in her face that might corroborate Kent's remark—that it was none of his business—but there was nothing but hatred in Dorianne's eyes.

"Dory, should I go?" he asked her.

"No," she replied. "Not without me."

Kent intervened gracelessly. "Dory, you're making a big mistake. When are you going to quit being so naïve? You're in over your head with a guy like him. He'll dump you so fast your head will spin. You read the papers. You know what goes on with him. He's got a different girl every week. When are you going to figure that out? You're heading for disaster. "

"No," she said, whirling around to face him and shut him up. "I was heading for disaster with you, Kent. Because I was in our so-called relationship alone. I was naïve about you from the very beginning; about your ever really loving me."

Dorianne motioned to Evan to follow her back to her bungalow.

"Dory, I'm going to come by later and finish our talk."

"I won't be there later, Kent. I have nothing left to talk to you about."

"Can you believe I loved him once," she sputtered at Evan before they were even out of earshot. "Can you believe he was everything to me? That I lived for him? That I wanted to spend my life with that bastard?"

Her eyes were brimming with tears now. Evan didn't really know what to say. The best he could do for the moment was take her hand and hold it.

"Wait 'til you hear what he told me back there, the load of crap he's been dumping on me for the last few hours. You'll really get a kick out of it."

Tears were streaming down Dorianne's cheeks now. She was too drained to pretend she wasn't crying.

"Why can't we come equipped with little red warning lights that signal to us like crazy when we're getting ready to be a fool?" she wanted to know. "Save us from all this wasted time and effort? These tears?"

Evan put his arm around her shoulder and held her close.

They were at her bungalow now. "I don't have an answer," he said. "I don't know how to make it better. If I could work a miracle and make it all disappear, I would because I don't like to see you so distraught. I know how it feels to be let down by someone; to be deceived."

"I suspect you do," she said, looking into his eyes. "I'm learning a thing or two about you, Evan Crane. You're a very considerate human being. I think you've had to learn a lot of things the hard way."

Evan didn't answer. Instead, he smoothed the hair out of Dorianne's pretty face. "Let me get you a tissue," he finally said.

*   *   *

Dorianne sat on the edge of her bed. She was calm now, yet filled with the hollow acceptance that comes with knowing that a love has finally died for real, has moved beyond all hope.

She had stopped loving Kent the morning she saw him in the diner, before she left for L.A. But no longer loving a man, and acknowledging that a love had always been in vain and was now dead, were two completely different feelings.

"It's like he's invaded me by coming here," she said quietly.

Evan was leaning against the dresser, staring off into space. But he heard every word she was saying.

"It was bad enough what he put in the paper this morning. Making it seem like he was doing me a favor, protecting me somehow by continuing to lie. But the truth is, I felt denied, voided out. Like he was still trying to cover his tracks after all this time. What's the point in it? Does he really think Katherine believes him after all his years of fooling around on her? How pathetic can he be?"

"I guess he has a lot of pride."

"He does," she agreed. "An inordinate amount. His reputation is very important to him."

"It is to all of us."

"I guess so."

"It's part of how we justify our constant struggle to succeed; one of the masks we wear to hide the fact that we're workaholics, afraid of finding our own hearts."

Dorianne smiled in spite of herself. Sadly, she recognized her behavior in Evan's words. She knew he was right—she and Kent were very similar when it came to pride and worrying about their reputations—although it didn't make her any less eager to succeed. She liked her success. But her heart was troubling to her and always had been. Why was she so afraid of being vulnerable? Of taking that risk, of getting over Kent once and for all and allowing herself to fall in love again even with the odds stacked against her? What did it really mean to lose at love? It didn't make her less of a person. So she had lost now, so what? She was still who she was, with her career intact, free to move whole-heartedly into the next adventure.

She never could control Kent, she knew that. And she knew she couldn't control *life*, didn't she?

"Some of us," Evan said thoughtfully, "expend an awful lot of energy trying to control the tiniest details of our day to day lives, because we feel that if we don't, life will spin completely out of control. When we do that, when we stay on top of every little thing," he explained, moving to sit next to her on the bed, "we fool ourselves into thinking that we're in control. That there won't be any curve balls. It'll just be one smooth stairway to the stars or something. When in fact we're just making ourselves, and maybe everyone around us, insane. We can't control life. We just need to expect the best and go with it."

"You're always reading my mind, Evan. How do you do that?"

"Just lucky, I guess."

"Evan, what am I going to do? It's not like I can force Kent to go home. To leave this hotel."

"No. But my offer still stands. You can move into my place. You can have all the privacy you want. I mean it. Kent doesn't know where I live."

"That's true. He doesn't."

Dorianne gave it some thought. She had thought about it all night, in fact. What would be the harm in moving in with Evan? It was only temporary, only until she went back to New York. Why was she hesitating? Because she didn't want to feel like she owed him something? Or that somehow he would be in control of her, or in control of the situation?

There it was again, the issue of control. What was there to control? Who was she fooling? After all, Evan was the only person she wanted to be with.

"I'll give you a room of your own," he said. "It's larger than this whole bungalow. I'll give you space. I'll let you work in privacy. I have to get some work done, too, you know. *Blast* is already in pre-production. I'm going to have to go to work right after the holidays."

"You make it sound so simple, Evan."

"Life can be very, very simple, Dory. Oddly enough, I learned that the hard way. You just have to learn to let go."

*　　*　　*

As Dorianne packed her things, she repeated it over and over again, like a mantra: *just let go, just let go.*

Yet part of her still felt trapped. It was because of Kent, lurking so close to her in that bungalow. Even though it was still daylight, although it was still a bit gloomy and gray, she felt as if she were preparing to sneak past the enemy in the middle of the night.

Evan was already in the lobby, settling her bill. She was really doing it, moving in with Evan Crane. Only a month ago, if someone had bet her that this would eventually happen, she wouldn't have put any money on it.

She took her cell phone out of the night table drawer and turned it back on. She knew that she was going to have to start behaving like a person who had a career, a job to do. She was going to have to snap out of all this dreamy-eyed stuff soon. Maybe being in the same house with Evan, night and day, would help diffuse the constant erotic tension she'd become a slave to.

"Fourteen messages!" she gasped out loud. "They can't possibly all be from Kent."

Dorianne felt a little overwhelmed and decided she'd play the messages back later. After the move, after she was settled in and could concentrate.

At the front desk, Evan signed for Dorianne's bill and made a mental note to have Henry come out with him later to move Dorianne's rental car, and then to call John and alert him to the move. Evan wondered what John would think of it, Dorianne coming to live with him. There hadn't been a woman living in Evan's house since the old days with Lisa. And that had been a different house altogether. The house Evan had owned in Whitley Heights. But that Mediterranean architecture never suited him.

Evan was heading back toward the bungalows when he spotted Kent just inside the doorway of the lounge. He had a miserable scowl on his face. Evan pretended not to notice him and kept on walking.

That could be trouble, Evan thought. From that vantage point, Kent will see that Dorianne's leaving. But maybe it'll convince him to just go home.

"Crane!"

Evan heard his name being called. He didn't have to turn around to know who it was.

"Just a minute, Crane! I want to have a word with you."

Evan tried to be civilized. He turned and faced Kent. "I'm in a hurry," he said calmly. "What is it?"

"Who do you think you're trying to kid, Crane? Why even bother with this charade? There are a million fish in the sea and you can have your pick of them."

"I have no interest in fish," Evan pointed out. "I'm only interested in one woman."

"But why does it have to be my woman? When are you going to learn to keep your hands off what doesn't belong to you?"

Evan studied Kent guardedly and quickly surmised that he was completely drunk.

This is going to go nowhere fast, he decided.

"Look, she's a human being. She doesn't belong to anybody but herself. She doesn't want to be with you anymore, Kent. Just accept it and go home."

"I'm not going anywhere."

"Well, whatever," Evan sighed. "It's a free country."

Then he turned around and continued on his way, leaving the Pulitzer prize-winning Kent Cryer standing alone in a drunken, impotent stupor.

CHAPTER TWELVE

The more Dorianne saw of Evan's home, the more she was in awe of it.

"This will be your room, if you like," Evan said, opening the door for her. "If you don't like it, there are a few other rooms to choose from. But they're done up a little masculine."

The room was directly across from Evan's and had originally been decorated with Evan's mother in mind. But his mother had passed away without ever once staying in it.

It was an enormous room, similar to Evan's. It had a terra cotta tiled terrace overlooking the swimming pool, the jungle-like garden, and the grounds surrounding Henry's quarters. And it had a large connecting bathroom, with a Jacuzzi and a walk-in shower—though nothing as exotic as Evan's shower was.

The bedroom was mostly white, with a regal king-sized bed, and it was formally decorated with vintage art deco pieces. It reminded Dorianne of the kind of room a fading movie queen from the thirties might have dwelt in; blithely petting her white afghan hounds and as she watched her reign over Hollywood fade into the celluloid sunset.

"I love it," Dorianne told him. "It's absolutely unreal."

"I don't usually try to impress people," Evan admitted. "But I have to confess, I was always trying to impress my mother. And she remained steadfastly unimpressed with just about everything. She didn't know how to be happy. I don't know if she would have liked this room or not. But I've always liked it. I know it looks old-fashioned, but it's actually very state-of-the-art."

Evan showed her where she could connect her modem and then showed her the controls that raised a fake wall and turned her boudoir into her own private screening room.

"There are tons of videos and DVDs downstairs in the study. And don't worry, I don't star in all of them."

Then he showed her the *piece de resistance*: a bookcase the pulled back to reveal a fully stocked wet bar.

Dorianne was delighted. "I can't imagine your mother wouldn't have been impressed with this, Evan. You didn't miss a trick."

"You know, my mother wanted to be a movie actress, long before I was born. She had high hopes, aspirations. But she eventually gave them up and settled for marrying a man with money. That wasn't my father. She was married to the rich guy, though, when she got pregnant by my illustrious dad."

"You're kidding."

"No. Crane was not my biological father's name. It was my mother's first married name and she passed it along to me, but that man, Edward Crane, wasn't my father."

"Who was your father?"

"Some mechanic. He worked on luxury cars, mostly. I was born right here in Los Angeles, you know, but we moved east soon after

I was born. My mother took me and deserted her husband. I think she was following my dad, who'd been hired to work on a luxury car collection on some rich guy's estate on Long Island. I don't know if my dad loved my mother or not, or if he even appreciated her following him out to New York. She told me I met my dad a few times on Long Island, but I'm not sure I remember him outside of a couple of snapshots. He was killed in a car accident when I was four."

Dorianne sat down on a beautiful white upholstered *chaise lounge*. She wished she had her tape recorder. Evan was really loosening up now.

"You've always told the story that your dad *left* your mother when you were four."

"I know. But when I was first starting out, my mother was still alive. I didn't think she would have appreciated it becoming common knowledge that I was conceived out of wedlock—after she took the trouble to give me her husband's name and everything."

"Wow, Evan. Is this something you want in the book?"

"Why not? It's me; it's part of who I am. I don't know why my father didn't marry my mother once she was in trouble. I'm a little undecided about whether he was a decent guy or not. But I'm ready to sort of 'claim' him publicly either way."

Dorianne wondered if any of the old photos of Evan's father had survived and would be reprinted in the book. She thought he'd probably been a very good-looking man, judging strictly by how Evan had turned out. Dorianne started to think this book project with Evan was going to be very surprising.

"Hey," she said suddenly. "What is this news about the book being called *Hollywood Upstart*? Whose idea was that?"

"I don't know," Evan laughed. "This morning's paper was the

first time I'd seen it. I don't know where Fribane came up with that bit of news. I don't like it."

"Me neither. We'll have to come up with something a lot better."

"Maybe something will just jump out at us while we're working."

Dorianne shot him a mischievous look. "You mean, instead of what usually jumps out at us while we're working?"

He laughed again. "Are you trying to start a fire, Dorianne? Because I'd be very happy to oblige you, if you are."

She looked at her suitcases that needed unpacking. She thought about all those messages waiting for her on her cell phone. Forget about her email, she hadn't checked that in days. But she looked at the fully stocked wet bar, the crystal stemware glistening under the perfectly placed track lighting. She looked at the king-sized bed, so regally appointed in white. And she recalled what an expert Henry was in the kitchen, and how impeccable his timing could be when it came to delivering food on a tray.

"This is much better than that bungalow," she said.

"You're not answering my question."

Dorianne sighed in defeat. "I'm going to work very, very hard tomorrow," she said.

"I know you are," he replied.

"Can you lend me a match, then? I'm ready to start that fire."

"You're very cute, you know that?" Evan said, leaning down and giving her a quick kiss.

"And you're an enabler, you know that?"

Evan dismissed it. "The book will practically write itself. Just wait and see. Now, can I get you a beverage of some kind? Perhaps something to fuel the flames?"

Dorianne got up and followed Evan over to the bar. "Fix me something like they used to drink in all those old movies."

"A martini, a highball? A gin ricki, perhaps? Maybe a stinger? Or maybe I can get you something a little more hardboiled, like a shot of whisky straight from the bottle."

"I think I'll have a martini. At least I know what that is."

Evan started fixing the cocktails.

"Was your mother a drinker?" Dorianne asked.

"Is this an interview?" he answered. "I mean, is this off the record?"

"I don't know. I was just wondering why you went to all this trouble to put such an elaborate bar in a room that was designed for your mother."

"Yes," Evan finally admitted. "She drank. She drank a lot. And she smoked a lot and she slept around a lot. And she was almost always drowning in broken dreams. I used to feel it was up to me to make her dreams come true—sort of by proxy, if you get my drift. Her dreams became my dreams somehow. But I don't regret it. I love my life, my success. I love what I do. But I don't think my success fulfilled her need to accomplish something of her own. She was proud of me before it was all over, but I think she would have preferred her own success. That's the kind of mother she was. She didn't live vicariously through her only child."

Carefully, Dorianne took the cocktail glass Evan held out to her. It was filled to the rim.

"To us," Evan said. "No qualifying ifs ands or buts this time, either."

"To us, Evan," she said as their glasses clinked. "Thanks for persuading me to come here. I feel like I've been living in a dream world ever since my plane landed—except for a few detours into a nightmare, of course. But you promised me I was going to get used to that."

"I sure hope so," he said. "I'd hate to see you give up and go back to New York."

Dorianne glanced at Evan over the rim of her cocktail. She wasn't sure how he meant that remark. "Well, eventually, I'll have to go back to New York."

"Well, eventually, we all have to go back to New York. For one reason or another. But we don't have to stay."

"Okay, I give up," she said. "What are you driving at? What are you trying to say?"

"I'm just saying you could stay here. If it works out and you're happy here, why not stay? Why go back to all the ice and snow? You see how much room I have."

"Evan, I just got here. We might make each other nuts, living together."

"We'll see," he said. "We might not."

"Plus I have a job."

"But you don't work out of an office. You work out of your home. I know that about you. You and your laptop could live anywhere in the world you wanted to live. You can't fool me."

"Okay," she conceded. "You win that round."

"Good," he said, downing the remainder of his drink. "I'm going to go round up Henry and see what he's up to. Why don't you take a little time for yourself and do whatever it is you gals do in that damn powder room. I'll be back in a few minutes."

*   *   *

Dorianne unpacked whatever she thought she'd need for the night and then she took a quick shower.

The hot water felt good. Her mind was reeling, but that was becoming a normal thing for her in Hollywood. She still felt bad, leaving Kent the way she had at the hotel. He was tying one on in the lounge when she left and he'd looked old and beaten down when she'd passed him on her way out of the lobby.

"We need to talk, Dory," he'd called out to her, drink in hand. Until a security guard ordered him back into the lounge.

"No drinks out here," the guard had said, as if he was talking to an unruly child.

The conversation they'd had in Kent's bungalow had made her sick to her stomach and had frayed her nerves. To have to listen to his crying about Gretta, the redhead who had now dumped him because of all the gossip about Kent and Dorianne in the papers.

"What do I care about Gretta?" Dorianne had shouted in disgust. "She's not my responsibility. Nothing about Gretta is my fault. You should have thought about that sooner, if she was so precious to you. You should never have even called me when you came back to New York. It's like you're addicted to cheating, Kent. Addicted to sleeping around."

And then Kent had pulled out a whole file's worth of paparazzi shots of Evan with more women than Dorianne could fathom. Most of the photos, she'd never seen before.

"What are you trying to say, Kent? What are you trying to prove? That Evan likes women? The guy's single, okay? He can date whoever he wants to date."

"But you accuse me of being addicted to sleeping around. Look at this. This is proof that the guy's just a player, Dory. You're just his latest number, that's all."

"So what?" she'd practically shrieked. "Don't you think I know that? I don't care. We're having a good time. And you know what? He can be seen with me in public if he wants to. He has nothing to hide, Kent. He's not caught up in some endless web of lies.

He likes me; I like him. We're working together."

"That's what you call it? How cute."

"And sleeping together, yes. And having an incredible time of it. Is that what you want to hear? You want me to spill it all? We're fucking our brains out. He makes me feel things I've never felt before, Kent. He makes me come in ways I could never have imagined. No one, I repeat, no one, has ever made me feel how Evan makes me feel."

"You're in love with him, is that it?" Kent smirked, sidestepping her insult and firing back some of his own. "You're really that gullible, that stupid? You're not a kid anymore, Dory. Your reputation might not bounce back from this one. Look at that Miles girl, booted right out of a job for making an ass of herself with Crane. It's not like the guy's going to *marry* you."

He spat the word marriage as if the thought of anyone marrying Dorianne was an extremely distasteful idea.

"You make me sick, you know that?" Dorianne had told him through her tears. "I can't believe I ever loved a man as hateful as you are." And then she stuck in the knife. "I really feel sorry for you, Kent. All you are is bitter and old. And you used to have so much promise."

It had been clear that Kent had wanted to go for Dorianne's throat for that remark, but instead he'd gone to the mini bar and things had deteriorated from there. It was then that Dorianne had left the bungalow, Kent following on her heels, and had run into Evan outside.

Evan, she thought now, the water cascading over her, hot and comforting.

It had been a very long day. She just wanted to think about Evan, about the evening ahead of them.

"A love child," she said to herself. "Who would have thought it?

One of the most sought after men in the English speaking world was an accident."

She turned off the water and dried herself off. She stepped out of the huge shower and took it all in. The bathroom that was meant for Evan's mother was very impressive. Truly fit for a queen. Then Dorianne wondered what that had been like, Evan's mother deciding to take her accidental pregnancy to term when legally she didn't have to, and she faced the added scandal of being married to somebody else.

His mother must have been hopelessly in love to go through all that, Dorianne thought. Evan's father was probably quite enigmatic.

And Dorianne found herself feeling profoundly grateful to both of them that Evan had been conceived at all.

What an inauspicious beginning for such a successful man, though. To be the product of an illicit coupling between a car mechanic and a failed movie actress, she mused. They make movies out of stories like that.

"Dory." Evan knocked on the bathroom door. "I'm back. Would you like another cocktail? I think I'm going to have one."

"Sure," she called out. And she opened the bathroom door, wearing nothing but a fluffy white towel. "Evan," she said.

"Yes?"

But then she lost her nerve. "I like you an awful lot," she said instead.

He smiled. "I like you, too," he said. "Come on out and we'll get that drink." When Dorianne came out of the bathroom, it became immediately apparent that Henry had been hard at work in the kitchen while she'd been in the shower. She could hardly believe her eyes. There was quite an assortment of appetizers set out on one of the coffee tables and she hadn't been in the shower that long. "Evan," she said, with a mixture of envy and admiration, "do you live this lavish life all the time?"

"No, not really," he admitted. "It's just that Henry loves to cook. He's always in the kitchen fooling around with something. I used to be very impressed with him, too, with his ability to pull these gourmet productions out of thin air. Until one day I discovered by accident that he has tons of this kind of stuff tucked away in the freezer. It goes right to the microwave and, then, voila. I have an Asian man, Cheng, who takes care of my house on Maui. He's also a pretty spectacular cook. I'm pretty lucky, you know. I can afford to pay people to just hang out and get creative."

"You are lucky," Dorianne agreed. "But you also had to work really hard."

"I did and I didn't," Evan said, setting their cocktails down in front of them and then sitting down next to Dorianne on the *chaise lounge*. "I have a certain amount of talent and drive, the rest of it is looking good on film. My talent has only taken me so far. I know that. I'm very aware of it. And it isn't that I don't keep trying to get better. But on film, I have a look that women like to dream on and that's been worth a fortune to a lot of people, including myself."

Dorianne wondered if that comment was off the record. Again, she wished she had her tape recorder handy. Evan was much more candid when the interview wasn't official.

But then I suppose everybody is, she realized.

"You know," Evan said, switching gears, "you look very fetching in that towel. It's a good look for you."

"Thank you, I'll try to remember that on those nights when I haven't got a thing to wear."

"I'm glad you decided to come here and stay, Dory. So much of this house never gets used. I'm always either in my room or the kitchen, or away on location. Having you here makes the house come alive. It makes me appreciate it all over again."

Dorianne wasn't sure what to say. She was touched. "Someday, you'll have to come see my apartment in New York," she said. "It only has a small kitchen, a living room, a bedroom and a bathroom. And yet it's considered a luxury apartment, by New York's claustrophobic standards."

"I'm sure your apartment is just as beautiful as the lady who lives in it. But I don't want to talk about New York right now. I don't even want to think about you going back there until you absolutely have to."

Dorianne was beginning to hope she would never have to. But she didn't want to say it. She didn't want to break the magic spell they both seemed to be under since she'd come to Los Angeles. And that stack of tabloid photos Kent had showed her that afternoon hadn't helped her feel encouraged. He had over ten years' worth of pictures of Evan with different beautiful women on his arm. In the end, maybe she, too, would be just another photo; another number that Evan Crane had played. But for now, she didn't want to worry about it. She didn't want to think herself right out of a chance at happiness, even if it wound up being s hort lived.

It's okay to lose at love, she reminded herself. Maybe one day I'll regret the things I've done. But I sure don't want to regret the things I was too afraid to try.

"Evan," she said, removing her towel. "Aren't you starting to feel a little over dressed?"

"God, you look beautiful," he said softly. "Do you know that? You were made to be naked in a room like this. Or maybe the room was made to have you naked in it. I'm not sure which." Evan leaned over and kissed her.

She smelled captivating, fresh from the shower. But what else was it that she smelled like? Evan couldn't place the fragrance, but it made him want to devour her. He buried his face in her neck. He greedily licked her ear lobe, and then kissed his way down her throat. Between her breasts—there it was again. That scent. Whatever it was, Evan thought, she knew how to enhance herself.

His erection sprang up full and hard. He needed to get his pants off in a hurry. She was already pulling his shirt off of him. He stood up and quickly undressed the rest of the way.

"Do you want to move to the bed?" he said, remembering the morning they'd spent making love in a chair. "It might be more comfortable."

She followed him over to the bed and together they fell on the soft, deep expanse of it.

Evan lost no time; he grabbed her long legs and pushed her thighs apart, and then he buried his face there. Between her legs, where she had the unmistakable taste of a woman but where she smelled vaguely of soap and expensive perfume and vexing flowers that grew in a world he could only remember from dreams.

His passion was completely aroused now. Who was this woman who tormented him so, that even while she was in his arms, he felt a hunger for her that he couldn't satiate? A desire that seemed to emanate from a place larger than himself, his mind, or the tangible world. It was lust for a woman's body, yes, but a lust that confounded him. The more he made love to Dorianne, the more he was consumed by his need to make love to her again.

The taste of her on his tongue was primal. It made his already aching hard-on swell. He wanted to get his cock inside her tight pussy; he needed to feel that relief. But at the same time, he loved to have his face between her legs, the taste of her in his mouth and the smell of her filling his head.

As if she was reading his mind, she solved his dilemma.

"Scoot up this way," she said. "I want to suck your cock."

And that's how they coupled for several entrancing minutes, with Evan straddling Dorianne's face, his erection easing in and out of her wet and willing mouth. While he kept at her with his tongue, tormenting her tiny clitoris until he could feel it stiffen and could suck it between his lips easily.

Entwined like this, they each fueled the other's desire, driving each other deeper into that seemingly insatiable realm of pleasure, until they both reached that peak of sexual arousal.

"I have to fuck you," Evan said urgently. "Right now." And he swung around to face her.

She was engorged now with lust and ready to be mounted. Her knees were raised, her thighs spread for him. He got on top of her, his slick, glistening cock sliding snugly into her hole. They kissed passionately as he fucked her. Dorianne's taste was on his lips and the smell of her filled both their heads.

She held to him tightly, clutching his muscular ass as he worked his cock in and out of her soaking pussy, going deeper with each thrust. Pushing in, pulling out, opening her and filling her.

"Evan," she gasped softly, "god, it feels so good."

And she held to him tighter, lifting her legs higher, helping him to get in there as deep as he could go, their rhythm increasing, their pleasure mounting, until Evan couldn't take the intensity of the pleasure.

"I'm sorry," he said. "I have to come. You're making me too crazy."

His climax was sudden and vigorous. Dorianne lay beneath him, impaled by his thick cock, as his orgasm shot out of him in strenuous bursts.

"Jesus," she cried, as he continued to come. And she held on, keeping up with his passion, taking it all in.

*   *   *

The evening sky was crystal clear and a cool breeze blew in off Dorianne's terrace. The light in the room was dim now, making the room look even more enchanting than it had seemed by daylight.

Evan and Dorianne lay in bed together, panting in the tangle of sheets and pillows.

"Why is it," Evan finally spoke, "that the minute I finish making love to you, I want to start all over again?"

"I don't know," Dorianne whispered, "but I feel that way, too. All the time."

They kissed, their passion enveloping them again quickly. Their heartbeats still rapid, their pulses racing from before, as if they didn't know what it meant to savor the moment or to bask in the luxury of time.

Evan mounted her again and her long legs parted. Her body accepted him readily. Once again, she threw her arms around him, pulling him as close to her as possible.

This is heaven, she realized, surrendering to his renewed rhythm immediately. This is paradise. Nothing could ever get any better than this.

Evan was working up a sweat now. Dorianne took so much out of him. He had to have her and he had to please her. Her beautiful body underneath him, the sight of her naked flesh provoking him, pushed him into reserves of physical endurance he rarely tapped into when he was with other women. With Dorianne he could come all night, he was driven, like a machine, an engine; tough as railroad steel. He couldn't feel satisfied until his passion had exhausted her, pushed her past that even and made her cry out. He needed to hear those sounds she made. His ears needed to hear that, to know for sure that he was making an indelible impression; that he was irreplaceable.

That was what drove him; that need to feel that it wasn't a mere part he was playing. No other man could take his place here. No younger, newer version could come onto the scene and play this role because this was beyond the realm of theatrics; this was destiny. That slot only one man was born to fill.

"I love you, Dory," he said without even stopping to think; without realizing he was saying it, revealing his final card.

Dorianne wasn't sure she'd heard him right. But something inside her knew that she had. Still, there was that unwritten rule that every woman learned the hardest way: a man can tell a woman he loves her, but if he says it only while they're making love, it means next to nothing. That was how it had been with Kent. It was more a hormonal thing than an offer of commitment.

Dorianne thought it was best to ignore it, to ignore Evan's remark and give him the benefit of the doubt. He hadn't meant it. It was just something that had slipped out. A line from an old movie, a part he had once played. Like Evan himself, the words were an accident. A beautiful accident that tormented Dorianne's heart.

He knows who he is, Dorianne reminded herself. He's an image that women like to dream on. He's just a player. He's playing a part.

And so Dorianne kept her mouth shut. She protected her heart from words that could betray her. He'd said he loved her and she let it pass, as if she hadn't even heard.

WHEN HEARTS COLLIDE

CHAPTER THIRTEEN

True to his word, Evan left Dorianne alone in her room. He gave her the space he'd promised even while he would have preferred spending the night with her in the same bed.

"Are you sure you want to go back to your own room?" she'd said, when they'd exhausted themselves with sex, with food.

"That's what we agreed on," Evan had answered. "I want this arrangement to work for both of us, Dory."

So they each slept in their own rooms, alone in their own king-sized beds. Dorianne had a fitful sleep, wondering why he had said it—that he loved her. Wondering why she was so reluctant to believe him.

And Evan barely slept a wink. He argued with himself. Why had he said it? Why had he told Dorianne he loved her when he'd only known this woman a handful of days? Worse yet, why had she completely ignored him?

She was a hard woman to figure out. She seemed hopelessly

romantic and yet hard as nails at the same time.

Evan left his bed and sat on his terrace in a tee shirt and a pair of jeans. He smoked cigarettes. Then he wandered the house aimlessly—a thing he hadn't done since his mother had died. He didn't bother to turn on any lights. Through the French doors in the living room, he drifted outside to sit by the pool. In the darkness, he looked up at Dorianne's terrace and it was as if she were standing there. He thought he could see her looking down at him, wearing a gown of white. He lit another cigarette and stared up at the apparition while he smoked.

But it was no apparition. Dorianne stood on her terrace, wearing a white cotton nightgown. She looked down over the dark garden, the surrounding grounds, and it looked to her as if someone were sitting down by the swimming pool. It spooked her. A chill shot through her heart. When a match was lit, she saw that it was Evan.

He can't sleep, either, she thought.

She toyed with the idea of going down to the pool to sit by him, to talk it out. But maybe they needed this space and Dorianne wasn't sure she felt like talking.

The thought of revealing herself to Evan, of admitting to him that she was in love, too, that she didn't care if she ever saw New York again, that she wanted to stay here in Hollywood and live with him indefinitely. The thought of being so candid only to learn that he hadn't meant it, or that to him, being in love was a frequent and transitory state of mind, made her bowels clench.

But it's okay to lose at love, she reminded herself as she watched him smoking in the dark. It's okay to fall in love alone. The important thing is to love, no matter how brief. To not be afraid. To be vulnerable. To be honest, human.

But he was too famous. Falling for a man like Evan Crane was a common and ordinary thing for a woman to do. And Dorianne had never considered herself common or ordinary.

This is my ego talking, she realized. These are my control issues again. What is my problem? Why can't I just let go?

With a start, Evan saw the apparition in white move slightly and he realized Dorianne was really up there. He wondered if she was watching him, if she could see him sitting down below her by the pool.

She can't sleep, either, he thought.

He took it as a promising sign.

But maybe she couldn't sleep for other reasons. Maybe it was Kent Cryer causing Dorianne to lose sleep. It could have been a number of things that had dragged her from bed out into the night air. She had a lot on her mind right now.

Evan wanted to go to her. Or at the very least, call out to her and ask her to join him. But maybe they needed space. He wasn't sure what he would say anyway.

I love you, he could say.

But he'd already tried that and it had yielded less than stunning results.

He thought about Maui. He pictured Dorianne standing on the terrace of his house there, overlooking the ocean at night, the black rocks, the endless sea. He had once seen Lisa in a similar pose at the house on Maui, solitary, reflective. Staring off into the night. She looked so feminine, so pretty. Like Dorianne. But Dorianne was a strong and determined woman. Nothing like Lisa Wilson. Lisa could have been lifted off the balcony in a strong wind and gone sailing off into the magnificent sunset, never to be seen again. And in a way—that Hollywood way—that's just what had happened to Lisa Wilson. The pressures of being so famous so soon had swept her into a world of insecurities and bad judgment that devoured everything that had been beautiful about her.

A thing like that wouldn't happen to Dorianne Constance. Evan could tell. Even in the dark, watching her from a distance, he thought he could see the strength in her. The steadfastness. The hard-headedness. A woman like Dorianne was only going to grow more insightful and levelheaded with time. No mere wind was ever likely to carry her off. A *tsunami* could break over a woman like Dorianne Constance and she'd find a way to still be standing when the waves washed back out to sea.

And she would be wearing a perfect little black dress, Evan thought with a smile. Her handbag would match her shoes and every hair on her head would be in place.

She was the kind of woman he'd dreamed about having for a partner, a wife. Until now, Evan hadn't realized that God had actually made a woman like her. He had begun to think she was only a fantasy. Yet here she was.

In my house, Evan thought.

He stubbed out his cigarette. He was going to do whatever it took to keep her in his house. He wanted her for all time and he was going to find the right moment to tell her.

When he looked back up at her terrace, though, the apparition in white was gone.

* * *

It was barely six a.m. when Dorianne decided to get out of bed. She wanted to check those messages on her cell phone and answer her email.

Quite a few of the phone messages were in fact from Kent. A couple were from her mother—she'd seen the items in the newspaper and didn't sound very happy and when was Dorianne going to call her back? But more than a few of the messages were from a co-worker at *Babylon*.

Strange, Dorianne thought.

The messages didn't sound urgent, but they were persistent. From a woman named Gertie who had worked at the magazine since it had launched fifteen years ago. Gertie had started at *Babylon* as a receptionist and had worked her way up to being a department manager. But at middle management, her meteoric rise up the corporate ladder had stalled. And there Gertie had stayed. But she seemed content. Gertie was a worker bee, a drone; a woman who valued job security and benefits over a shot at the title of Executive, or even at the title of Executive's Assistant. She was a woman satisfied by a decent paycheck and two weeks' vacation a year, foregoing the risks involved in aiming for the fat paycheck and a cushy home office.

Did I remember to proof my interview with Vera Randolph? Dorianne wondered. Did I forget to turn in an assignment? Did I bounce a check on somebody? This is so weird. Why is Gertie leaving so many messages?

Dorianne looked at the clock. It was after nine in New York and Gertie had probably been at her desk for over an hour already. She dialed the office.

"Good morning, Media Publishing. Where can I direct your call?"

"This is Dorianne Constance calling from Los Angeles. Can I speak to Gertie?"

"Dorianne!" the operator gasped breathlessly. "It's me, Connie. You lucky duck. Are you really going out with Evan Crane?"

"What do you mean? We're working together. You know that. We're doing a book."

"That's not what I heard. That's not what everyone's saying around here."

Dorianne was beside herself. "Well, I don't know what everyone's saying around there, but out here, I'm working. Can I please speak to Gertie? She's called me a million times."

Sufficiently chided, Connie put through the call and after a moment of silence, Gertie was on the line.

"Hey stranger," she said. "Looks like you really hit the jackpot in la-la land. Are you ever coming back to us commoners?"

"Gertie, of course, I'm coming back. When I'm through with the book. But I just got here. What's going on out there?"

"Nothing much," Gertie sighed sarcastically. "But we do read the papers, and we get the AP wire. And we've seen some *photos*," she added, with so much innuendo in her voice that Dorianne wanted to scream.

But she tried to remain calm.

"What photos? What are you talking about?"

"You and Evan Crane, holding hands, kissing at Casa Hollywood, hob-nobbing with the stars."

"I'm not hob-nobbing with the stars, Gertie. Evan Crane is a star. It's his job. I'm working with him."

"Really? Do you kiss everybody you work with right on the mouth?"

Dorianne was losing her cool. "Gertie, why were you calling me? Is there something you need? I'm really busy here you know," she lied.

"I wanted to warn you that Kent Cryer has been nosing around. He called me the other day and seemed intent on flying out to L.A. to confront you about, well, you know what."

"No, what?"

"The stuff in the papers. You, him, his ex-wife."

Dorianne was mortified but she put up a good front. She couldn't pretend that the whole world didn't know her secrets now.

"Well, thanks for trying to warn me, Gertie. But it's too late. Kent's already here. He arrived yesterday and checked into the same hotel. I already had words with him."

"That must have been ugly, judging by the mood he was in when I saw him."

"You saw him? I thought you said he called you?"

"He did call, but then we met after work for drinks. He was in a real state, I must say. I tried to call and warn you that he was on his way to Los Angeles, but you weren't answering your phone. Of course, I'm not sure I'd answer my phone either," she added, "if I had the option of going out on the town with Evan Crane."

There was something unnerving in Gertie's tone. "I appreciate the effort, Gertie. But I shut off my phone to keep Kent from calling me non-stop. He's been out of control."

"I guessed that. But at least he's over that Gretta tramp. She was a waste of his time."

"What do you know about Gretta?"

"Plenty. I know you never met her, but she's just a gold digger, Dorianne. Kent's better off as a free agent. And it's about time, you know. Katherine was a weight around his neck since day one. He needs to spend some time just being available. Single. You know, free."

"I never knew you had such strong opinions about Kent Cryer."

"Of course I do, Dorianne. He and I go way back, to before the beginning of *Babylon*. Who do you think hired me? The same married man who hired you, my dear."

Dorianne wanted to be sick. She tried hard to hide her shock, to stay civilized as the full effect of what Gertie was saying hit home. "I never knew that."

"Don't worry, Dorianne. There weren't that many of us. I'm the only one who lasted, who's hung in there. But you're the only one who can say she truly made it—who made something of herself."

"What do you mean, there weren't that many of us?"

Gertie seemed to be delighting in having it out on the table at last. "There weren't that many of us at *Babylon* who were sleeping with Kent Cryer. Sleeping our glamorous ways to the top. Don't tell me that naïve act of yours was actually genuine? You knew what kind of track record he had. You must have always known."

"No, I didn't."

"Well, now you know, Dorianne, but what's the big deal? You're sitting very pretty now and Kent Cryer is old news. It's about time he realized he can't just walk on everybody—everybody who wears a skirt, that is. It's time he tasted some of his own medicine. And frankly, I'm really sick of the competition. I'm not getting any younger, you know. You know it and I know it."

"Are you trying to tell me you're still sleeping with him?"

"Honey, it's going on twenty years already. That skunk had the nerve to pay my way to his own wedding in Miami, and I was the first one he invited to Paris when the divorce from Katherine was final. I've been all over the world at Kent Cryer's expense. I've been in every one of his beds. Sometimes we barely had time enough to get the sheets warm before he had to dash off somewhere—tape a TV show, or do an interview."

Dorianne had never felt more humiliated. This revelation was worse than seeing her secrets spilled in a nationwide gossip column.

"Gertie, why are you telling me all this? What's your point? What do you want from me?"

"I don't want anything from you, Dorianne. You're a good person. You deserve more than a dog like Kent. You need to see him for who he truly is and get over him once and for all. I used to be jealous of you, in the beginning, in the old days. I felt the competition. You were smart, young. You were pretty and Kent wanted to be your mentor. He saw a lot of potential in you.

But I saw to it that you got out of the running, at least in the bed department. I convinced him that you were going to be trouble for Katherine and he dropped you like a hot potato. I'm not sorry I did it, either. You've been much better off without him. You're a success. You wouldn't have had that if he'd stuck around and 'guided your career,' as they say. He would have had you too worn out to get any work done—worrying about who else he was fucking."

"Oh my god."

Dorianne's voice was barely audible. She couldn't mask now that she was in tears.

You are a demon from hell she wanted to say to the voice on the phone. But mostly she felt sorry for Gertie. What a pathetic life she had chosen for herself. And maybe she had done Dorianne the biggest favor of all by taking away the man she had loved right from the beginning, before he could do too much damage.

"Listen, Dorianne, you just send him packing. Tell him it's over and that he should come back to New York and behave."

"I should tell him that he should go back to you, is that it?"

"That's it, honey. Why not? You have Evan Crane now."

"What makes you think I 'have' Evan Crane? We're just working together."

"Knock it off, Dorianne. I've seen the pictures. I've got a whole stack of them on my desk as we speak. The one I especially like is of you two out on a terrace in the Hollywood Hills. It's kind of fuzzy, with more than a few trees in the way, but it's clear enough to see that he's wearing a pair of under shorts and smoking a cigarette. And you're wearing what looks like a man's tee shirt and that's about it. Is that how you're spending your afternoons, you lucky girl? And you call that working on a book? That's going to be some book, honey. Well, only in L.A."

"What are you doing with pictures like that? How did you get those?"

"On the *Babylon* expense account. It's for a side item: 'Handsome' Evan Crane takes on Babylon's own Dorianne Constance. Is it finally love for the sexiest man alive?"

"You can't be serious."

"Why not?"

"Because I work for *Babylon*. You're invading my privacy."

"Just tell Kent to come home. He's making an ass of himself. I'll even hang on if you want to go next door and tell him right now."

"I can't, Gertie. I'm not at Casa Hollywood anymore. I'm staying at Evan's."

"Well, well, well. That's a step in the right direction, I must say."

"I don't want to be anywhere near Kent. I want nothing more to do with him and he knows it."

"Then why is he still there, drinking himself to death? He had me up until three in the morning, babbling over the phone about you and Crane."

It was all clear to Dorianne now. Fritz & Conway's source had been Gertie. Evan was right; the culprit had surfaced. Gertie was bitter enough to do it, and probably wanted the extra cash.

"Well," Dorianne said, having had her fill of all of it, "if I run into Kent again, I'll be sure to tell him to go home, Gertie. But I'm not likely to run into him here."

"Why not? You think he can't find out where Evan Crane lives? Hell, these photographers had no trouble finding the right house. And I can certainly clue him in."

"Well, I hope you don't. I don't need Kent Cryer around here. And I promise you that if there's ever a photo of me in *Babylon* where I'm anything less than fully dressed, I'll hold you responsible and I'll sue the hell out of that magazine. I would hate to see you lose your pension over something this stupid. You've been a slave for that magazine for too long to lose everything now."

Dorianne clicked off the phone. She was seething.

*   *   *

Evan and Henry were having a late breakfast. The sun was shining. It was a beautiful morning.

"Should I take something up to Dorianne?" Henry asked.

"I don't know. I hate to disturb her. I don't think she slept well. She'll come down when she's ready."

Evan was planning on spending most of the day going over the working script for *Blast*. And when Dorianne was ready to do some more work on the book, he would spend some time with her. He was going to be vigilant. He was going to make an extra effort to help her stay on schedule, to get her work done.

"Do me a favor, Henry," he said. "Make the arrangements for Maui today. And get two tickets this time. I'm taking Dorianne with me. I want to leave on Friday morning, right after Thanksgiving. Find out from John when I need to be back in L.A."

"You're taking her to Maui with you? You're sure about that?"

"I'm sure," Evan replied.

"Did you ask her already?"

"I did."

"And she said okay?"

"She said okay." Evan put down his fork and looked at Henry. "She said she thought she would go anywhere with me. So we'll start with Maui. We'll give it a try and see what she thinks after that."

"Well, what female wouldn't go anywhere with you?"

"I'll tell you something, Henry. There are places this woman has already gone with me that aren't on any map. I'm not sure what to do about it."

"What is there to do? You'll go to Maui. You'll find out."

"I think I want to go to Salvatore's for Thanksgiving dinner this year. I want a quiet table. Would you call and make us a reservation?"

"Does that 'us' include me?" Henry joked. "You know I hate being a third wheel, boss."

"You're getting the night off, Henry. Not that I don't find your company utterly charming."

"You're serious about this one, aren't you, Evan? I can tell."

"If you can tell I'm serious about her, why can't she?"

*   *   *

Evan's bedroom door was slightly ajar. Dorianne tapped lightly on it.

He was in there. "Come in," Evan called.

"I hope I'm not bothering you, Evan."

"You're not bothering me."

Evan was sitting on his unmade bed, wearing his usual black tee shirt and black jeans. He was surrounded by a pile of books and a script was open in front of him.

"You're working," she said. "I can come back later."

"No, what is it?"

"Nothing much. I called my parents, finally. Of course, they'd read about my affair with Kent Cryer. And they wanted to know all about you. I assured them I hadn't done anything to destroy your relationship with Norma Pearl."

"You're kidding."

"No. I think that mattered more to them than the story about Kent."

Evan gave a short laugh of disbelief. "People are strange. What can I tell you?"

"They sure are. You know what else?"

"No."

"I found out who Fritz & Conway's source was. A woman who works at *Babylon*."

"Really?"

"Yes. She's worked there forever. She's not a writer or anything, but she's a long time friend of Kent Cryer's. It sounds like she knows everything about me and I'd never had any idea. I never really knew anything about her, except for her name."

Dorianne was beside herself. She felt like such an idiot, such a fool. She started to cry and she'd promised herself she wouldn't.

"Dory, what is it?" Evan got off the bed and went to her.

"It's nothing, really. It's just that I think I want to quit my job."

"What?" He was incredulous.

"I want to resign from the magazine. Do something else with my life. Write about things besides Hollywood and movie stars."

Evan went for a tissue and brought it to her. "What did I do to make you feel this way, Dory? Tell me and I'll try to undo it. I swear."

"This isn't about you. I still want to do the book. I just don't want to work for the magazine anymore. What that woman did to me—to us—it makes me sick to my stomach. I don't want to be a part of it. Selling secrets and all that paparazzi crap."

Evan didn't know what to say. "If you quit your job, it won't make it go away. Too many people are making a ton of money."

"I know."

"And you've made such a great career for yourself."

"I know that, too. But there's got to be something more rewarding to write about than this."

She plopped down in one of Evan's upholstered chairs and tried to pull herself together. She couldn't admit to him, at least not yet, what the real trouble was—Kent and his womanizing. That she'd been a fool in too many ways for so many years, and she hadn't even known she was doing it. And that now the very magazine that she'd been so proud of working for, the magazine that had helped her forge such a stellar reputation for herself, was threatening to publish pictures of her with next to no clothes on. All because she had fallen in love with Evan Crane and couldn't keep her mind, or her hands, off him.

"It's hard to love you," she said in despair.

"What?"

"I'm sorry, Evan. I didn't mean that. I meant to say, it's hard to live in your world."

"I know," he said. "What can I do to make it better? Should I quit my job, too?"

At last a smile lit up Dorianne's face. "No," she said. "I don't want you to quit your job, too. I just want to figure myself out. Why I'm always such a naïve fool."

"But I like you this way."

Evan knelt down in front of her. "Seriously, Dory. I don't think you're a fool. People can be creeps, that's all. And you can't change that. But you've got to figure out what's going to make you happy, and then do it."

And he wondered privately to himself about what she'd really said, that it was hard to love him.

Hard or not, she's admitted it, he told himself. She loves me.

The rest was just a matter of patience.

CHAPTER FOURTEEN

Salvatore's restaurant was as upscale as it got in L.A. An unassuming entrance with no windows, where reservations were required, and most reservations were flat out refused.

"We're booked solid for the next three months," was the pat answer given over the phone to anyone who wasn't 'somebody.'

And the true somebodies never made their own reservations. There were highly paid people who did it for them. All that was required of a 'somebody' was to show up, and they didn't even have to bother themselves about being on time. Being there on the right night was good enough.

But Evan Crane wore a watch and was usually pretty good about keeping his appointments. He and Dorianne had dinner reservations for eight o'clock on Thanksgiving night. And a nine a.m. flight to Hawaii out of LAX the following morning.

To please Dorianne, Evan had dispensed with 'L.A. casual' for the evening and was decked out for dinner in a black tailored suit, a pristine steel gray tailored shirt, and a gray and black silk tie.

He waited for Dorianne at the bottom of the stairs.

"What a complete surprise," he said, when he saw her come down the steps in a perfect little black dress. But tonight, she wore her hair swept up and pulled off her face. She looked radiant.

"You look stunning." Dorianne said to Evan before he could open his mouth to speak.

"I was going to tell you the same thing."

She kissed him when she got to the bottom of the stairs.

For the last two days, since her conversation with Gertie, Dorianne was feeling better about herself. She'd gotten a lot of work done, both on her own and with Evan. And she'd sent her resignation to *Babylon* magazine via Overnight Delivery.

Evan had been afraid she was making decisions too quickly, but it was her life and she needed to live it. Besides, who was he to point fingers at people who made decisions too quickly? Wasn't he off to Maui with her tomorrow, a woman he hardly knew, with an engagement ring already in his suitcase?

Evan walked Dorianne to the garage and helped her into his car. He pulled slowly down the drive, stopping to wait for the electronic gate, and then he zipped his Mercedes down through the hills to the boulevard.

In the rearview mirror, Evan noticed a metallic blue sedan. He didn't think anything of it, until he kept noticing the car in his mirror. At traffic lights, he noticed it. Left turns, right turns—there was the metallic blue sedan behind him.

He thought it best not to mention it to Dorianne, but he felt in the breast pocket of his suit for his cell phone. It was there. He made sure it was turned on.

"What are you doing?" Dorianne asked. "Are you expecting a call?"

"Maybe. From John. You never know. There might be last minute changes in the flight tomorrow."

"I sure hope not," Dorianne said.

She wondered what it was going to be like, flying all the way to Hawaii with Evan Crane. The fewer people they had to interact with, the better. The photographers, the fans, the people gawking wherever they went. It wore her out.

But after the trip, a trip she knew would fray her nerves; she would be alone with Evan in paradise. For four solid weeks. She wasn't even going to pretend to work. She would bring her tape recorder, in case Evan suddenly felt garrulous. But the laptop and the cell phone were being left behind.

She and Evan had barely made time for sex during the last few days. And Dorianne was looking forward to changing that trend. She imagined them having sex during every waking moment on Maui. She wasn't even bothering to bring many clothes. She didn't think she would need them. She wanted to be naked as much as possible—

"Are you missing not being with your parents tonight?" Evan asked.

"Not right this minute," she answered with a gleam in her eye. "I'm happy right where I am."

Evan pulled up the drive to Salvatore's, stopping under the pink stucco portico and, to his dismay, the metallic blue sedan had followed him up the short drive and was coming to a stop behind him.

"Dorianne, I don't like this," he finally said. "Someone's been following us since we pulled out of my driveway. It's probably somebody who's harmless, but you never know."

The parking valet was coming up to Evan's window.

Dorianne turned around to get a look at the car behind them.

A man was getting out of the car.

"Oh my god," she cried sickly. "It's Kent!"

"For Christ's sake," Evan swore under his breath. "How the hell did he find out where I lived?"

"I have a good idea," she said.

Evan opened the door for the valet and said, "Don't take the car just yet. I'm not sure we're staying."

"Evan please," Dorianne said.

Evan got out of the car and he faced Kent Cryer under the well-lit portico. "What do you want, Kent?" he said. "Don't you take holidays off, or are you a pain in the ass 365 days a year?"

Dorianne opened her door.

"I'd rather you stayed in the car for a minute," Evan called to her. "I want to find out what's going on."

The valet was very attentive. It was better than watching a movie. This was the real life Evan Crane and he was obviously upset.

"Crane, I don't know what you're trying to prove by keeping Dory a prisoner up there in that compound of yours, but I'm sick of it. I want to talk to her—now!"

"How many times do we have to tell you, Kent? She doesn't want to talk to you. Now, if you don't get back in your car and drive out of here, I'm going to call the police. You're harassing her. You're harassing both of us."

Dorianne opened her car door again and this time, she got out.

"Dory," Evan snapped at her, "I told you to stay in the car."

"There's something I want to say to him, Evan."

The parking valet took a few steps back. The drama was getting good.

Another valet came over to where they were standing. This one had a cell phone to his ear, but he wasn't calling the cops.

"Let the lady speak, Crane, okay?" Kent shouted. "You don't own her."

"I know I don't own her. But sometimes she doesn't know what people are capable of—the jerks they can be."

"Evan, please," Dorianne intervened. "I just want to tell him to go home. Go back to New York, Kent. Go back to Gertie, she's waiting for you."

Kent stared Dorianne down.

"I know all about it now, Kent. You don't have to look so wounded and shocked. And don't for a minute try to tell me I don't know what I'm talking about. You don't want me back because you love me, Kent. You just don't want Evan to have me. Because he's got more money than you do. And he's younger than you are. And, let's face it, better looking. But Gertie still wants you. God only knows why."

Then all hell broke loose. It suddenly seemed like cameras were everywhere. The flashes were popping in their faces. One of the valets had alerted a few of the photographers that stalked Salvatore's nightly for scoops just like this one.

"Dorianne, get back in the car this minute," Evan hollered her. "We're going home."

Dorianne was quickly overwhelmed by the bright flashes of light in her face. She felt out of her mind with rage.

But I don't want to show it, she tried to warn herself. I *can't* let it show. This will be plastered all over the damn papers by tomorrow!

When Dorianne was safely back in the car, Evan hit the automatic locks and sped off—carefully—hoping not to run over anybody as he pealed out of the drive, leaving Kent behind them somewhere in a thinning swarm of cameras.

Neither Evan nor Dorianne looked back.

"Thank god we're getting out of here tomorrow," Evan said. "Maybe now he'll go back home."

But Dorianne didn't respond. She sat motionless in the front seat and stared out the car window.

CHAPTER FIFTEEN

Behind a ten foot privacy wall of solid rock, stood the most unusual beach house Dorianne Constance had ever seen. It was a testament to modernism, all angles and concrete, teak wood and glass. And yet there was a serenity to the structure, a simplicity that belied its massive size and various shapes. Its perfection, the way the house gleamed and sat so harmoniously amid the delicate landscaping atop the black rocks of the Maui coast, reminded Dorianne of a flawless pearl.

"Evan, it's beautiful," she said. "I've never seen anything quite like it. 'Seen' isn't the right word. This is a house you feel with all your senses."

Evan was relieved that she was talking to him again. Not that she'd been completely silent since the plane took off at LAX, but she hadn't been her usual self. She'd been withdrawn and distant since the episode with Kent and the photographers the night before. That was almost twenty-four hours ago.

"Thank you," Evan said. "It's a very special house. I fell in love with it the moment I saw it."

The limousine driver unloaded the luggage at Evan's entryway—a massive set of cathedral-like doors. Then Evan signed for the brief rental of the luxury car and sent the driver on his way.

As if their suitcases touching the front step of the entryway had set off an alarm, the massive front doors opened almost instantly and there stood a calm, peaceful, perfectly centered older Asian man. He was attired in a simple white polo shirt, a pair of khakis and slippers, and a long white apron.

"Evan," the man said with a warm and genuine smile. "It's good to see you. It's been too long. You need to come home more often."

"Cheng!" Evan said with gusto, as if greeting his long lost father. "How are you? This is Dory. She's the woman I told you about on the phone. Dory, this is Cheng. My caretaker and a sort of spiritual mentor."

"Hello, Cheng."

"Hello, Dory. It's good to finally meet you. I've heard such interesting things."

Dorianne was a bit taken aback. "You have?"

"Indeed I have," Cheng said with a comforting twinkle in his eye.

"Cheng," Evan cut in, "Let's get the bags inside so we can all relax. It's been a long trip."

Dorianne eyed Evan curiously as he and Cheng gathered the luggage. Then she followed them inside.

The house was as magnificent inside as it was on the outside. Dorianne felt spellbound. She wasn't sure where the feeling came from—the uncluttered spaciousness; the blending of angles and lines that connected one room with another invisibly; or the fact that most of the rooms had no walls to speak of and were in the open air, surrounded by little man-made pools and tropical foliage?

She felt as if she shouldn't make a sound, or disturb the perfect balance of the atmosphere.

In the near distance was the soothing sound of the ever-returning waves. And a light breeze filled the living spaces with the fragrance of tropical flowers.

Evan called to her. "Would you like to come in here and see the view from the bedroom?"

Dorianne followed the sound of his voice.

The master suite was splendid. A high parquetry ceiling and a swirling overhead fan gave the room an airy look straight out of the movies. One wall opened onto a highly polished teak wood lanai that looked out over the ocean. Palm trees dotted the horizon in spare clusters and the sky went on forever.

At the other side of the room was the master bath, complete with an outdoor shower situated inside a private garden. Here, the foliage was dense and lush.

"You take a shower outside?" Dorianne marveled in disbelief, privately thinking about the revealing photos that had been taken of her and Evan on his terrace in the Hollywood Hills—she hadn't told him about that yet.

"There's also an indoor shower, if you're too chicken," he teased her. "It's very quiet out here, Dory. No one has ever bothered me."

Cheng set the remaining suitcases on the bedroom floor. "Does anybody feel like eating?"

"I'm starved," Evan said. "How about it, Dory? Are you hungry?"

What Dorianne really wanted first was a shower. But she opted for the more private, indoor one. She told Evan she would join him in a little while.

Everything about the house spoke of subdued luxury, even in the bathroom. It was much more regal than the house in

Los Angeles and for the first time, Dorianne got a full sense of just how wealthy Evan was. No detail was too expensive to be overlooked. The elegance of the house seemed effortless. Hadn't Evan himself told her once that he had more money than he could spend in this lifetime?

That's a whole lot of money, Dorianne thought with a shiver, as the water sprayed down around her and she wondered about what she'd gotten herself into. How does anyone get comfortable with this much wealth? What if it all disappeared one day? Then what? How would you handle the extravagant loss?

After her shower, Dorianne slipped into a peach silk dressing gown and a pair of slippers. The weeks she vowed she would wear next to nothing were beginning now.

She found Evan sitting at a table in the dining area, which was an open-air space off the living area. He was having a cocktail. The night air around him was aglow with torches. Beyond him, the glorious sunset was about to disappear.

Dorianne noticed a small spiral staircase leading up through the living room ceiling. "Where do those stairs lead?" she asked Evan.

"To an observation deck. I have a telescope up there, to watch the stars."

"You're kidding!"

"No, you want to look?"

"I'd love it," she said.

She started up the staircase with Evan close behind her. So close, that his body brushed against hers.

"You look really pretty in that color," he said quietly, sliding his hand along the peach silk that sensuously outlined her rear end as she climbed.

Dorianne felt his heat. Every touch of his hand was like an erotic caress to her. She hoped that particular sensation would last a lifetime; that his hands would always find her on fire for him.

At the top of the staircase, the view was breathtaking—three hundred and sixty degrees of tropical night sky. The stars were visible in multitudes.

"Here, let me adjust it first and then you can have a look."

Evan fooled with the telescope until he had it just right.

"Now you come around this way and see it for yourself."

Dorianne leaned into the telescope, and Evan stood behind her, pressing his body close against hers, his arms around her waist.

"It's startling. It's so clear," Dorianne sighed. "I've never looked through a telescope like this one. This must have cost you a fortune."

"To be honest," Evan said quietly, "I don't even remember. I just like having it."

Evan moved his hands up toward Dorianne's breasts. He stroked the silky material lightly, feeling her nipples come to stiff points underneath it.

Dorianne sighed again, this time for a different reason.

"I'm so sorry about last night," Evan said in her ear. "I'm sorry I ruined your Thanksgiving. You haven't given me a chance to properly apologize."

"But it wasn't your fault, Evan. It was Kent's. And those photographers come with the territory. It's part and parcel of your life, of who you are. You said it yourself; you're a public personality. When you're out in public, nothing is private. I'm the one who either has to get used to it, or go back home."

Evan was breathing quietly in her ear, his hands lifting her breasts through the sheer material of her robe, his fingertips brushing lightly across the points where her nipples protruded. "I hope you're not planning on going home anytime soon," he said, holding her very close now. "Or ever, for that matter."

Dorianne didn't know what to think. Was that an invitation, or just fleeting romantic talk?

"I still have an apartment in New York, you know. My whole life is there."

"Maybe your possessions are there and your parents, but you don't have a job there anymore, remember? The only job you have right now, for this moment, is right here with me. Wherever I happen to be on any given day. Or evening. Or night."

Dorianne could feel Evan's hard-on growing inside his trousers as he pressed it against her behind. His teeth sank gently into her neck. She groaned as a shiver of delight spread down her spine.

Evan parted her robe slightly, enough to expose her naked breasts to the tropical night air. He pulled lightly on her stiff nipples, knowing this would make her quite amenable to anything he proposed.

Her body squirmed gently against his, her ass pushing determinedly up against his covered erection.

"You want to make love right now, up here, Dory? A quickie?" he asked.

"Right here?"

"Sure," he encouraged her, his thumbs stroking her captive nipples. "Just lean over and look into the telescope again."

She did as he suggested, already stirred and feeling wet between her legs. He let go of her breasts and she heard him unzip his trousers; felt him lift the back of her robe and expose her behind to the open air. She spread her legs a little as he tried to find her hole and then he guided his cock up into her.

"Yes," she groaned quietly, her eye focused on the exquisite vision of a fiery, leaping star.

Evan held tight to her hips and worked his cock in and out of her slowly, methodically. He leaned down close to her as he fucked her.

"What do you see out there?" he asked softly.

"A beautiful star."

"Really? How beautiful?"

"He's breathtaking. He's right out of God's heaven, starring in the movie in God's mind. Everything about this star is perfection."

Evan didn't say anything more. Her words had taken him to another place—a place where all that mattered was satisfying her and getting his cock into her deep.

She moaned repeatedly as he labored to please her.

"Oh god, Evan, that feels good."

He hiked her hips up higher against him and she gave up all hopes of focusing on the star. She let the telescope slide from her grasp and clutched at the railing surrounding the small observation deck instead. Then she leaned over the railing, steadying herself, getting her ass up high for him so that he could push his cock way up inside her, to where she felt positively impaled, stretched and filled completely. She spread her legs wider as he picked up his rhythm and pumped his thick shaft up into her hole, over and over. Slamming it to her hard.

Dorianne's tits were out of her robe and swinging vigorously in the open air with each rugged stroke. She might as well have been completely naked, she was that exposed. And suddenly, that's what she wanted, to be as naked as she could get for him. She let the sash of her dressing gown give way. The robe dropped open and slid down her shoulders. Her bare ass was up high and her tits were hanging down over the railing.

Not too far below her, she could see Cheng hard at work in the kitchen area, chopping and chopping. Some kind of meat was blazing on the grill.

All he would have to do is look up, she realized, and he'd get an eyeful. He probably hears us.

She and Evan were both grunting in pleasure. Groaning, moaning, their voices were hardly being masked by the crashing surf.

As if reading her mind yet again, Evan leaned over her and said quietly, "Don't worry about him. Cheng is good people. He's very unobtrusive. You can be yourself. Come on, baby, give it to daddy. Let me hear you."

Then Evan drove his cock in hard and deep, determined to shake her free of all her propriety. "Come on," he said through his clenched jaw, working her hard, fucking her vigorously. "Come for me like you did that other time. Squirt out all over my cock; open your pussy up all the way, give me that hole, Dory, let it go and come all over me."

Dorianne was in utter ecstasy, clutching tight to the railing and bearing down hard on Evan's relentless cock. That feeling was building in her again, that intensity, that ominous wave of pleasure. She was pushing down and pushing down and opening herself to his furious fucking.

"Oh," she cried. "Yes," she whimpered. "Yes, I'm coming. It's happening. I'm coming."

And from her swollen, stretched, impaled hole, Dorianne spurted her come all over Evan's cock, his trousers, her naked legs. Her body brimmed with that sensuous, searing fire, and more and more fluids spurted out of her.

Dorianne's hole was so open, so engorged, Evan felt like it was swallowing his cock whole. He couldn't remember ever being in her this deep. "We have to fuck like this more often," he sputtered. "This is incredible."

And then the feeling snaked up from his balls. The liquid fire was shooting through him. He was coming and coming. And she was taking it, working his cock with her soaking hole. Working it, working it.

"Jesus," he said finally, coming down to earth and back to his senses. "God, that was good."

Dorianne, still leaning over the railing and clutching it tight, laughed in spite of herself. "That's putting it mildly," she said. "God, what was that?"

"Your first orgasm on Maui," he said, uncoupling from her. "That's what it was."

The front of Evan's trousers was soaked. "I need to change before dinner. Come on," he said. "Let's go clean up."

Together they slipped down the spiral staircase and Cheng never once looked up from what he was doing. He seemed to be quite entranced with his dinner preparations.

In the bedroom, Dorianne felt brave enough to shower outside with Evan. After all, she'd just been naked on top of the world and nobody else but Evan had seen her.

The shower was just off the bedroom. It had a small area of tiled flooring with a drain and a tiled archway overhead, from where the water sprayed down. But other than that there was nothing but the night sky and foliage, barely illuminated, along with their naked bodies, by the dim light of a lamp spilling warmly from the bedroom.

"This is a nice life you have here, Evan," Dorianne admitted, passing him the soap. "I can see why you cherish this place. It's hard to imagine it overrun with loud, careless people."

"I know. But at the same time, it gets lonely being here alone. Although I really like spending time with Cheng, talking with him about life and the universe, whatever's on his mind on any given day. That man thinks an awful lot. I've learned a lot from him. Still, this is a little better. Being here with you."

"Don't get mad at me, Evan, but I just have to ask. I have to know."

"What?" he said, grabbing her under the steaming spray and pulling her close.

"It was true, wasn't it? That story a few years back about some wild sex party here at your house."

Evan smiled slyly. "What can I say? People screw their heads off around here. There's something in the air, I think. It makes people feel very uninhibited. But it got too crazy, the drinking, the noise, people copulating in every corner. I finally had to boot everybody out and start from scratch. I completely redecorated and tried to create a sense of calm here."

"Were there a lot of famous movie stars running around naked, acting disgracefully?"

Evan shrugged. "Maybe," he replied with a smile. "I'm not telling. That's not my style."

"You're too funny," she said. "You're a nice guy, Evan Crane. I like you."

"I like you, too," he said, looking her dead in the eye. "In fact, I love you."

"Evan," she said and faltered, not knowing what to say next.

"I do," he insisted. "I love you and you can pretend all you want that you don't hear what I'm saying, but that doesn't mean I'm not going to keep saying it. Because I mean it. I love you and I don't want you to go back to New York."

"I can't work on the book forever. I know it seems unlikely now, but we're eventually going to finish it and turn it in. We have a contract, you know."

"I know, but this isn't about work, Dorianne. It's about you and me, here and now. And staying together. Don't be so stubborn. You know what I'm really talking about."

Dorianne's heart was racing. She didn't say anything more. She held Evan tightly, pulled him very close.

What would she do without a life of her own? Her own apartment, the city she knew so well? She'd had the same job since she'd gotten out of college. She didn't even know yet how it was going to feel to live without it, that safety net of everything being exactly the way it had been the day before. She was going to have a lot of money when this book was finally over, but what was she going to do with her future? And add to that unknown quantity, the prospects of a Hollywood life in a fish bowl with Evan Crane; Dorianne didn't know if she could handle it.

"Come on," Evan said, rousing her from her thoughts. "Let's dry off and go get some dinner. Wait 'til you taste Cheng's cooking. He's a certified kitchen magician."

Dorianne and Evan got out of the shower and he helped Dorianne dry off.

"I don't want you to be disappointed in me, Evan," she said.

"I'm not," he assured her. "We're here to relax and I have to remember that, not to pressure you."

The dinner was everything Evan had intimated it would be. Flavors that were new to Dorianne mingled with flavors she was familiar with but hadn't been expecting. Her mouth was in its own ecstasy. And the wine came from Evan's private cellar, a cellar he'd added to steadily and conscientiously from all the cities he'd visited around the world.

Still on California time, they retired to the bedroom soon after dinner, exhausted and satiated. They slipped between the cool sheets and lay together in the welcome comfort of the bed, as the steady sound of the surf just beyond the lanai filled the sacred darkness and lulled them to sleep.

It was still quite dark when Dorianne was awakened.

Evan was lying along side her, his elbow propped up on a pillow. He was watching her. The sheets were pulled down and he lovingly stroking her naked body in the darkness.

"You're up," he whispered.

"How long have you been touching me? I was having a very dirty dream."

"Long enough to think you were never going to wake up. You were sleeping pretty soundly."

Evan leaned over and kissed her. "Tell me about your dirty dream," he said. "Inspire me."

Dorianne snuggled next to him, her body still heavy with sleep. "I can't really remember it now," she said, "but it had something to do with water. I was having sex with water and looking at myself in a mirror at the same time. You know, between my legs. The water was rushing between my legs and I could see everything in the mirror. I used to do something like that when I was a little girl, not with a mirror, though. I used to lie in the bathtub and let the water rush right between my legs. I'd position myself so that my clitoris got pounded by the pressure and I'd stay like that until I had an orgasm. I guess I was pretty limber when I was little. God, I don't know why I just told you that."

"You were trying to inspire me," Evan said.

"Are you inspired?"

"Well, I'm intrigued. I bet you were a very interesting little girl."

"I guess I was like every kid. I was in my own little world. What about you, Evan?"

"That would be putting it mildly, that I was in my own little world. I had a lot of problems dealing with reality. My mom was always getting married and zipping me off somewhere, to live in a new house, go to a new school, and get used to having a new guy around who was supposed to be my father. I hated it. Nothing ever stayed the same. So I would go to a world in my head where my father was still alive and married to my mother and we lived like a perfect, loving family and nothing ever went wrong. I spent many, many years living in that make believe place where my father hadn't died, where he worshipped my mother and me. Where we were everything he wanted us to be and he hadn't abandoned us."

Dorianne put her arms around Evan and laid her head against his chest. She wondered why he always chose to make his revelations when her tape recorder was nowhere in sight. In fact, she hadn't even unpacked it yet and wasn't sure where it was.

"You're a curious fellow," she said. "You make a fortune making movies that, for the most part, are very superficial—big block-busters with no intellectual depth. But you're a complex man in real life. You have a way of seeming very accepting of your circumstances, like you just go with the flow. But at the same time, you're tough as nails. You're very driven underneath it all. You seem like you really have your head together. Lately, I feel like I'm falling apart at the seams. How do you do it?"

"I don't feel like I have it together, Dory, any more than you do. I know how to go after the things I want. It's a skill I've developed. Beyond that, I feel like I never have a clue what's going on. I'm feeling my way."

"Well, you're very convincing, Evan. You play the part well."

"Don't say that."

"I meant it as a compliment. You always seem so calm and cool and I want to be like that, I want to be like you."

"But I'm not playing a part when I'm around you, Dorianne. I hope you understand that. Don't make that mistake about me."

The sudden urgency in Evan's tone startled her. There was a hint of a reprimand in what he was saying and the seriousness of it jerked her wide awake. She pulled back from him.

"Evan what is it? What did I say? I didn't mean to insult you."

Evan got out of bed and felt on the night table for his cigarettes. "I need a smoke. I'm going to sit out on the lanai for a few minutes."

Dorianne watched Evan move through the darkness, out to the lanai, where he sat down on one of the rattan chairs and lit a cigarette. It reminded her of watching him smoke alone that night by the swimming pool.

She got out of bed and went to him. There was a cool breeze. Not uncomfortable, but cool enough to make her aware that she had nothing on and she wondered if she should grab her robe. But she let the thought go. She approached his chair in the darkness. "Evan, what is it?" she asked. "Talk to me. I'm right here for you. You don't have to retreat into that world in your head right now. Or let me in on it, at the very least."

He felt her delicate hand on his shoulder. He turned to look at her.

"I don't know what it is about you, Dorianne. You intimidate me sometimes. You're so smart. You're so disciplined and serious. You can set your eye on a target and you're going to hit it, I know that about you. You're that kind of woman.

"I don't know what it is I'm trying to do. Sometimes I feel like I want to own you—that I want to absorb the essence of you and make you a part of me so that nobody else can have you. I want to devour you sometimes. I crave you so much, my cock aches just thinking about you. I'm in love with you and I want to be the kind of man you want. But sometimes I'm not sure what kind of man I am. I'm confused.

"I brought you here to Maui because I wanted to share the serenity of this place with you, help you get to a place inside yourself where you can be calm and think clearly again and be ready to do some good, solid work on the book when we go back to L.A. But I also wanted you to see the kind of man I can be when

I'm calm, when I'm out of the chaos of Los Angeles.

"A woman like you can have any man in the world she wants, Dorianne. And I want to be the one man you want. It's driving me nuts that you don't take me seriously."

Dorianne sat down in the chair next to him. She searched her heart for an answer. It was time to be honest with him.

"I'm guilty," she admitted softly. "You're right. Part of me hasn't taken you seriously. But it's not because of you, it's because of me and my huge ego, my need to protect myself, to try to make sure I don't wind up looking like a fool. And I've wound up looking like a fool anyway. Not because of you, but because I'm so naïve. And because of Kent and *Babylon* and my Pollyanna world. I've learned a lot of ugly things about people in the few short weeks I've been with you, Evan. I don't know how you can stand being in this kind of world, being exposed to the weaker sides of human nature all the time. The jealousy, the greed.

"But when I think that I should just go back home, I realize that part of what's been exposed to me here is the lie I was living with back there. There were layers and layers of lies that I was blithely ignorant of. So it's not that easy to be smug anymore and say that Hollywood is just an illusion. Everything's an illusion."

Evan stubbed out his cigarette.

"Come here," he said. He reached for her hand in the dark. "Come right over here by me. Sit here," he told her, scooting over to make some room for her on his own chair. "Let the fact that it's dark out and that I can't really see your face be your security blanket if you still need to have one," he said. "I want to know the truth. Do you love me, Dorianne? Answer me without qualifying it, without answering a question with a question."

"I love you," she confessed. "I do. I love you. I'm in love with you. But it makes me feel ordinary, Evan. Everyone's in love with you."

"No they're not, Dory. They're in love with their own idea of me. Their love for me doesn't involve me whatsoever. It involves their own empty needs, their unfulfilled aspirations. There's a big difference between that and what I feel coming from you."

The waves crashed methodically against the shore in the knowing night and filled the silence that grew between them. A silence that planted seeds now, that would bind them, each to the other's destiny. It was an eternal love, just beginning—laying its roots down deep. A love that would endure the callousness and insensitivity of other, more ordinary human beings. A love that would withstand the animosity of the lesser creatures that were waiting in the wings, waiting to tear at their love with sharp teeth and tough talons.

But destiny was no joke when it took hold of two people with their eyes wide open. It was not a fragile thing.

Evan knew what awaited them in the press if they weren't careful. They would have to be vigilant, resilient. They would be hounded mercilessly and Dorianne would be unscrupulously eviscerated by the press. Until the onset of wedding bells—then, for a while, she would be able to do no wrong. After the wedding, though, it would start again with a vengeance, as the press planted story after story of false infidelities and disharmony and disillusionment. It was going to be up to them to know what was real.

But he was rushing things. He hadn't offered her the ring yet.

"Do you want to go back inside and lay down?" he said.

"Yes," she said.

She followed him back to the dark bedroom and they slipped back into bed.

Evan pulled Dorianne on top of him, pulling her face down close to his to kiss her mouth.

Their tongues met and they kissed with renewed purpose and intensity, their tongues exploring each other's mouths, back and forth; creating the rhythm of kissing and pulling them into its flow.

Dorianne moaned softly while they kissed and Evan kissed her more determinedly, pulling her head closer to him in the dark, his fingers digging in and gripping her hair. Then he eased her over onto her back and whispered down in her face. "Let's make love tonight like lovers do, with our hearts wide open in the dark. You think you can do that, Dory?"

"Yes," she said, feeling sure of herself and the choice she was making. This was the man who, when his heart was beating up close to hers, she wanted to follow to the ends of the earth. She wanted to be with throughout all time.

She parted her legs for him and he entered her slowly, his full weight on top of her, his mouth close to her ear.

His face was rough against her soft cheek—he hadn't shaved in hours. But the roughness appealed to her tonight—his masculinity tempered her, reminding her of her own femaleness. Giving her a place she was comfortable in, that she understood, maybe for the first time. She received him.

In, out. His cock's rhythm was steady as it grew stiffer, thicker, and more insistent.

Dorianne wrapped her legs around his waist, lifting her hole up higher for him.

In and out he continued, with a full hard-on now. His thrusts reached in her deep. Then he hooked her legs up over his arms; higher still, until her thighs were up around his shoulders and her vagina was raised to him as high as it could go.

He steadied himself on his knees, now. He planted the center of his weight directly at the opening of her hole and, to her surprise, grabbed each of her wrists in his hands and pinned them down against the pillow, up above her head.

"I just want to feel what it's like when you're completely open," he explained to her. "When you can't hold back. When you're giving everything to me, letting me have your sex unconditionally. And letting me give it pleasure in return."

Dorianne knew this was about trust. About loving him with her heart wide open in the dark.

Evan's cock felt enormous now and when he pushed it into her vagina, it filled her, past the point where it usually reached, past her cervix he went. But he eased up there slowly, finding his way in.

"Oh god," she groaned quietly. "God."

No one had ever been in her that deep. She felt herself opening around the head of his cock, making room for it somewhere very deep inside her.

Over and over, she took him all the way up.

He kissed her mouth hard while his cock opened her. And he held firmly to her wrists, even though she didn't struggle.

She liked to be in his power, giving herself to him. She liked the feeling of his hands holding her, pinning her down and keeping her breasts vulnerable, her heart on display. It was a posture of surrendering and Dorianne succumbed to it blissfully.

"Oh god, Evan," she cried softly, feeling him up there inside her again.

"Yes," he whispered, "what is it?"

"God," she said.

"What is it? Tell me."

"It feels so good," she gasped.

He eased out. "What does? What feels so good?"

"Your cock inside me. It feels so good. God. Fuck me."

"I am, honey. I'm fucking you." He pushed up into her again, opened her all the way.

"Yes. Fuck me."

"I'm fucking you."

"God," she groaned. And it was more guttural now, coming from her chest. Not her throat. "God, Evan."

She felt split open, his cock was so thick, so relentless.

"You're taking me clear up to my balls, you know that, Dory?"

"Yes," she gasped.

"You feel them?"

"Yes," she tried again. "Yes, I feel them. Keep fucking me. Promise you'll keep fucking me."

"I promise," he said, increasing his rhythm, taking her to the edge of endurance. "I'm going to fuck you harder now," he said. "You think you can take it?"

"I can take it," she cried. "I can take it. Fuck me hard, Evan. Fuck me hard."

He gave her all he had then, every ounce of his strength. He held tight to her wrists and centered himself at her hole, kneeling over her entire body, lifting her spread thighs higher with each powerful thrust up her vagina.

He was working too hard to kiss her. Her face was buried somewhere in his neck. Her cries came out rhythmically against his throat, somewhere down there in the darkness she was crying up to him, "yes, yes, god, yes" with each of his quick and vigorous journeys up through her. "Fuck me, yes, god, Evan, yes," she went on, as he came closer to coming, to emptying out the fruits of his labor into the very depths of the vagina that received him. "Oh, I think I'm coming, I think I'm coming," she chanted, as his sperm shot out of him in short, hot bursts and filled her. "I'm coming," she said. "I'm coming," she cried. Her legs jerking, her body convulsing, her hole in spasm around his pulsing, spurting cock.

"Oh," he cried out. "God. Yes."

The come triggered out of his cock like shooting fire. And her pussy contracting around it while she came only made him come more.

"Oh," they grunted in unison now, in utter exhaustion, but their bodies kept coming, rapture enveloping them as each of their orgasms fueled the other's ecstasy.

Then their bodies collapsed against each other; depleted, spent.

"God, that was good," Evan gasped.

"I know," Dorianne panted. "That was good."

*   *   *

Dorianne opened her eyes in the morning light and what she looked upon was breathtaking.

The bedroom was filled with a gentle fragrant breeze and the world beyond the lanai was bursting with color and life. The ocean looked to be an indelible blue, matching the brilliant hue of the endless sky. The palm trees swayed lightly while birds glided overhead, calling to the earth to wake up already. The highly polished wood floor of the lanai gleamed brightly and reflected the morning sun everywhere she could see.

She saw Evan sitting out there in a chair, drinking a cup of coffee and that's when she realized she was alone in the bed. She sat up. She was going to call to him, to say good morning. But instead she watched him quietly. He was lost in thought, staring out at the distant waves, out past the black lava rocks, the white beach.

It's all his, Dorianne thought.

She wondered what that must feel like, to own paradise. Or even a small chunk of it.

She'd slept soundly. She felt great—happy, content. They were having some incredible sex already and they'd just gotten here.

She saw Cheng bring Evan a tall glass of juice. As Cheng turned to go back to the kitchen area, he saw Dorianne sitting up in bed. He smiled and waved at her then kept on walking toward the kitchen.

Dorianne smiled, too. Then she realized she was sitting up in bed completely naked.

That guy's unshakeable, she thought. Nothing nudges him off center.

Dorianne got out of bed and went over to her suitcases, which she hadn't even bothered to unpack yet. She rummaged through them but felt thoroughly disinterested in her choices. She pulled on a pair of panties and grabbed one of Evan's white tee shirts instead. She walked out onto the lanai to greet him.

"Good morning," she said, apparently startling him.

"Dory, you're up. Good morning. Did you sleep well?"

"Like a baby," she said, grinning broadly, feeling as sunny as everything around her. "How about you?"

"Me too," he said, eyeing her a little strangely. "Want some coffee?"

"Yes, but just sit there, I'll get it."

She walked over to the kitchen area, past the little reflecting pools, where fountains burbled gently and splashed the water up and over the carefully selected polished stones. Whereas the night had made the house seem magical and sacred, the morning made it look idyllic, peaceful, safe, serene.

"Good morning, Cheng," she said.

"Good morning, Dory," he replied cheerfully. He handed her a glass of juice, as if he had been expecting her. "You want some coffee, too?"

"Yes," she said.

"This is a big day for you," he said almost cryptically, that twinkle in his smiling eyes again.

"It is?"

"Well, it's your first full day of vacation. You just relax and take it easy. I'll have breakfast ready in a little while."

"Dinner last night was incredible, by the way. You disappeared before I could thank you."

"You don't have to thank me. Cooking for me is like meditation, like art. It's a creative outlet. I cook like that even when Evan's not around. I just do it in smaller portions. You'll see."

Dorianne noticed now that Cheng had a slight British accent. "Where are you from, Cheng? Did you grow up around here?"

"Oh no. I'm from Singapore originally. I came here when I got out of the army and never left. That was many years ago. I'm a naturalized citizen now."

"You were in the army? I can't picture you doing something so regimented and severe."

"It was compulsory where I came from. I didn't have a choice. But the discipline was good for me. And, thankfully, there were no wars."

Then Cheng gave Dorianne a cup of coffee and shooed her away.

"Now you go look after Evan. He needs somebody to hold his hand this morning. He has a lot on his mind. I work better when I'm alone anyway."

That was strange, Dorianne thought.

She walked back over to Evan and she noticed now that he did seem preoccupied.

She sat down next to him with her cup of coffee. "What's up?" she said.

"I was thinking, Dory. Do you like it here?"

"Of course I do. It's incredible. It's everything you said it was going to be. Thank you so much for bringing me, Evan. I know this place means a lot to you."

"How would you feel about owning a little piece of paradise?"

Dorianne looked at him curiously. "Well, I suppose I'm going to have to do something about all this money I'm getting. Invest it somehow, but I hadn't really thought about it yet. Why? Is there a house you want me to look at?"

"Boy, that came out all wrong. Let me try that again."

Evan set down his cup of coffee and faced her squarely. "I'm asking you to marry me, Dorianne. To share it with me; this place, life, everything, kids; the whole nine yards."

Dorianne was dumbfounded. She stared at him over her cup of coffee. She swallowed hard, her throat suddenly dry.

"Are you serious? You're asking me to marry you?"

"I'm very serious. Here," he said, nearly forgetting, digging into the chair cushion and retrieving the black velvet box. He opened the box and handed it to her.

A diamond solitaire set in platinum sparkled exquisitely in the bright morning sunshine. It was a flawless stone, full of ice and fire.

Dorianne set down her coffee cup and gingerly took the box from Evan. She stared at the beautiful ring, unable to speak.

"You don't have to answer right away. You can take some time and think about it. But I had to get it out; I had to ask you. I couldn't take the tension anymore. Of course, if you decide right away, we can get married right here on the island if you want. Here at the house. Just something private, no press. Just you, me, Cheng, a judge. Something like that. Or we can wait and have a big wedding, the white dress, everything. I don't know. It's up to you. God, I'm babbling, I'm sorry."

Dorianne took the ring from the box and slipped it on her finger.

It was a perfect fit, like everything else about Evan and her.

She looked over at him. "Thank you, Evan. It's beautiful."

He looked back at her and waited.

She shook her head in disbelief.

"I love you," she said. That much she was sure of, but everything else seemed unreal.

If I say yes, she thought, that means I'll be defined as the woman who married Evan Crane. Nothing else I've done or achieved will carry much weight. Everything else about me will slip from people's minds. Can I be comfortable with that? Being a mere extension of a myth, a cultural icon, a movie star?

I can keep writing, though. I'll always have my work. And what does it matter what other people think, as long as I feel loved and can give love? And feel fulfilled.

But how can I be enough for a man like him? Marriage is a commitment; it's about forsaking all others. And every woman in the world will always be throwing herself at him, regardless of whether or not he's married to me. People don't respect other people's boundaries or values, especially in this seedy business of dreams.

"We'll give it our best shot," he said quietly, reading her mind again. "We'll learn how to let go, how to trust. I think we know what's out there, Dory. And I think we know how it compares with what we have right here. Nothing compares to what we have right here, between us. And what we have, we take with us wherever we go."

Dorianne stared out at the steady, washing surf. How glorious it all was—eternity, destiny.

Could it really be this simple, she wondered. You meet a man, you desire him, you fall in love, he loves you back? You're born into the world to find your way, like anybody else, and then, for no apparent reason at all, God hands you the pick of the litter, just like that. Why?

Maybe I shouldn't ask why, she cautioned herself. Why do those waves keeping coming back to the shore? Why is this island so extraordinarily beautiful? Because life knows how to thrive without any answers at all.

"Yes," she said suddenly. "I'll marry you, Evan. I want it; the whole nine yards. I'll give it my very best shot."

"Oh, Jesus," he sighed emphatically, his whole body relaxing at last. "Thank you, Dory. You've made me incredibly happy."

"Kiss her," Cheng called out on his way over to them. "Don't forget that part. Although the two of you," he added as he came closer, "don't need any encouragement in that department. I'm surprised you aren't already on top of her. She's been awake a whole twenty minutes."

Dorianne laughed in spite of herself and blushed crimson.

"You two are *noisy*," Cheng went on playfully. "My goodness. I thought the whole house was coming down last night."

Evan was blushing as much as Dorianne was now. "I'm sorry," he said. "We get a little carried away."

"Come on, you guys," Cheng said seriously. "Breakfast is ready. And congratulations," he said to both of them. "You're going to be very happy. I know it. I have the inside scoop." Then he headed back to the kitchen area, giving them their space.

*   *   *

True to her word, Dorianne wore next to nothing on Maui, day in and day out. What she did wear, however, that she hadn't planned on wearing, was a beautiful diamond ring on her finger. Other than that, she wore whatever came off easiest, and most of the time, they were Evan's tee shirts.

"We should go in to town and buy you some new clothes," Evan said. "You're too pretty to hang out like this. You need some flowered dresses to wear."

When they went in to town, the people stared. The tourists' cameras clicked away. But nobody mobbed them; the world was somehow under control. And Dorianne felt happy and at peace.

Before heading back to the beach house with their bags and packages, they made a small detour to a tiny white, one-story clapboard building where a state licensing agent nearly fell over herself when they walked in the door.

"We'd like to apply for a marriage license," Evan explained.

"You're Evan Crane!" the agent gasped in reply.

"I know," he said.

When the license was ready, they had thirty days to use it or it would expire.

In thirty days, Dorianne realized, they would be back at the house in Los Angeles and Evan would be hard at work on the set of *Blast*. She would be writing his memoirs at the desk in the huge white room across from Evan's. It was going to be her office, they'd decided, even though the king-sized bed would remain there.

One quiet evening, when the sky beyond the lanai was streaked with violet and crimson and gold, and on the horizon, the palm trees cut a soothing silhouette in the tropical breeze, Evan and Dorianne decided to get married. They would do it the following day. They would have Cheng locate a judge. It would be simple, private, and quick; and then eternity would be wide open for them.

"Cheng," they called, like a couple of exuberant children. "This is it! We've decided. Tomorrow's the day, get ready."

That night, they celebrated with a bottle of champagne from Evan's cellar. Cheng joined them in a toast.

"To your happiness, your lives," he said. "They will always be precious. I have the inside scoop on that."

He winked at them and smiled, and drank his glass down. Then he left them to wander with their re-filled glasses up to the observation deck alone, to look at heaven with their own eyes. At the multitude of stars above and the ocean that stretched forever before them, the same ocean that had brought destiny to other lovers in other dreams, throughout all time.

And when they'd had their fill of drinking down the expanse of stars and toasting the blessings of heaven, they retired to their bed and honored lovers everywhere.

They were magnificent in their naked splendor; in their rapport as lovers; in their courage and grace. And they woke Cheng with their rambunctious lovemaking, but they knew he wouldn't mind.

"You're burning the house down with all that love," he'd teased them once. "But that's okay," he'd added. "There's always room in paradise for a house on fire with love."

Other Magic Carpet Erotic Romances

THAT CERTAIN SOMEONE	Shauna Silverton	0-9726339-46-3
THE ESP AFFAIR	Alison Tyler	0-9726339-45-5
DREAMS AND DESIRES	Laura Weston	0–937609-35-8
BLUE VALENTINE	Alison Tyler	0-9726339-0-1
WHEN HEARTS COLLIDE	Marilyn Jay Lewis	0-9726339-1-X